BIRD ALONE

SEAN O'FAOLÁIN was born in 1900 in Cork city, the son of a member of the Royal Irish Constabulary. He studied at University College, Cork, before travelling abroad, first to Harvard and then to London to teach in the teachers' training college at Horace Walpole's Strawberry Hill. When he returned to Ireland in the 1920s, he became involved with the IRA, and was for a time their Director of Publicity. Later he worked with W. B. Yeats at the Irish Academy of Letters. He has written about thirty books: novels, including *A Nest of Simple Folk* (1933) and *Come Back to Erin* (1940); short stories, including *Midsummer Night Madness* (1932); biographies, autobiography, travel books, criticisms, and translations from the Irish.

BENEDICT KIELY was born in Dromore in County Tyrone and grew up in the county town of Omagh. After graduating from University College, Dublin, he worked as a journalist on various Dublin papers. Later he lectured at UCD and at several American colleges. His novels include *The Captain with the Whiskers* and *Call For a Miracle*, and he has written a number of books of short stories, among them *A Journey to the Seven Streams*. His non-fiction works include a study of William Carleton, *Poor Scholar*, and *All the Way to Bantry Bay*.

ALSO AVAILABLE IN

TWENTIETH-CENTURY CLASSICS

SEAN O'FAOLÁIN

Bird Alone

➤➤◆◄◄

INTRODUCED BY
BENEDICT KIELY

Oxford   New York
OXFORD UNIVERSITY PRESS

Oxford University Press, Walton Street, Oxford OX2 6DP

Oxford New York Toronto
Delhi Bombay Calcutta Madras Karachi
Petaling Jaya Singapore Hong Kong Tokyo
Nairobi Dar es Salaam Cape Town
Melbourne Auckland

and associated companies in
Beirut Berlin Ibadan Nicosia

Oxford is a trade mark of Oxford University Press

First published 1936 by Jonathan Cape Ltd.
First issued, with Benedict Kiely's introduction, as an Oxford University Press
paperback 1985
Reprinted 1986

British Library Cataloguing in Publication Data

O'Faoláin, Sean
Bird alone.—(Twentieth-century classics)
I. Title II. Series
823'.912[F] PR6029.F3
ISBN 0-19-281906-2

Printed in Great Britain by
The Guernsey Press Co. Ltd.
Guernsey, Channel Islands

INTRODUCTION

BY BENEDICT KIELY

SEAN O'FAOLÁIN, who is of an age with the century, had his first book published in 1932. It was a very notable collection of short stories and it immediately placed O'Faoláin among The Masters in Ireland, or in any country or age you care to think of: a position that he has held and steadily fortified over the last fifty or so years, as you can readily see for yourself by consulting the fine three-volume edition of his collected short stories (Constable). These volumes are an ornament to any shelf or any civilisation: 1,315 pages, and a good round total of ninety stories, if my addition, seldom as reliable as my subtraction, is correct.

Thirty-five years ago when I was attempting, with great impertinence, to write about his short stories, I came up with something like this:

It is not easy to find the exact description of O'Faoláin's mastery of the short story. There is easiness and grace, and a preference for the significant moment which can frequently be the contemplative moment, and more important for O'Faoláin, or for any other wise man, than the platform called plot or the unreality called a central character. Life, O'Faoláin has always maintained, has no central characters—and life flows through his stories so easily that it is pos-

INTRODUCTION

sible to lose sight of the art involved. Humour breaks like coloured bubbles on the smooth flow, a whirling twist of the water reminds us that life can be cruel and terrible and heedless of the results of its own cruelty. There are moments filled with contemplation, silent like some lost valley in Muskerry but alive with the life of silent places. There are stories as crowded with jostling characters and words and ideas as any lane in the city of Cork—and the city of Cork is very important in much of what Sean O'Faoláin has written. Life began there and exile begins where life begins. Reading his stories you can get, at times, the feeling that for him memory is neither a locked box nor a tidy room with objects on orderly shelves, but a living body still growing and capable of intense pain. Frankie Hannafey, one of three significant brothers in that novel of exile (actual exile in the States, spiritual exile in Ireland, and ironically entitled *Come Back to Erin*), remembering his childhood, feels, 'as if death works on us by gnawing away the beginning, creeping after us daily, eating away the road over which their is no return, until at the end there is one last day or two left; and then— the pit.'

That was thirty-five years ago. Now that the third volume of the collected stories has appeared, I find I am still struggling to describe or define this most urbane and learned man who, after William Yeats, the poet, has been the greatest encouragement and inspiration to Irish writers of our time.

Stories, novels, biographies, autobiography, books about travel in Ireland and Italy, criticism, translations from the original Irish, and even, on the side, one play

INTRODUCTION

for the Abbey Theatre. The achievement is awesome and, perhaps, even disheartening to those of us who are doing our best to follow his lead, even if the example he has given us is inspiring. One book I miss from the list because, for all I know, it has never been put together. That is a collection of, or at least a selection from, the leading articles written when he was editing the literary magazine the *Bell*, and giving most invaluable support to what we may still be bold enough, or antiquated enough, to describe as the cause of civilization in Ireland.

The first time I heard Sean O'Faoláin speak in public was at a bookfair in the Mansion House in Dublin sometime in the 1940s. It was a most impressive occasion. At that time he was at the height of what I may call his Bellism; eloquent, provoking to those who provoked, as the old Spaniard might have said in the movie of *For Whom the Bell Tolls*, even provokingly civilized, a state of being that can rattle a lot of people. With his friend and fellow-Corkman, Frank O'Connor, he maintained a most reasonable and ultimately effective attack on the quite absurd literary censorship of the period: a wearisome business and even wearisome to look back on.

He had also then about him the stormy reputation of having upset many accepted ideas on history and politics by his biographical study, *King of the Beggars*, of the Liberator, Daniel O'Connell, who, Balzac said, incarnated a nation. That notable book appeared in 1938 and had been preceded by a lively study of Constance Markievicz, one of the dear shadows of the poem Yeats wrote about the light of evening and Lissadell, a lady of the gentry who took to the cause of the people and to the streets with a pistol—to the misfortune of one policeman. His study of the great O'Neill who had fought the armies of the first Elizabeth was to follow in 1942 and later still, and perhaps to balance the boat, a study of John Henry Newman who, like the others, had some misfortunes in Ireland and who might, by some, also be regarded as a rebel.

O'Faoláin's first novel, *A Nest of Simple Folk*, appeared in 1933. The title is a courtly salute to Turgenev, but that is the only connection. For the novel is very much out of Ireland. In his autobiographical volume, *Vive Moi* (1965), he said of that novel:

It was a historical novel, or family chronicle, based on everything I had known, or directly observed in the countryside, of my mother's people, and the city life of my father and mother away back . . . in Cork City. So that, in this book that I am now writing, that novel . . . links these last pages with my earliest pages describing my childhood. It was a child's view of the world brought into relation to a grown man's view of the world. The grown man was, in his cave of Self, explaining to the child he once had been what it really was that he thought he saw as a child. It was a relating of aspirations nourished in innocence to the world experienced in knowledge. While I was working at it a friend might have asked me, 'What are you writing about?' And I might for

INTRODUCTION

short have said, 'About Limerick and Cork between 1840 and 1916.' But it would not have been true. Just as a critic reading the novel might have said 'He here describes life in Ireland over three generations', and it would not have been true. I was writing about dreams . . . I was hearing every time—no matter what I was writing about—the drums of my boyhood dreams.

The novel here before us came two years later and the drums of boyhood may have beaten off into the dim distance. The novelist is in conflict with himself, and with his country and people. He considers that Henry James writing on Hawthorne didn't know the half of it, that a few more conflicts would not have done Henry James any harm, might even have made him as good a writer as Hawthorne who, 'faced so many problems—and kept sweet'. He might have said to Edward Garnett that the real problem of the Irish writer was to keep sweet about his material, not to go sour on it: and Garnett would have roared at him to give Ireland hell: and that he would have had to reply that he didn't want to do that because in his divided heart he loved his people. Corney Crone, surrounded and perhaps entrapped by the lights, colours, odours, and sounds of the sanctuary, thinks here that it was not that he did not believe in men but that he could not believe in what men believed.

Then thirty years after the writing of this novel O'Faoláin looks at an old notebook of the years that formed the basis of the novel—'odd thoughts, wonder-

ings and problems of the soul, and I am not surprised
that they all look slightly daft to me now'.

Socrates, looking backwards, must have thought
that he had wasted a lot of breath. Yet it seems to me
now, on my fourth reading of a novel that I have long
admired, that for a man at variance with the ideas on
life and history accepted by many of his countrymen,
the inevitable place to begin a statement was with the
betrayal by bishops and politicians of the Uncrowned
King, Charles Stewart Parnell, the man who for a brief
few years was even more than the Literator. Few Irish
writers, or few Irishmen who gave thought to anything
but were not, over a half-century, affected by that
agony.

*

WHEN Conor Cruise O'Brien first printed his brilliant
essay on 'The Parnellism of Sean O'Faoláin', I felt that
the work in biography of O'Faoláin would not be complete until he had written a study of Parnell. It was, as
we know, Conor Cruise who was to write the study: he
also had meditated much on that classical tragedy.

The agonising love-story in this novel is not, as
Cornelius Crone early realises, simply the surrender
of lover to lover, but a war between the two worlds in
which they suffer, separate and apart. There was
example for 't, not in Cork but in fair Verona. Corney,
with Parnell in his mind, and even more potently with,
from that grandfather, Fenian, revolutionary, anti-

clerical instincts in his veins, cannot accept the suffocating cloistral atmosphere of the house of the beloved. The act of love might seem to be, as I once heard it said of an affair that began in a somewhat similar fashion but did not, fortunately, last long enough for disaster, like tossing the tall candle-holders off the high altar.

For a brief moment the living, fighting figure of Parnell helps to hold the young lovers together:

There were two . . . places where we used to meet, and one was when, with Christy and my grander, we tore after the warring factions who turned the city into a bedlam at every political meeting. For, however much her father grumbled and disapproved, she loved to watch the stones flying, and the stub-legged police crashing their batons on flesh and bone, and women screaming, and the tar-barrels sending their black smoke into the sky. She and I were mad Parnellites in those days and when we shouted his name as we swayed back and forth in the mêlée, we felt every shout as a blow for the old cause; it was a triumph for us if we saw old Phil, my grander, up on the wagonette, his badge in his coat, his stick waving down to the surging sea of faces, and behind him in his place the pale face and the burning eyes of The Chief.

Then the Chief, the Uncrowned King, is betrayed and dead, and desolation and death follow as the night the day, and Cornie is a bird alone, a heron without a mate in an expanse of grass, an exile among his own people. There are echoes of the young Yeats giving a

INTRODUCTION

tongue to Aleel, the poet, who must out where wind
cries and water cries and curlew cries: 'How does the
story go that calls them the three oldest cries in the
world?'.

In the words, above-quoted, from Frankie Hannafey, in the novel, *Come Back to Erin*, there was more
than the echoing of a phrase to remind one of the
Book of Job. Three of O'Faoláin's four novels deal
with old men. The fourth and latest novel is, as we shall
see, a special case. One of those three old men comes,
at times, close to the God-permitted sufferings of Job.
Corney Crone, in *Bird Alone*, acquires Job's patience,
although he applies it not in relation to the will of God
but in relation to 'those little accidents' (Hardy's
Chance) that prevent some men 'from taking part in
the affairs of their city, or from marrying a little wife
and bringing up a family in the fear and love of God'.
It might seem that for Sean O'Faoláin the genuine
rebel against the beliefs of other men is always an exile.
Frankie Hannafey is left, in the 1920s, isolated by the
end of a revolution, an exile in New York, an exile
when he comes back to Erin. Corney Crone never
holds a gun in his hand and never apart from that journey all the way to Wapping Wall, seems to have left Ireland. But his life ends in exile, brooding upon his first
and last and only rebellious love-affair. The old age of
Corney Crone, his old man's love for morning and
evening, has a place among the classical stories of exile:
the exile of a man from his people, of man's spirit in

the world of men:

> For I am become an old man and my friends are few, and that new faith I set out to find I never did find, and because I have sinned all my life long against men, that whisper of God's reproof, who made men, has been my punishment. I have denied life, by defying life, and life has denied me. I have kept my barren freedom, but only *sicut homo sine adjutorio, inter mortuos liber*—a freeman among the dead . . .

The irony, for which we all in Ireland have reason to be grateful, is that the man who wrote so feelingly of exile and alienation, has devoted a very valuable life to his country's welfare. To compound that irony, and with a sardonic humour of which only he would be capable, his latest novel, *And Again?* (1979), was the life-story, or the two life-stories, of a man who, by a double trick of the gods, finds himself growing backwards or whatever into youth and boyhood and worse. When I began to read the novel I thought, simply, that the novelist couldn't get away with it, that nobody could, not even the gods themselves. But the novelist is so plausible that once you begin to check statistics the laugh is on you and you have accepted the monstrous impossiblility that provides him with the framework for an amazing, amusing, learned, wise, human book about life, as we call it, and love, as we call it: and a lot of other things if, that is, there are a lot of other things.

And talking of the gods one of the ladies in the double life of that man may be allowed the last, courageous word:

INTRODUCTION

My own feeling is that the gods have long since forgotten the whole thing as they often seem to have forgotten this world they idly made one supernal morning when playing with a handful of Olympian cloud, out of which, boredly, kicked into limitless space, man has through millions of years created every speck of the splendours and miseries of civilised life.

BIRD ALONE

Factus sum sicut homo sine adjutorio, inter mortuos liber

I am become as a man without help, a freeman among the dead

PSALM LXXXVII

CONTENTS

PART ONE

THE DARK CAVE

Two parts of the day I love, morning and evening —
old men's time for walking—because they cannot sleep,
because they would sleep. And two walks out of the city
I love, the one to see the sun rising, the other to see it set.

An hour before dawn in winter, if the weather is
good, an hour after it in summer, I go down along the
river where I can see the formless fan of daylight
up-spreading below the lochs of the Lee, while about
me the mist is barely beginning to move from the
sluggish mudflats — that dull, whispering, sheeny
mirror to the houses across the water, to the limestone
castle, to the ball of light risen for another day's toil.
There I turn and look up the stinking river at the cold
chimneys of the city where two spires of a triad —
broken trident of a cathedral — catch the light. They
mark my house, just beneath, and as I look I picture
the Fort beside, and the slums beneath the Fort, and the
sleepers, and the down-beds hot with heavy bodies as
yet unaware of the lovely coolness of the morning.
Farther still up the river where the stink has ceased, and
where I walk in the evenings, I know the mist will be on
the meadows, and the cattle stumbling from their
knees, and the water, over the stones, pure and cold and
untroubled and aloof. North and south, as I return
slowly, the city is still asleep on its bastions and nothing

for a man to hear except a lonely heel-click on a pavement, or a cock loudly crowing in a backyard, or a churn rattling in an early milk-car, or if it is summer, and the sun is early, the little rondo of the angelus-bell kept up for a few minutes between the three churches — the Capuchins, the Dominicans, the Friars — that acknowledge the sun. I hear the gulls driving one another mad with their squawking over the quays. If it is one of my happy days, I may see, high up over the river-basin in one of the few lovely Georgian houses that we still retain in Cork, a window opening noisily in the silence of the morning, and two soft hands beneath the wood of it disappearing behind the tallow-coloured blind; and when the blind has jerked upwards, some brown-haired girl, still warm with sleep, catching her nightdress about her neck, will look out over the early fog. In the evening I go in the other direction, where I spent so much of my childhood, out the field-paths beside the upper reaches of the Lee to hear the evening sparrow-call, to see the mists sinking down again and the cattle returning to their knees. And if the sky is fiery, I return to see the golden mosaic in the arch of the cathedral doorway burning its tympanum to the night.

These are the hours that comfort age; for youth, though sometimes excited by these lovely extremes, measures life by what lies between — day, when old men find time heavy on their hands, and night, when old men have no love and cannot sleep. Only children do not think of the sun-god. For them it is day at one moment and night at another and they are so busy in all that brings them sleep that they never see time move; like birds they cry out when the sun comes, and they cry out when the sun goes, and at once for them the day is dead. But as we grow older and become foolishly busy, all our days are either too long or too short, and our lives have no even flow. Until, suddenly, the sun, as if weary of being chased, stands still and we realize that where there is no night nor day, no swing of work and rest, life hardly exists at all. Is it any wonder that youth and age see different meanings in the same things? Or that old people love those hours that give sense to too-long life? All life hangs on heavenly order that all may sense in the rhythm of a turning world, that the child obeys, and men forget, that old age discovers just as it begins to feel the stopping of the wheel.

So, whereas now I find it an ease to be out of the glare, when I was a boy I used to complain that this corner of Cork, especially the timber-yard where I worked, was a great deal in shadow; as it is — for in winter the sun does not come from behind the Fort until noon and begin to pass behind the towering spires. And this sun appears to me to move very slowly now, whereas it seemed to me, sixty years ago, to leap from prong to prong of the great trident overhead and I was always surprised when I returned from school to find our house of Cork brick, crusted and vermiculous as a worn clinker, like all the little houses about, red as wine. My young day ended when the Fort sank back into the dusk. Now, long after the day is down I can see daylight evaporating from the valerian on its rocky side and night means so little to me that I am just as pleased when the great bulk goes jet against the sky and all the hundred lighted lane-cabins underneath reflect the stars.

No! Time's wheel is stopped for me. Time has become for me like the mist that often floats in layers across the Fort and the mildew-green of the cabins, so that the cock on the spire seems to move, and yet nothing really moves and even the mist is only a shaken veil. Those very lights in the cabin-windows measure me out no hours since there are always one or two yellow until daylight under the rock, as if there, too, some old man could not sleep or feared the dark.

The day gives me, however, one great joy, one perpetual variety that I never heeded sixty years ago. In the hot blazing summer this nook of the city is bright from cockcrow, and the whole street and even the faces of the passers-by are tinted all day long by the lovely wavering light from the brick. That warms me like a fire and when I see this wine-red house at sunset, or watch the old purple Fort changing colour in the light I think this the only corner of the city fit to live in.

And it isn't just because I am a builder like my father and my grandfather before me — I have been in the trade since the year 1890, when I was a lad of seventeen —

that I have this fondness for coloured stone. It is simply that stone comes out of the earth and the earth is nothing but stone pounded beyond a sand and that nothing so becomes a city as to retain the quality of the earth that made it. Brick does that, granite and sand-stone. Whereas a white glimmer, like a tombstone, is at all seasons the light of limestone cities at sundown even when the rain darkens them until they are sodden; most of all when a long summer dries every crack and cranny until the walls and the wide streets are only a dusty clay. Look at Dublin, made, every foot of it, of small, tidy brick — there is a city to look at! Though, of course, if I had my way I'd build every town in the world of scarlet marble.

It is a good nook to live in, for other reasons. All Ireland, and we knew it even as children, is in those two buildings, the cathedral, built, burnt, rebuilt on the site of a hermit's church: and the Fort that our people held in 1788, and the militia-boys held for England in my day, just a hundred years later, tramping heel on heel under the great archway, their bodies shaking with the 'old-sweat's' swagger and the weight of the pack and helmet they had carried all over Africa and Asia under the green flag — a heel on heel learned on such famous treks as that three-hundred mile march for Roberts from Kabul to Kandahar, or Wolseley's 'too-late march' of three-thousand miles from Cairo to Khartoum to save poor Gordon. Youngsters hardly even hear of these things, nowadays — that Ireland is gone — but I lived them. I saw my mother crying when the news came that Gordon was dead, and my grandfather go off for a booze with the Fenians down the city because England had at last got wiped in the eye. So, on Sundays we used to hear the bugles calling the swaddies to church-parade, our church, and the organ from the English nave across the road booming over the Irish mass-bells in the flat of the city. We used to see the Proddy-wodds, all so neat and clean and in black, with their prayerbooks as fat as ledgers and red ribbons out of them, coming out in twos and threes, solid and sour. How different to the crowds that tumbled out of the Lough Chapel, the lane-people, the hucksters, the working-men, pulling on their caps outside the porch, and in their eyes the look of a girl who has been kissed.

Oh, Gilabbey was a good place to live in, all right, the very names a history of Ireland: Saint Finbarr's, Dean Street, Bishop Street, Cat Fort, the South-Gate Bridge a stone's throw away, Wandesford Quay (some Lord Lieutenant or other), Hanover Street across the river, Saint Mary's-of-the-Isle at our back-door. As a boy, I need hardly say, we accepted it all in the too easy acceptance, the lovely too-innocent acceptance of childhood, although my old grandfather was always trying to bring the names to life — talking of the wild Irish outside the city walls, the Earl of March at the convent, the cannonball smashing into the old cathedral from the bastions of the fort, the marriage of Elizabeth Boyle in the Cathedral, and Spenser writing about her 'lips like cherries charming men to bite, and all her body like a palace fair'. I can see the old devil, my grandfather, sitting up there under the slates in his attic with his green-globed lamp alight and the dim crown of flickers from the rock, thinking of it over and over. 'Her breast like to a bowl of cream uncrudded ... her paps like lilies budded ...' As I can see in his earlier time Bishop Berkeley, who said that nothing exists unless it exists in the mind, and he, beside his green-globed lamp, too, in one of those old red-brick houses behind the cathedral, looking down the little slope, hearing the squawk of the marsh-birds in the evening air, seeing the moon rise over Cork Harbour, slow as a poem.

But, even if all that was hidden from us, it was still a grand place for kids. We had the Bishop's Marsh; we had the timber-yards where the rafts came floating up from the quays; we had the weirs and hatches roaring below Gilabbey Rock; we had the hill-fields opening up and out beyond and behind the lanes — away to the farthest horizon of greenery by Lehenagh that looks down from the south on this Lilliput of smoke; we had our own timber-yard behind the Red House; and in each of all of them a particular group of familiars — bird-catchers, lollers, strollers, ex-soldiers, corner-boys, wood-gatherers, idlers, whom we came to know and talked of as if they were our friends; who, indeed, took the place of relatives so far removed from us by distance that we might be said not to have any at all.

It was my grander, Philip Crone, who built the Red House when he was only a few years in the city: though it was not his own idea and he had never intended to live in it. He was at the time living a little farther back the hill towards the fields, barely on the edge of the city. For he was a Skibbereen man who had married in Bandon and sent his son before him to the city to learn a trade: in other words he was one of the wild Irish who always settle down gradually, as by ancient habit, near the edge of a town. Later, as we did, they move into it. It is a form of siege.

It was his son's idea to build the Red House, because it was his secret intention to marry and live in it. I often heard the story of this manœuvre from old Tom Scanlon, the foreman, and how my grander fought tooth and nail against Pidgie Flynn. But, as old Tom would say, it's not for me to judge her. If she was not the best of wives to my father I have no cause to complain of her as a mother, and I have long decided that the real reason my grander didn't like her was that she was far too like himself.

She was fat and buxom and warm, the kind of girl that, as they say, wouldn't come in the door for you, the kind that made my grander say of her that she 'was as lazy as sin and as slow as a hearse'. Whereas my father was known to his men as Christ-on-the-cross-Crone and had the sharp look of the Famine about him: he had a furrowed brow like a man who was always saying, in his heart, 'I'm only a worm — O God, don't stand on me'. What with his long narrow black moustaches and his hollow cheeks and his high celluloid collar, a dog-collar on a gander, and his curious cold, long hands, he always reminded me of Simon Legree in *Uncle Tom's Cabin*. If he had only stooped his back and said Fee-fo-fum to a child in the street I swear you wouldn't see that child's backside for dust. He always dressed in black and he took us for long walks on Sundays and gave us the best of advice. No wonder five of us ran wild and abandoned him, the sixth was poor Bob, and he was a natural.

I doubt if he had a friend in the city of Cork. Though afterwards, I met two or three men who knew him well and they told me he was one of the best fathers and husbands they ever knew — reliable and upright. But as my brother Barty said once when he heard tell of a saint whose deathbed confession was as innocent as the confession of a child of seven — 'That would be just like our da — innocent before God and disliked by every man that knew him'.

One Sunday, for example, Barty, Micky, and I were playing in the kitchen-garden behind the house, and we heard him opening the little squeaking gate that was hidden from us by the rose-bower. At once we fled down the garden, for he hated us to be there, damaging the plots, and as we ran we left a swathe of broken potato-stalks behind us. We climbed up a willow that hung over the stream below the garden and I have to chuckle every time I think of how he came down, looking at the damage, and peering right and left to find us. At last he went away and we whistling with our lips at one another to hear him complaining to my mother. That night when he came in for tea he just gave us one look, took down a cane he had for the purpose, said, 'Corney, your hand', 'Micky, your hand', 'Barty, your hand', and gave each of us three cruel slaps on each palm. Then, never saying a word, he read his paper while we whimpered in a corner.

Another time, my mother was giving a birthday party for Vicky, my sister, upstairs in the room, and we singing and laughing and enjoying ourselves when suddenly in the middle of some loud joke or other we heard the haw-haw-haw coming up to us through the floor, and every time we laughed loudly that night we would hear his mocking bray from the room below.

When we grew up he changed completely and was always wanting to be near us — but it was too late; we left him to himself as we had always done since we were children. Bob responded to him, I think . . .

Anyway, he married Pidgie Flynn and my grander gave him the Red House as his wedding present, and it was like the old man to be impulsively generous and to repent too late. He drew up an arrangement at the last moment whereby the top half of the house was to be kept for himself and his wife, my grandmother, as long as they lived. And it was like him to make a mess of it too, for a bare month after the wedding my grandmother died and the half was reduced to a room, a fine long attic under the slates from whose window you could see all Cork and its harbour, and there he was at the mercy of a daughter-in-law who had every reason to dislike him — or he was as much at her mercy as such a firm-jawed flat-poll could ever be.

He and old Tom Scanlon must have been right about her in many ways, and I well believe all they used to say about her — that within two years of her marriage she was streeling around the house in her petticoat, that she had a chest a man could sit on, that the rest of her went east-west whenever she moved, and so on and so forth ... But she did no harm to me that I know of and what matter if she was fat, and the house was always upside-down, and she did take a sup of whisky now and again. I know few things out of my childhood more pleasant to remember than how I used to lie sometimes, as a little shaver, on her great bosom, warm as a kitten against a cat's fur, and both of us dozing off by the fire into a deep-breathing snooze after our little sup of winter punch. What did I care, then, if the red glow between the bars of the range was the pyre of the best mouldings out of the yard? Or if the whisky-punch was part of a bill as long as my arm at the grocer's? I could have stayed there for ever cocking a blind wink at the fire, listening sleepily to the talk with some old gossip of my mother's — hearing bits and scraps in the shuttle of the wind: 'terrible weather, all moiling and toiling, the river in flood, the end of the world, went off in a flash, and may the good God rest all poor souls, with a pinch of snuff, will ye listen to that rain and the Lee rising, me tush of a fire, Janey Martin, snuffle and scratch and windy latch . . .' until I felt, too, rising and falling on a mighty swell, that I was out on the wild white sea beating its storm through the harbour-mouth into our little rain-washed town.

No more did I think of that side of the story when with Barty and Vicky and Micky and Maurice — poor Bob always played alone — I sat with my grander up under the rattle of the slates before his little fire and his green lamp on the floor to warm him — barely lighting his under lip and he telling us the story of Faust; or think either that he was a wifeless, ageing man. That I think of now as I see him writing in the book from which the story came, in his slow, firm hand-writing:—

Philippo Croneo, The Red Houseo, Gilabbeyo, Corkio, and after it, in pencil, the strange entry, *Je souffre tant, O Jésus,* and on the back fly-page a list of long words such as *labyrinth, simultaneous,* or *homologation,* with his favourite hard word, which he possibly invented, *transbansmagnificanslansubstantuality.* To us he was simply our grander who would, of nights, let us into his bed, shoving into him, snuggling into him, while he recites the story of that book, beginning with:

'This great play of Faust, my young auditors, was written by George W. M. Reynolds, M.D.'

His rough hand steals under my nightshirt as he speaks on and on, stroking my little belly round and round, his bald poll on the pillow, his beard cocked up to the ceiling, his large O of a mouth reciting to the glow of the lamp over our heads. I only remember bits,

now, of this saga — how Otto Pienella arranged a
meeting between Faust and Beatrice by a canal in Rome
— we had a print of that famous picture in the sitting-
room — and how Faust lived on the tip-top of Shandon
Tower, right under the weather-fish, and how when a
light shone from his little window in the belfry it meant he
was studying over old books, and when no light shone
it meant he was meeting Beatrice. Then there was the
terrible part where Faust was down in the dungeons.
'. . . and one day, as his eyes grew accustomed to the
dark he saw a most terrible thing. And, Corney,
doyouknowwhatitwashesaw?'

'Nnnno, Grandaddy?' I'd whisper, glad to feel his
hand round and round my belly-button.

His white mouth in his little pointed beard, rising
and sinking, would say very slowly and solemnly:

'A terrible incantation on the wall.'

Then the part came where 'His Satanic Majesty'
bought Faust's children, and 'The Quare Fellow'
appeared in a ring of fire, coated with pale blue flame
'like methylated spirits', his tail waving like a cat with
a mouse, and he said in a little growl:—

' "Faust, me bucko. Yer time is come." '

At which the three or four of us would dive right
under the bedclothes clutching him in the dark. We
would peep out, like mice in hay, for the end:—

' "O-o-o," moans out Faust then, "Gimme wan
minute till I say an Act of Perfect Contrition." '

' "Nah," says the Ould Lad, "nor half a minute," and

with that the floor opened beneath them and the fire glowed and Faust was thrust down for ever, and ever, and ever, into the pit.'

'Go on to bed now, Corney, you little monkey,' he would say in his natural voice, but I would not and he would have to let me rest in his arms until, sleep-drenched and limp-limbed, he carried me in his shirt-tails down the bare stairs into my cot. That he might remain awake, for hours and hours afterwards, I did not consider.

It is more rich now, to think of him, knowing more of him, in the dewy frosty evenings when the reeds of the Bishop's Marsh make a whistling and the moon is exactly over the spire, up in his attic, with his shiny poll like an egg crushed by the spoon, and his little beard stuck out from his big jaw, and something in his brilliant eyes of my father's melancholy and in his voice of his softness, but with a hardness and a cruelty in him that came out of the hard and cruel coast-farm behind Skibbereen. 'He was a vain man,' somebody who knew him once said to me, 'and ambitious; but very weak in the carnalities.'

I must say all the 'carnalities' I ever saw in him at *that* time was when he would be with his friend Arty Tinsley, and I after him with young Christy Tinsley, in and out of every pub in the city of Cork, and rain, hail or snow, every third Sunday of the month galloping out the country in wagonettes, decorating the graves of the Fenian dead. Then we would be, the four of us with his friends, over a pub fire in Kilcrea or Ovens or

Kilcroney, the talk floating up the chimney with the steam of our legs, while the rain hissed into the misty grass and the pokers hissed in the mulled stout, surrounded by a procession of names, hour by hour, corner to corner, Rossa and O'Neill-Crowley, Land and Labour, Davitt and the Tory 'hoors'; a drink to Lomasney who was found in his own clots of gore on the mud of the Isle of Dogs after floating down from London Bridge that he had tried to blow up — nothing less would appease his wild imagination, I suppose: and a drink to the men who swung for the agent they sunk in a bog near Tipperary: and a drink to His Lordship of Cashel who talked up to the Pope when he went to Rome *ad audiendum verbum* . . . all ending with the road thick with night and a singing born of liquor, and Christy Tinsley and myself wrapped into one another with cold and sleep.

Then came the day when old Arty Tinsley died. It was a wretched rain-down of a southern evening when my grander and myself set off to the cemetery on the Douglas Road, that was for some crazy reason called The Botanic Gardens, to fix about the burial. I was not sad but frightened, for this was the first real death I knew. But my grander took my dread for sorrow and as a reward he packed me with Shandon Mixtures and Peggy's Leg until I was sick in the stomach and sticky around the mouth as I stood under the yews of the graveyard. In the Gothic porch of the gate lodge — smelling of laurels and wood-smoke — my grander was discussing the details of the funeral with a long dreep of a caretaker who kept on remembering all the Tinsleys who ever came in the gate on the flat of their backs. Then we went into the lodge itself, very small with its red and black tiles and even more odorous of the fallen leaves and the damp wood-smoke; and I was looking at a photograph of a bishop, and at the framed photos of the red-coated sons holding their arms very stiff to show the sergeant's stripes, when I suddenly felt a strange silence and saw my grander over the book, making slow circles with the pen in his hand.

'That's the way, sir', the foxy caretaker was saying, 'that's grand, now, Mister Crone, religion now, sir, enter the religion of the deceased.'

'He was born a Catholic,' said my grander.

'Down with it, sir,' said Foxer.

'But . . . I don't know what he might be, now?'

The man looked at him in surprise, as if he was asking himself, 'Does the ould lad think there's no religion in Heaven?'

'Fill it in, sir,' he said politely.

'Yes, grander,' said I. 'C — A — T — H . . .'

'Go out, boy, and wait outside,' says he very shortly.

But I was soon sick of the misty hills and the swaying wet yews around the marbles — ever since I have hated that white Carrara marble for outdoor monuments — and I returned to the porch. There, inside, was a terrible argument going on between the two of them, and my old grandfather shouting:—

'What I say is, if an unfortunate Fenian isn't left in peace by the clergy when he's alive then they should leave him in peace anyway when he's dead.'

And the man crying out:

'For God's sake, now, Mister Crone, fill in the two words — R.C. — and be done with it — the church is wise, Mister Crone — the church have to look after us all, dead and alive — and for God's sake and God is the best judge of all those things and God will judge you and me . . .'

'What I say is, the church wouldn't admit he was a Catholic when he was alive, so why should the church want to say he's a Catholic because he's dead?' (I knew what he was at — the Church had banned Fenianism in Ireland.)

'My dear good sir,' said the man, beyond all patience, 'I'm not the church and you're not the church and if the church says he was a Catholic then it's dogma, and a Catholic he is, and no wan can get behind that. Write it down — R.C.'

'The church never admitted he was a Catholic. It denied him the sacraments. It now wants to deny him Christian burial.'

The foxy man held out his index finger, as if he was balancing a pin on the ball of it. Solemnly he looked at it; solemnly he looked at my grander; he tapped that finger with the tip of another, saying quietly but finally:

'Did the church say he was a Protestant?'

'No.'

He tapped his second finger. 'Did the church say he was excommunicated?'

'No!'

The man drew out a sail of a handkerchief and blew his nose.

'Write down R.C.,' he ordered, like a pope.

'NO!' said my grander and he flung down the pen in a fury. 'The church never said yiss aye or no to Arthur Tinsley. But you know and I know and everybody knows that no Fenian could get absolution in confession or the sacrament from the altar unless he retracted his oath to live and die for his country. And . . .'

'Mister Crone . . . '

'And . . .'

'Excuse me, one moment, mister . . .'

'AND if Arthur Tinsley was asked here and now whether he would retract that oath . . .'

'There's nobody asking him . . '

'. . . whether, to obtain burial in this bloody cemetery, he would bow the knee to the church, and the first question they'd put to him would be, Do you admit that oath was a sin? — what would he say? What would he say?'

The man walked away to the door.

'What would he say?' roared my grander. 'He'd say "I wo'NOT!" And what would they say?' he bellowed, with a great sweep of his hand through the air. 'They'd say "Then we'll have nothing to do with yeh, and yeh can go to hell!" '

'This cemetery,' said the caretaker loftily, 'is a Catholic cemetery.'

'Then,' sobbed my grander, 'where will I bury him?'

'Look here,' said the man in a kindly voice, and he picked up the pen. 'I'll sign it, R.C.'

'NO!' cried ould Ten-to-Wan. 'NO!'

'Very well,' said the man. 'You can put it to the Cemetery Committee. I won't have anything to do with it.' And he walked out about his business.

'Come on, boy,' said the old lad, and away we went, I with big eyes and beating heart, he muttering his rage:

'Damn the Committee! Damn the Committee!'

We took the tram, damp and mist on the windows and horses' coats shining, out to Douglas. I did not ask any questions but when we came to the Protestant cemetery and I was sent off up the little village street I guessed there was something wrong. After shivering under the thatch of a cabin-end for an hour I began to search for him — as by instinct among the pubs. Sure enough I found him gosthering with some old toady in the Royal Hotel and the upshot of it was that I was soon sipping my cherry-wine over the snug-fire and watching the usual smoke and steam of talk and damp and peat curling up the maw of the chimney, but this time it was all — British Foreign Policy, the Vatican, diplomacy, cardinals in their robes drinking wine with English lords, pulling strings to the ends of the earth, and, 'where will I bury him now? — dogged even to the grave — no rest nor pity for Ireland's bravest sons', ending with another fierce, 'Come on, boy!' (Actually I do not believe he went near that cemetery at all.)

It was late afternoon when we were back down in the flat of the city and into a covered car and the cold rain in torrents following us along the empty streets behind the step. We halted in Grattan Street before a dirty cave of a shop, full of dry rusted irons. In the dim inwardness of this cave, all hung with useless iron junk, was a stove, and almost embracing it was a small bearded Jew. Flecks of down steamed about his surtout; a tin of water, crossed by a butcher's knife, steamed at his feet before the fire. He barely glanced at us over his half-moon iron-rimmed glasses, took the knife and spoke in a queer language.

'Shah go deimhin,' says ould Ten-to-Wan in Irish. 'Ta sin go maith, but what I want is for to bury a man.'

A Jewboy ran into us.

'Vat is it you vant, mister,' says he in English. 'I sell you vat you vant?'

'Go out, boy,' to me.

'I wo'not,' says I. 'I'm cold. I won't go out for no wan.'

'My God this day,' cried my grander. 'I'm pestered from you. I'll never bring you out again, you little caffler! Sit down there and hold yer gab. I want,' says he, to the two Jews, 'to bury me old friend Arthur Christopher Tinsley.'

'Ah,' from the Jewboy. 'He vas a Jew?'

'JEW?' shouts my grander. 'You bloody . . . here, it doesn't matter to you what he was. I want to bury

him. Decently! And no nonsense about it. No penny
in his mouth, either. No crossing the Jordan. No
standing up in the grave. Dacently — like a Christian.
Now. How am I to do it?'

The two Jews argued and argued for about ten
minutes and then, when old Ten-to-Wan was beginning to burst out at them again, the young Jew spoke
in English.

'He vas not a Jew?'

'Certainly not.'

'Vas his father a Jew?'

'NO!'

'Vas his mother a Jew?'

'NO!'

'Vas his grandfather a Jew?'

'NO!'

'Vas his vife a Jew?'

'No, nor his uncle nor his aunt nor no wan on earth
here nor there unless we all goes back to Adam and Eve
in the Garden of Eden where we were all Jews. Can't
ye see,' he implored, 'the position is that my friend
Arthur Tinsley, may God look down on him this day,
is the victim of the foreign policy of the British Government. The Vatican,' he took the Jewboy by the lapel —
the old Jew paid no earthly heed — 'the Vatican is,
what, engineered, manœuvered, deceived.'

The Jewboy shrugged his shoulders.

'Tell it to your ould fellow,' pleaded Ten-to-Wan,
'tell it to him. He'll understand the situation.'

He turned himself to the old rabbi who was gently waving his palms to and fro before the coals, or holding the fingers close together to see the tender glow of the fire light up his bones.

'Look,' cried my grander, and his stick stamping and his eyes piercing the old man's skull. 'The Foreign Policy of the British Government. Il est le Vatican — Roma? — Italia? — Vaticano? Do you understand me?' he shouted.

The rabbi opened and closed his fingers and shrugged with boredom. My grandfather shoved back his hat and enveloped the rabbi with his arms.

'Governmente Inglese,' he pleaded in a tender whisper of cajolery, 'has, you know, Vaticano — eh — manœuvre. Oh, Jasus, what do you say?'

His hands grasped for the missing words as he looked into the fire and back at the rabbi. I heard the rain pounding the tin roof like drumsticks. I felt as I once felt before when, sinfully, I stole into the Protestant Cathedral during a service. That time they told me I would have to go to the Bishop to be forgiven. This time we would all be damned by the Pope himself.

'Diplomaticato!' cried my grander with satisfaction. 'Have yeh me knife?'

The rabbi smiled and rubbed one finger across another. 'Cutty cut,' he chirruped.

At that my grander clapped him on the back and laughed with delight, while the rabbi rubbed again and smiled with vanity.

'I knew ye'd understand. Now yeh can see why he can't be buried at any crossroads. He has to be buried with honour. Con honore. Iralandiso sepulto in Irelando con honoro. Have yeh me knife?' he cried joyously.

Again the rabbi chuckled and said 'Cutty cut', and grinned at the Jewboy and took his knife to make a nibbling incision on an imaginary kosher fowl.

'He don't know vat you talk about,' said the son. 'You vaste your time.'

Grander rubbed the perspiration from his neck and looked at the rabbi through whose transparent skin the fire shone like watered blood.

'You don't understand?' sighed my grander.

'Oh, yes, understand', said the rabbi. 'Ver good. Cutty cut!'

'Come on, boy!' he ordered.

The jingle was on its way, down the Marsh, and over the glass-factory bridge where the river, far below, was pocked with rain. But we passed our house and went onward up the hill to the University grounds. It was dark evening and there were pools of water in the quadrangle and the thud of a football sogged through the air somewhere to our left. I was shivering with cold and fear when we halted by a dirty green door, my grandfather speaking no word. I could smell the pungent stink of what was, no doubt, formalin, coarse soap, and iodoform. Up the stairs the gaslight was like a candle in a tomb.

'Wait there, boy,' he said, but as the door of that room opened I turned and flung myself down the stairs and hell for leather across the rainy grass into the dimness of the waiting car. For I had seen a table in the centre of an immense hall and from that table there dangled a brown human leg. I was crying when I saw him return slowly — his short, pot-bellied body, his bone-ridged hands, his little beard. The river was roaring far below the grounds. The birds were singing because the rain had stopped. Maybe it was then, for the first time, when a gas-lamp scooped his temples and made caverns of his eyes, that I thought I saw in his face and look the damned look of another Faust. Or perhaps, I often thought after, it was then the souls of those damned ones entered him for the first time when he realized that by the mortality of his friends he was condemned to the sentence of too-long life. For behind us the tower-bell tolled and the tower itself rose, like a Faustus tower, against a drying night, and over in the dissecting-room the gaslight rose and sank in the wind, and it was the colour of rotting grass.

Of course there was a terrible scene when we got home, and the funeral had to be postponed by several hours while Arthur John Coppinger, who was now Christy's guardian, arranged for the proper burial of poor Arty Tinsley. But it was never forgotten for my grander, and to his dying day he was talked of as the man who sold his friend to the cut'em-ups. Local gossip, as usual, preferred fantasy to truth.

Some of these things it would be wrong for me to
recall at this point, since I did not at this point first
observe them, if I had not in my years discovered that
what a man observes about himself refers always to
times long gone before, when he was being fashioned
unbeknownst. To me, apart from such a day as that one,
whose effect I could not have realized, life ran to a
perpetual cuckoo-call, spring-flash and warm sun. Or
am I again fooling myself, knowing as I do that we
live two lives at the same time, one in daylight, one in a
darkness of self? I don't know. I only know there come
back to me days upon days of playing in the sunlit yard
with my brothers and Vicky; or down in the marsh
where the log-rafts floated slowly on to the saw-mills;
or out along the fields — peepshow bits, seen through
pinpricks of memory, interrupting me perpetually and
uninvited — a doorway, a handful of coins given me by
my mother, a Sunday walk after Mass with the family.
With difficulty, however, I drag less sunny things from
the well of the past, such as that Christmas morning
when we had all been to Communion except my grandfather; and how after it, as we drank the ritual glass of
cold water, my mother, full of unction, started to rub
him sideways with her tongue, saying, 'Oh, there's
some people can go without God all their lives, but

they'll die, yet, roaring for the priest'. And when I came to read *Gulliver's Travels* for myself I noticed that the only part my grander had ever told us was about the horseheaded men and he had called them all by names like Paddy and Shawn and they all lived in Skibbereen, so that it came as a surprise to me to find that the story had nothing at all to do with Cork or Ireland.

But now I see a great deal more of that kind of thing and how the old man was for years dragging me before my time, secret and timid though I was, into the world. Once, even as a child I saw it — or it seems to me that it was as a child I saw it. That once was of a Christmas Eve when Christy Tinsley and myself were guiding him home through one of his usual rampages. As we came out of the Young Ireland Rooms he bought a pig's ham in the bacon shop round the corner, and all the way home he carried it under his arm while the grease melted through the newspaper like sweat. In the tram he was particularly garrulous, and he called the conductor a 'parrot-nose bastard' because he charged full fare for myself and Chris. To distract him I said — after much colloguing with Christy on the best way to do it:

'Grander, that's not an Irish ham there you have.'

To my shame he held it aloft for the whole tram to see and began tearing the paper right and left and crying out in a loud voice:

'Irish? What's not Irish? Look at it — burnt on

33

his ass with red irons. *Denny's Best Home-cured.* Good God, do yeh think I'd pay as much as a lop for an English pig's crubeen? Not Irish . . .'

And so on and on, until at long last Christy and myself got him in home and I looking forward to a restful end to the night, maybe with a bit of cake and a glass of lemonade, while across the fire my grander and mother would, in respect of the season, exchange in peace their stories of old Cork.

On this night, however, immediately I got indoors — with Christy Tinsley racing home across the river to his aunt — I could feel there was something in the air. My da was in the front parlour, without a fire, groaning over his accounts, my sister and brothers in bed, and my mother embracing herself in her big arms before the fire, nicely warm with punch and tears. With his eyes averted, as if he were the executioner offering the henbane, grander held out the tattered pig's ham to my mother, and she took it as if it were the body of her only child, snuffling her thanks. Then she had to offer him punch and I begged my jorum and the three of us sat to the range with our glasses set in a line on the iron fender.

My mother was clever enough that night, as I now see it, in the way she led the talk by devious ways to where she wanted it. For she had received that day a Christmas letter from her sister Virginia, in London, about — of all people — an uncle of mine whose name had never before been mentioned in our house. Virginia, who had married well in London, wrote to say that she had met Mel Crone, that his wife was still alive, that they were very poor, and that Mel had been ailing for a year. It was only when the night was finished that I discovered who and what his wife was — an actress out of Johnny Gooseberry's play-tent on the quays of Cork, Mel had married her when he was twenty-five — I no more than a crawler at the time. That, I now reckon up, must be nearly sixty years ago, and that onion-scented, fish-stinking tent where the Corkites of the day could, for a penny, see Shakespeare and hear a new ballad, their only newspaper, is long become part of the half-baked antiquities of this little city. And yet, for all anybody knows, Melchisidek Crone and his Ophelia might, though very old, be still alive in some London poorhouse, or some London slum, or in any rural field of all England. (You see how my mind wanders when I think of him. Even so my mind wandered that night for the first time out of Ireland and Cork when I heard his name. It was like the day, later, that I heard somebody talk of the Seven Seas, and as they tried to list them I swam from my own body — the Red and Black, they said, the Sea of Marmora, the Atlantic, Indian, Pacific and Mediterranean . . . Had they said Sirius and Cassiopeia I should have died.)

When we were comfortable and grander's pipe drawing like a steamship:

'I suppose,' sighed my mother, 'the streets are alive

with people. It's grand when Christmas Eve comes of a Saturday night.'

'There's a great number of people abroad,' said my grander unsteadily.

'Ah, but, sure', says she, 'the gaiety isn't like old times. God be with the good old days.'

And she shuffled herself and rubbed her nose horizontally with a fat finger.

'Shandon bells!' says she then. 'They'd ring the Christmas in and they'd ring the Old Year out, and they were like heaven in the sky.'

'Yes,' growled ould Phil, very proper, 'and what was it like on earth? Before Father Matthew came you couldn't hear a bell with the bellowing in the street. Drink', he gasped, puffing easily, 'has been the ruin of this country for a hundred years.'

'Or more,' says she, poking the fire until it shimmered in the three glasses at our toes. 'But sure the young must have their day, too. Isn't it nice for me, and you, too,' says she, 'to be thinking now of the times we spent in Batty's Circus, say, oppósit' the Courthouse...'

'Psha! Batty the name and batty the man. Once only I went to that kip of a place, and then I came out before I'd get sick in my belly.'

'Ah,' says she, shivering with a thought of age and time, 'but they had lovely girls in it. 'Twould raise the cockles of your heart to look at them.'

'Oh?' says I. 'They were acrobats? They were flying in the air like angels?'

Like a guinea-fowl she chuckled with delight, and slapped my bottom, and took me on her lap.

'Yeh divil. It's the Crone blood in ye. But, for all that, Philip, they were a lovely sight, only I terrified they'd break their little bones, the poor creatures.'

'And is it true, grander,' I asked, 'that they have their souls sold to the devil like Faust?'

He growled.

'Ah, it's not them, boy', explained my mother. 'What are they but gipsies earning their living like Batty the Bitch with his fiddle. Or the Blind Harper. Some say it's the actresses in the plays are a bad lot, though.'

He took his drink and he glowered at it.

'Down the play-tents', she prodded, 'with Johnny Gooseberry', she prodded. 'For it isn't like them others that sort lives — not in tents and caravans.'

'Have sense, woman!'

'Oh, and Hoho!' she prodded. 'I often heard it. Dressed in finery and not a shift to their backs beneath the frippery and the froppery.'

'They're intelligent people, woman. Learned in the drama. Imbibing the poet's words, night and day. Not like your Batty's strollers. The mouth of the poet. The voice of the writer. The wisdom of ages.'

Her eyes lit as she raised her own jorum.

'Yes,' she said, 'and where does the finery come from? It isn't their pay. What them sort gets wouldn't break a bank or bankrupt a parish, and yet they out in silks and sateens like Lord Rosebery!'

'Woman,' he cried. 'You have no knowledge. Keep to yer clowns. Keep to yer clowns.'

'One time he took me to a play,' she appealed to me. 'And a dirty brute of a fellow there with a whip and he hitting a poor woman. "Is it the moon?" says he. The brute, and he knowing well it was the blessed sun! "No," says she, for she wouldn't lie. "Now," says he, and he lambasting the poor creature, "is it the moon?" "Oh," says she, and the lie in her mouth, "it is the sun, moon and stars and whatever you like," says she, "only don't bate me!" There you are — there's little else in all them plays but lies, lies, lies,' went on my mother, and she winking at me, 'and the brutality of men.'

'Psha, and thrash. You don't understand the play, woman.'

'And then there was a poor woman,' winked my mother, 'and she going mad for the love of a fellow in black and he teasing and tormenting her and giving her no peace. "Go and be a nun," says he. "Oh, but sir," says she, "and is this what you say to me now after all the presents you gave me." "Go and be a nun," says he. And sure the poor soul went off her rocker, and had flowers in her hair and drowned herself. Is that what you call wisdom? Is that nice or proper for men to be looking at?'

'Silence, woman,' he cried. 'You're only making a fool of yourself.'

'It's the way all men treat all their women,' says she. 'I nearly cried for the poor girl, even if she was a bad woman itself.'

'She was not a bad woman,' he roared. 'She was not a bad woman. She was an innocent girl. She was wronged.'

'And who wronged her?' cries she. 'Who wronged her? Maybe you'll say it was Melchisidek Crone. . . .'

'Silence,' he roared at her, and he was red with anger as she jumped up.

In came my da, at that point, and he too was annoyed, and he became doubly annoyed to see us at the punch.

'Three times, this blessed and holy night,' he wailed in his sorrowful voice, 'I asked you to stop that drinking. Isn't it a holy night for the like of that boy to be in the company of two people like ye! And how can I settle my accounts if there's noise and contention? . . .'

'Oh, for God's sake,' says my mother, 'go back to yer accounts. Amn't I only trying to soothe and console myself for the sad and sorrowful news I heard this day from my sister Virginia in London.'

'What news?' says my da and my grander together.

'News about your son,' she says to my grandfather. 'And he sick and maybe dying in London. And his wife . . .'

'Not another word,' orders my grandfather, and he white as his whiskers.

'Oh, father,' said I, to keep the peace, 'will I get the holy candle and light it?'

I ran off to the scullery and brought it out. It was all ready in its turnip and jam-jar and the frilly green paper crackled in my hands. As I went and returned the argufying grew louder in the kitchen.

'I suppose I am entitled,' my father was saying when I came back, 'to hear something about my own brother.'

'The oldest in the house,' says I, 'must light it. Get the Holy Water, mother,' says I.

'It's upstairs,' says she.

Off I ran and down I ran with the bottle, and the green stuff floating about in it.

'. . . and one second ago,' my mother was crying out to my grander, 'you wouldn't have one word said against her. Imbibing the wisdom of the poets,' she mocked, losing her cunning in her temper.

'Here, mother,' I implored. 'Shake the Holy Water, now. Light it, grander,' I begged him, offering a match.

'But men are cruel,' she wailed, taking the bottle. 'Light it, child, you're the youngest. The light of heaven to our poor souls, now and at the hour of our death, amen.'

Lavishly she spattered the water from her palm all over us. It hissed on the candle. My grander puffed himself from it and he brushed the drops from his chest and face as if he feared it would hiss on him, too.

'Bless yourself, ye hathen. Ask God to forgive you for your hardness of heart.'

'In the name of the Father . . .'

My da blessed himself like a man about to be executed.

'Soften yer heart, ye hathen,' she ordered my grander.

'Soften my arse,' he roared, and he rushed like an exorcised demon from the kitchen up the stairs to his room.

'Oh dear, oh dear, oh dear,' sighed my da and he returned to his cold parlour and his moneys: while I, seeing that the three of them would be holding the forts of their minds in silence against each other for the night, stole after my grander to his attic.

The streets were sunk in silence, and across the frosted roofs Shandon measured the first quarters of Christmas Day. We leaned over his old lamp — as usual on the floor at our feet to heat us — and he, greatly excited, began to lay into my mother and Melchisidek.

'Sending us home, now from London, how are yeh, his loving messages! Psha! Cockawalla! Nothing else would do his Lordship but an actress! Ophelia, if you please.'

Then in a mean whining voice, like a Cork whore, he snivelled:

> ' "My lord, I have remembrances of yours,
>   That I have longéd long to re-deliver;
>   I pray you now receive them."

'Well, I'm not giving a reck about her. I'm no Polonius behind no scenes. Mark that, boy.

> ' "No, not I.
>   I never gave you aught . . ."

No, boy, no. Not a bloody make. Not a lop or a tosser. No! Not a pin's fee, as Shakespeare says.'

'Grander, you'll wake Barty and Vicky,' I whispered.

'Do you know what comes after that?'

'No, sir.'

The lamplight picked out only the peaks of his face, and the cruel underlip, snarling, were all over the ceiling. He resumed:

> ' "My honoured lord, you know right well you did,
> And with them words of so sweet breath compos'd
> As made these things more rich; their perfume lost,
> Take these again; for to the noble mind
> Rich gifts wax poor when givers prove unkind." '

He was deepened of voice.

'Ah, yes, is that the way of it? That's her line. But,' he thundered at me, rising over the lamp and sweeping his beard out like a horn, 'but the power of beauty, aha, ould Shakespeare was the boy for them, he knew them, the power of beauty will sooner transform honesty to a bawd — a BAWD, boy — "than virtue can transform beauty to its own likeness. I did love you once." '

I still hear the whisper of that last sentence. He saw me looking, wild-eyed, at him across the funnel of foggy light.

'Do you understand, boy?'

'No, sir.'

'It means ... it means ... She was a good-looking girl, yeh know. Do you know ...? Them lassies in the circus ... they were handsome, too.' His voice trembled. 'Strong, you know, and well made. Did you say they were like angels? Ha. The way,' he remembered, 'the way their lace used to ripple around them, you know. Like angels. But, boy, BEWARE of the pretty eye, the red cheek, the glowing lip, the comely form! Good looks are the devil's passport! "Can sooner transform honesty to its own likeness ..." It's true! Shakespeare knew the world. 'I know it, too. "Get thee to a nunnery." It's true! Make them say it's the bloody moon. Make them say it, boy, and if they don't, give them the stick, the bloody bitches. Give them the stick. It's the only way!'

He strode across the garret into the dark.

'I am proud, revengeful, ambitious, with more offences at my beck than I have thoughts to put them in, imagination to give them shape, or time to act them in. Go thy ways to a nunnery. Where's your father?'

'Down in the parlour, sir.'

'Damn good. Let the doors be shut on him that he may play the fool nowhere but in's own house. Haha! God almighty, it's better'n a play. If thou wilt needs marry, boy, marry a fool, a FOOL.'

'Was she pretty, grander?' I asked.

He sank like a tide, away and away. He looked into the lamp. He went to a chest of drawers and pulled out a box and emptied it on the floor at my feet. In the circle of light he swept his long fingers through the rubbish and picked out an old tin-type photograph. It was spotted with mould but I could see her fair hair and the zone beneath full breasts. A sloppy, I said to myself, and a softy. He sat looking at it for a while and then suddenly, as I was just forming strange questions in my brain, he threw it on the floor, lightly, and said:

'Well, the night is long but young shavers must be in bed. Run along, boy.'

And when I delayed he suddenly began to cry in his drink and he got sick out the window, moaning at the moon. I ran, stopping on every step, and looking up in fright through the well to his door. Below, through the fanlight I saw the spire of the Cathedral shining, and as I looked up again my father's mumbling came from the parlour: 'Seventy-two and nine ... seventy-two and ...' I went into the kitchen.

'Mother,' I asked, when I was once more sitting for all my thirteen years on her lap, 'when did my uncle Mel go off with the actress?'

'Ah, you were only out of your eggshell, my lamb. Lemme see, now. Your poor grandmother, God rest her, was dead a year. Eighty ... It's thirteen years ago.'

'How old was my granda at that time, mother?'

'Old enough to have more sense.'

'More sense than what?'

'What do you mean? "More sense than what?"'

44

'That's what I was saying, More sense than what? You said he ought to have more sense. I said, than what?'

The way she looked at me gave me my answer and it went through me like an electric shock.

'Go to bed, Corney, my lamb,' she said, warningly. For it's all hours and the blessed Christmas morning. Don't be bothering your head with things that happened long ago.'

'Am I a slyboots, mammy?' I asked in vanity.

She flung a hairbrush after me while I ran, delighted with myself. I do not know where my waking night ended and my dreams began, or if I did hear from that attic room as I climbed towards it the murmur of:

> 'Indeed, my lord, you did,
> And with them words of such sweet breath composed
> As made these things more rich . . .'

In my sleep he was racing wild through the frosty streets in his nightshirt. From him fled an Ophelia with an angelic face and out of the Young Ireland Rooms there staggered, screaming, the figure of a man called Melchisidek Crone. He poured wine over his head and cried out that they had burned *Denny's Home-cured* with red-hot irons on his bare backside . . . At times Shandon tower boomed and there was warm punch in my veins. When I woke to Christmas Day it was raining softly and my mother calling the five of us to rise for Holy Mass.

45

I FIND it in an old pass-book, written across the pale red columns ... incomplete, written in the office when I was twenty-one:

> ... but keep it deep within its cave.
> Love is a girl that shuns the light,
> But try by night, if she's a shade.
>
> For know, Maeotis kills the girls
> Who cannot cold Maeotis shun,
> And cold Rhodope's light imperils
> The flowers that love the Afric sun.
>
> And if you bring in pomp of power
> Your flower to light in vanity,
> Her petals falling in a shower,
> Will feed the East Wind enmity.
>
> Fall they, then, like a falling dress
> When trembling fingers loose the zone,
> Except that this love's loveliness
> Is but the loveliness of bone.
>
> No matter if your heart's a bell
> Beating lest the others see;
> Beat it within its cave nor tell
> Where lies her blossom nudity.

For I, too, once in pomp of power
Brought out my flower from her dark cave,
I saw, like you, her stripling shower . . .

Ah, why do we not keep from the bright
Sun, for the hour before the stars embark,
Our girls that *are* girls by night
Our Venus that engenders in the dark.

But pride destroys our love and we
Must look on what delights us;
The secret's out. 'Tis dead. We see
A face . . . affrights us. . . .

Could they not have let me be a little longer innocent?
Or is every old man a vampire on youth like the Faustus
of George W. M. Reynolds who sold his children to
prolong his own life? Or do they all sell themselves for
pride and then cheat their children to retain it?

There was that school my grander sent me to. I
thought I chose it for myself, for my father wanted me
to go to the little gentlemen's school up the hill and I
wanted this one because Christy Tinsley was there. My
three brothers went there after me: Robert never went
to school at all. For years I was grateful to my grander
who took my side; but now I know the truth. If it was a
place where the innocence of me was forced and pampered, he wanted it pampered only because he could feed
on it. You don't believe that? Then why else did he send
me there—an old lecher who had long since lost the Faith?

Not that I am sorry I went there, really, into this bizarre, cobwebbed, dust-smelling cavern of a school that might have been in its earlier days a bedlam or a jail, that we called the Lancasterian School, thinking of the Tudors, when in fact it was one of the first Bell and Lancaster schools, unchanged since the days of Wordsworth and really as old as Carleton. For it was nothing but an enormous hedge-school, crowded like those stables under whose drip the tatterdemalion outcasts of the eighteenth century wept and shivered over the 'larnin'.' Though unlike their schools ours was pretentious but ignorant, with its poor little monks about whose greening skirts we crowded and who were the centre and the fount of all ignorance and simplicity.

By day we were all, a half-dozen classes of us, scattered about the Big Room that wealthier schools would have called the Aula Maxima — a lofty hall lit by a clerestory from which the cracked glass fell so frequently that as we toed the horseshoe line chalked on the floor we held open books balanced like little penthouses on our heads to protect ourselves from the penalty of a split skull. There every second boy was barelegged, with the mud drying between his toes and zoomorphic tracery on his mottled shins for sitting in the ashes of his laneway home.

At the centre of each chalked horseshoe sat the brother in charge of the class, and we found ourselves more than once, in our interest and eagerness, crowded in on him so tightly that nothing but a lashing sweep of

his leather sent us scurrying back to 'toe deh line' —
shuffling to it as meticulously as if a millimetre astray
would have landed us back or forward into a pit. Once
our Brother Josephus was so interesting about the
passage of the stars that the horseshoe was left abso-
lutely empty except for Chris Tinsley alone. There he
stood, meekly, 'when all but he had fled', as Josephus
said, adding: 'That boy is the only boy in the class who
will be a soldier.'

I remember it because it came true, and because I
wished I had stood my place and been prophesied for a
soldier, too.

I am sure Josephus told us a great deal of nonsense
about the passage of the stars because I have, in later
life, found out that much of what the monks told us was
entirely inaccurate. They were raw youths with red
hands and buttermilk complexions, and big hats only
prevented from extinguishing their faces by the Divine
prescience of ears, and their feet moved with the
memory of the clay. They commonly pronounced the
simplest words wrongly — saying Newfoundland, and
the Balearic Islands, thinking doubtless of other
Ballys better known to them; they said cathedAral, and
contrAry, and theather, and elum, and they said book
and home as slowly as if they wished us to know that
time was no object in a world that moved to eternity.
I cannot credit my memory that one good monk told
us that combustion was due to phlogiston, but I do
know, for I questioned Christy about it afterwards,

that another told us there were ten minerals, and gave us a list of them and that was that; and Josephus certainly told me — for in later life I told it to others who were ribald — that circumcision was a small circle cut in the forehead of Jewish children. His reading clearly misled him, and innocence of the foreparts of his own body. On the other hand I always think admiringly of old Brother Magnus who offered six-pence to anyone who would extract salt out of the sea-water in the harbour; and when one or two did it offered a silver watch to any boy who would extract sugar out of a turnip! I remember getting the milkman to bring me a turnip and wrapping it in a towel on the floor and pounding it with a hammer....

I am not recalling these things in pride, mind you, for though I am a well-read man who knows his Shakespeare and his Moore, and knows everything that is to be known about building and carpentry, I realize that as knowledge goes I possess only a modicum. And I know, too, that I am doing these good monks an injustice and doing injustice to those days that will not return again.

But it is another world, not only gone for ever now, but not to be recaptured even in memory. All I did and learned there was done and learned for the love of the thing. In the High School life and learning became and have ever since remained complicated by the impor-tunity of those two heritages of Adam, the conscience and the will. From that complicated world to look back on a world where these genii did not exist is to look into a blinding light.

Life there was a succession of dream-days which now — caught as I am in the icy splendour of the mind — I envy to tears because they were the only days of my life that were really lived. Then there were no such ambitious strivings as came later; no questionings, as in the conscience of the grown man, to annotate the joys of living by reminders of the seriousness of life. Then, far otherwise, all the seriousness of life was annotated by the sheer, unconscious joy of being simply alive. I was unaware of nakedness.

What of those wet southern days when few children dared to come to school and the feeling of comradeship among those that came was so great that we hated to return home? While the rain lashed the patched windows in the clerestory and we crowded over the fire to talk of the tawny rivers of the city rising in flood! When we rounded our cheeks and rolled our eyes and said Oooh! to the wind under the door! I could weep now because never again can I say Oooh! to the wind under the door. But then it was all sheer delight in the delights of Delight itself. And then there were days before breaking-up at summer-time, when all fear of inspectors was vanished, and we did nothing for days but clean the white ink-wells, and roll up the maps, and disclose on the walls behind them sudden stored blasts of light, and shoved dusters down one another's backs, and crushed closer than ever about the skirts of the

Brother to talk of our home, and our holidays, and their
homes and their holidays, and our future — which
meant next year — and theirs that meant, alas, so much
more. You looked back at the last moment at the crumb-
laden floors, and the dust under the desks, all empty, and
you felt the crumbs at the bottom of your school-sack
that suddenly having lost all its import smelt only of
vanished days; and you turned away as to a long exile.

It's the sense of wonder which is gone now, I suppose,
the capacity of enjoyment killed by too much thinking
of things instead of doing them. Even those casualties
from falling glass, or stones flung in yard-fights, even
they were welcome because you were led out by an
elder boy to be stitched or bandaged at the hospital, a
gorgeously terrifying experience during which you
wondered if you were going to die. These breaks
were typical of that school; it was a delight to be sent
making up the rolls, doing all the adding and sub-
tracting and compiling that the Head was too lazy to do
himself; to be sent out to the street just before roll-call
to see if any laggards were coming, in which case you
certainly told the wretch that Sloppy Dan would KILL
him when he got inside; magical to be sent in search of
a missing pupil down among the penthouse lanes of the
city, in and out of Featherbed or Cut-throat where the
shifts and shawls drying from window to window made
the colours of a canopy in a procession, and every dark
doorway under the thatch was shot by its blob of firelight to delay further your already lingering steps.

That was the school to which I went with my grandfather's help. And if it is a longwinded account I give of it I cannot help it, because he figured there in one of those incidents that shame me even to recall.

We were all — the whole upper school — all, that is to say, except the aisles, gathered for the singing lesson and there, in tiers, were the last rows standing on the desks, bawling away at the hymns we were to sing the next Sunday at Mass; when suddenly we noticed our Brother Angela blushing and stammering before us. The hymn wobbled. We on the desks, whose voices were cracked and who were the altos, saw him first. The tenors went on without us:

> 'To Jesus' heart all burn-ing
> With fervent lo'ohove fo-hor men,
> My-hy heart with fondest yearning . . .'

He stood by the entrance door and listened, his beard peaked, his hat — worst of all — on his head, his hand beating time.

'Who's th' ould lad?' the fellows around were asking.

'Jasus,' said one, 'it's Crone's ould fellow's ould fellow.'

'Look at Angela,' said another. 'He's hoppin' mad. God, Croney,' they said to me, 'you'll be murdered for bringing him here.' They were delighted to see me taken down a peg.

'I never brought him,' I protested furiously, but I

wished I could crawl under the desk as he advanced
and Angela went down to ask him what he wanted.
The whole school turned then.

'What do you want, sir?' says Angela.

'I sang that hymn — when I was a boy fifty-five
years ago,' said my grander. 'I heard it and I passing.
It's a moving hymn.'

'And what do you want, now?' asks Angela, red with
shyness.

'It's so lovely. Most edifying.'

And, my God, if he didn't begin to sing it with
Angela getting crosser and crosser at him, and trying
to edge him out of the door. Suddenly my grandfather
saw me.

'That's my grandson,' he said in a loud voice.

'Yes,' said Angela, 'do you want him? Corney
Crone.' he ordered. 'Come down.'

Before the school I climbed down.

'Go and show your grandfather the yards,' says
Angela, and I thought at the time that his diplomacy
was a finished thing.

'Sing that hymn for me, Corney,' orders my grander.

'Wouldn't you like to hear him outside?' pleaded
Angela.

'No,' insists my grander, and at once I smelt the
sup from him. 'Sing it, Corney,' he ordered.

'Go on,' said Angela, dying to get the scene over.
'"To Jesus' heart . . ." Go on, boy. Sing.'

'Sing,' says my grander crossly. 'Sing.'

' "To Jesus' heart . . ." ' Angela led me into it.

Under my breath I mumbled it, with my collar choking me and I sweating under my shirt.

'" . . . all burning
With fervent love for men,
My heart with fondest yearning
Shall raise each joyful strain.

While ages course along,
Blest be with lou-hou-dest so-hong"
. . . I forget.'
'Sing, you divil!' protests my grander.
'I forget.'
He raised it himself:

' "To Jesus with heart all bu-hurning,
With fervent lo-hove fo-hor me-hen . . ." '

He was enjoying it immensely — wallowing in it — actually crying when the door closed on us. But I hated him and contemned him from the bottom of my bloody heart. I sinned. I blasted him. I had no idea that such a sewer of words was in me and I ran from him all the way home. My next confession was an agony. That was the confession where I said:

'Forgive me, father, for I have sinned. Father, I said bad words.'

The priest was a bit deaf or drowsy for he said, 'What?'

I listed him six bad words — the usual words —

whereupon he threw me right out of the box, and I didn't go to confession for three months after. By that time I had said more bad words against my grander than I have said since in all my life.

Well, the place is gone, now; not a stone remains upon a stone, and a boot-factory in red-brick stands where it stood. A new, modern school replaces it, all white tiles and parquet, very anodyne and aseptic. That is all to the good but it is not that which gives it an advantage over the old place — it is beside fields and below it there are trees through which you see the flowing river with cows in the fields beyond. In our place there were a few ragged trees growing out of the gravel but not a blade of grass to be seen anywhere, and a school without a field is little better than a prison.

If I were a child again and both schools stood, to which would I go? If not to some sterner, more ambitious school than either of them? Certainly, if it is a matter of getting on in the world, to neither. For though that old ruin kept up by the cobwebs is a joke by comparison with the modern place, where there is no atmosphere, but where they have real equipment — real Bunsens and real gas where we had a painter's blowlamp that went on fire at every experiment and smashed every retort it tried to heat so that Magnus would say, 'Well, that's burst again, but I'll tell ye what would have happened if we could have done it ...' — still, both of them are very simple preparations for the business of 'getting on in the world'.

Even if you place more value on other things, on, say, 'the other world' — prefer Peace to Knowledge, Ignorance to Unrest, I do not know that that kind of school was ideal. Unless there is, indeed, a world where the tender and secret flowers of the heart can for ever blow and blow?

I can hear to-night beyond my window-curtains, as so many years ago I heard it often, the rain falling intensely from a townlit sky, the river mumbling in flood, the muddy city humming away to its sleep; and I hear a boy crying his evening paper against that windy rain. He is being raised as I was raised — another of the meek and humble of heart — thriving for his time on breast-pap. Through my heavy curtains, as he races past, a green ray from my lamp will fall on him. If he sees it as I saw it from the world of others, is he not, too, as I was,

> Doomed at last in pomp of power
> To bring his flower to light in pride,
> Its petals falling in a shower
> As when the Austers ride. . . .

> Ah, boy, bring not your flower to light,
> But keep it deep within its cave.
> Love is a girl that shuns the light.
> A fly-by-night. . . .

How can he? I could not. I had a grandfather and so has he, and poor boy, as I was, so is he — doomed to come from his Dark Cave out into the Jungle.

PART TWO

THE JUNGLE

I SHOULD have mentioned before that my mother had 'a voice', and not only had she a voice but she had a sister who also had 'a voice': and with that kind of folly that overtakes frugal but ambitious Irish homes like theirs (her father had kept one of those little sidestreet pubs where nobody ever goes) the two sisters had been sent to London to have their voices trained. Virginia, as my father was always telling people — he was a 'boasting' husband — had actually gone on to Paris and Milan, but my mother returned home after a single day in Paris, why we never knew. This singing, the one day in Paris — so often mentioned — and the mysterious sister in Milan, were most obnoxious to my grandfather. 'Bloody cod,' was his word for such foolishness. Just that, and no more.

Now, however, my ma's voice, such as it was, came in useful, together with her jolly ways, her lovely golden hair, and her six-children bosom : for she was always singing at charity concerts, and while her family were tearing wild at home, she would be in the wings with three priests around her, laughing and joking, or even joking with the other business-men who helped my miserable-faced father at these affairs. In this way she did for my father what he could never have done for himself — she made useful connections for him in

the way of business, and through her he became a
well-known figure in the city. She did something
else that angered my grandfather. She put ambitions
into my father until he, who had been content with
small but profitable job-contracts, now began to build
whole houses, even a terrace of houses, and she did not
rest until he began to think of using 'his connections'
to get contracts for churches and convents. It meant
endless quarrels with my grander as long as he
lived.

This search for 'connections' enlarged my world.
First there were the Hoares, whom we called the
Chaddys or Shaddys, after my great-aunt Charlotte,
an ancient creature, all black satin, snuff, and gold
chains, who lived with her married son, Tomeen, up
Lehenagh Hill, two or three miles outside the city and
so overlooking from afar off our smoky roofs. It was
a cold windy group of fields, part of the bastion roll of
hills that protect Cork from the wild sou'westers, and
I loved the place because I loved Tomeen and his son,
Dan Jo, and from every ditch I could see, after dark,
the cup of lights twinkling away and away below me.
My mother and father visited them only because
Tomeen was married to a Whitley, and in the Whitley
family there was a canon, and a reverend mother of a
rich order of nuns. They had no respect for the Hoares
themselves because Tomeen was only a cattle-buyer.

It is true that even when we first knew them both
father and son were already dwindling away their

substance like the froth of the river, regular harum-scarums who liked nothing better than to keep an open house with melodeon dances in the kitchen every night, and attend as many race-meetings as they possibly could. The great story of the pair of them was when they met face to face one morning coming out of opposite bedrooms in a Dublin hotel — of a day when Tomeen was supposed to be in Nenagh buying store-cattle and Dan Jo in Liverpool selling stock. Tomeen looked at his son and he said:

'Ha? So I have yeh caught? The Phoenix Park is what you're after, I suppose?' referring to the races.

Dan Jo, who guessed that it was also what his da was after, said humbly:

'Well, it is then. But, you see, I have a dead cert for the three-thirty.'

'Birdy Boy?' challenges his father, without thinking.

'It's not,' says Dan, and they began to whisper in a corner and the next thing they knew they were arguing across an oyster dinner in the Red Bank and across the well of a side-car as they bowled off to the Park.

In that kind of way they burned the candle at both ends; though, as I looked back at them now the only difference I see between them and us was that they lived more briefly in a brighter light. Now, Dan Jo is come down to a job with the County Council, and when you meet him he beats the side of the old trap and cries heartily: 'All I have left, bejase, out of the wreck.'

Though it is a good post, and like him to get it; the blooded horsefly!

Once or twice only did my grandfather visit the house. He disliked them. 'Ach, they have too much boasting!' And even though he had a relenting admiration for Dan Jo, the son, and would laugh at him and say, 'That fellow is a proper divil. Oh, a hardy boy!' — not even this much would he admit to my father who, after a night's talk in the parlour with Mrs. Hoare, would argue that 'On the maternal side the Hoares are very refined'. I never said much about that, but I did not agree with him. I could never forget what Dan Jo said to me once when I was patiently explaining to him the difference between a Gothic and a Roman arch. He had turned on me rudely and shouted into my face, 'Do you know what you'll do with your bloody Gothic arch? Well, I'll tell yeh!' And he did — a very coarse thing to say to a mere boy who was trying to be helpful!

I must admit this argument about who was and who was not refined came oddly from our house that was a kind of bedlam with six children tearing up and down the stairs all day long, or rolling like savages in the back-garden until it became a mere baldy patch of grass. And if, sometimes, we were as neat as the bishop's children who walked out every day hand in hand with their governess or their nurse, we were more often as ragged as boys from the Cat Fort lanes; until I do not know whether my mother the more shamed us with the slovenly way she reared us, or we her when we crowded around her in the street and she with some neighbour, quivering all over with sham politeness and grandeur.

Once, for example, the dean's wife, whom we called *Nuff-noff* because she stammered, met Maurice and Michael in their velvet clothes and she rashly asked them, on the spur of the moment, to a children's Christmas party. They went; but they never went again. For they had formed a habit of writing away to English firms for free samples of everything from foreign stamps to cures for reducing the bust, all of which they used to sell for pennies to the people about the place. At this party of the dean's they decided that there would be a good market for their wares and unhappily they took with them, among other things, a sample of a quack cure for the stammer. They sold it to poor *Nuff-noff*. . . .

Even Vicky, my sister who afterwards to our surprise became a nun, was often in disgrace. She was kept back a year from confirmation because on the day when she should have been confirmed, with the church crowded and the bishop on his throne, her voice was heard in shrill argument with another girl. It finally rose into a bawl and she was heard to say, 'Your sister's drawers are always coming down'. A nun whipped her from her place as you might snatch a wasp from a window-pane, and in the sight of everybody she was bustled from the church.

Still and all, in spite of my grander's disapproval of the refined Hoares we continued to visit them — even after the sad occasion of Virginia's return to Cork; and my grander's only retort was to take me out, as often, to Sherlock's or the Condoorums: though, there again, it was our connection with the disreputable Condoorums that people chose to observe and remember to our discredit. As for the Sherlocks — well, that is my story.

THEY lived — old Sherlock was a water-bailiff — a
goodly step from us out the valley of the Lee, snug in a
weather-slated house sunk in trees beneath the hill-road
that climbs behind it at that point, so near to the low
wall that you could drop a pebble into the roof-leads
and get an aerial view in ground-plan of the cow below
lumbering into the stables. On the river-level the
ancient fields were heavy with clay, good enough for
sheep or cattle but too wet and sandy to be ploughed,
and so filled with reeds in the lags, and ragwort,
thistles, asphodel, or even bog myrtle on the long
narrow flats (there is the width of one field between
road and river for ten miles out of Cork, and the hill-
slopes all the time by your side) that they held the
dust of the road by day, and by night the smell of the
wild plants and the stagnant ditches. But, except that
that barrenness reminds me of the ancient quality of
the place, almost demanding, as it were, the emphasis
of a ruined castle, what really dilates in the remembering mind is the drowsy meadow-sleep that hung over
it in the afternoons, or the rainy wind that seemed to
ravel the river until it was permanently combed like
the face of an old man: for a solid sameness about the
house and within it, a lovely sense of 'always', that
appeared to resist, even to ignore, change, is the true

quality of that part of the valley of the Lee in which they lived.

It is one of the most common types of Irish homes, and to visit them is less like paying a visit than making a pilgrimage, so powerful is their atmosphere of family life. You knocked: old Sherlock greeted you, or any one of the boys, or Elsie or one of the guests — in terms of welcome that were so constant as to be like a ritual: and there were no conditions — they even waited until the last visitor was gone before starting the family rosary, rather than impose that much on him; but somehow or other immediately you entered the house an invisible finger touched your lips. They had an immense circle of friends, so that the parlour was always full, and these friends, as by agreement, had fallen in so completely with the Sherlock way of life that to have differed even slightly with their inarticulated fellowship would either have been an outrage, or (more likely) a joke, the best in the world.

Not that they didn't argue, passionately, even angrily, bawling at one another. The very first Sunday night I went there, with my mother and father, we walked into a terrific argument about the rapacity of the Irish priests — a subject very important to them since they had, already, one priest in the family, Father Arty, and one young man within four years of the end of his fifteen years' preparation to be a Jesuit, and a boy, Tom, at Maynooth, as well as two girls who were nuns. Arthur John Coppinger was there, the chairman of the county council, a little ball of a man and a great admirer of theirs, and a Franciscan priest who gurgled with joy at their attack on the seculars.

'Still and all,' old Sherlock was saying, hunched up in his chair like a leprechaun, a pipe half-way into his mouth, his hat on his head (as always, even indoors), and it was so big that it made his face like a farthing, 'still and all, the priests must live.'

'Yes,' cried Elsie, with such spirit that I at once loved her for it, 'but so must the people. Forty pounds for a wedding! It's daylight robbery.'

The Franciscan growled comically.

'The only funeral I ever attended, do you know what I got? A pair of slippers and five shillings. That was in England. And I had to give them up to the Superior. He wore the slippers, the ruffian!'

'There you are!' stormed Elsie, furiously. 'There's the English mission. But here the priests bleed the people.'

'You couldn't live for long,' said Coppinger dryly, 'on two slippers and five bob.'

'It's two extremes,' said the old man, jigging his knee uncomfortably. 'Now twenty pounds wouldn't be bad.'

'Twenty pounds!' cried his son Tom, from Maynooth. 'Nobody ever gets twenty pounds.'

'They do, they do, they do,' cried Elsie, flashing.

'They don't, they don't, they don't,' he mocked.

'They do.'

'They don't.'

'They do.'

'They don't.'

They battled crescendo and ended in a roar of laughter. All night, cases were cited and contrary cases were cited. Like all good and pious Catholics, who really love their priests, they scourged the clergy. Even Tom, the cleric, still young, was willing to believe five pounds for a wedding would be a great deal. Only the father who knew what it cost to make a priest defended the system: the end of it was the departure of the guests, home through the fields, still arguing, and doubtless the family rosary murmuring in the room we had left.

And yet, they had no interest in money, and were so obtuse about worldly things that my mother, after several efforts, dropped them in disgust. They simply could not understand her hints.

It took me years to see that these Sunday-night arguments never touched on anything basic. It was, no doubt, the price of peace in a quick-witted family: even if it did mean that they could never, not if they argued to Doomsday, alter a jot of what they traditionally believed. Once, perversely, towards the end of a discussion on heredity:

'Is there freewill even in heaven?' I demanded.

'Of course there is,' said the old man, jigging away.

'Then,' I countered, 'there must be sin in heaven, too; otherwise freewill is never exercised and doesn't exist.'

Silence followed that pronouncement. I had broken the unwritten code. The next time I went Elsie triumphantly came out with:

'I wrote to Father Arty about freewill in heaven. He said, "There *is* freewill but you wouldn't want to exercise it." He also said I must be reading bad books or keeping bad company.'

They laughed with pleasure at that — I had been rebuked, with authority and with good humour, and everything was as it always had been. I think it is typical of them and him that my grandfather loved them. They took his 'heathenism' with a light touch.

'We know, Mister Crone, that your knees are crusted from saying secret rosaries.'

He cackled with joy at that, at its flattery of simultaneous belief in his wickedness and his goodness.

I loved the place from the very first; and it appeared so far away to my short legs that to my long legs the journey still had the charm of a pilgrimage. And when I became aware of Elsie Sherlock and she imparted to me, as to me alone, by a thousand casual words, the ways of the river and the long meandering valley, it all opened up and out before me, beyond sight, as a river of the imagination like those rivers in medieval pictures that meander into mountains. She did it with stories of poachers, or stories of floods when the water lapped the doorstep and the plain was a lake that in its subsidence became wrack-strewn as a beach after storm. You can have no idea how my brain dilated when, over the fire, with the wind in the chimney and the trees howling, old Sherlock took a pencil one night and made a rough diagram to explain the tides to me, distinguishing between Neap and Spring. He drew it like this, saying the words as he drew:

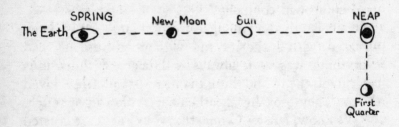

'Now! There you are, Corney. There's the earth and the water around it. The double attraction of sun and new moon gives you spring tides. But, d'y' see, with the first quarter of the moon, the sun is pulling *against* the moon. So spring high-tides are very high. Now, in January, say, when both sun and moon are near the earth, not to mention with rains on top of everything, we get the divil's own lot of water down the river and up the river. If you stood at that window now, of a night of full moon, in January, you wouldn't see a thing from here to Carrigrohane but black trees growing out of white water. And the same thing up the valley for miles.'

He turns then from his paper to point to the foot-stool by the fire, or a chair, or a front of a piano, all flotsam of those floods, commemorations of many winters. And then back to the earth with a bang — Elsie talking of the familiars of her childhood, from bad women who slept on the banks at night, in summer, like the Black Prince, to the tinkers who camped in the quarry; or their human clocks like Tony Lambkin, or Mail Dog, or Canadian Beans who 'hodded it' out along the banks every morning at regular hours to their pint at the Angler's Rest — each one with his legend wrapping him like a coat out of a folk-tale, even though his legend might be as humble as that of Mail Dog whose mother wore his breeches before he got up in order to warm the seat.

Inevitably, whether she talked like that, or of the dawns when, as she milked her cow, the plain was so thick with ground mist that you could not distinguish water from grass, or of nights when you heard nothing but the cackle of a bird or the gurgling weirs, she became for me the figure of what she loved. She was no more than fifteen when that happened. I was seventeen and a half.

We leaned over a gate and I saw a long dark hair caught in the splintered wood.

'That's one of mine,' she said, eyeing me archly.

'Oh, but yours is . . . is . . .' And I was immediately caught in its flaming coils. She laughed, and drew out of the wood the long strand from a horse's mane.

'And see how coarse it is!' she said, with a glint in her wild eyes.

I ran the thread through my fingers. She ran, laughing, before I could attempt a comparison.

She was never a beauty and she didn't grow any more beautiful with the years — too wide in the hips, not tall enough, her chin undershot, her nose too softly turned; and her throat, though it might in time make her swan-proud as a Roman mother was, when I knew her, too full for girlhood. But her hair — ribbed fire and smoke. Her waist — a greyhound. And her smile — wide, oddly twisted, quizzically mothering, asking you for everything that you could give. It curled into her apple-cheeks, and what with her faintly-furrowed brow and her wistful eyes, made you want to squeeze the life out of her. I have heard other girls wonder afterwards why men were so taken by her, saying that she had a poor figure, though she had lovely hair and good teeth, and so on and so forth — but of the power in that smile, its innocence, its quivering at the corners, the attraction of its softness, they had no idea. It was, at once, a sensuous and an innocent mouth because not until the end did she let any worldly knowledge — the thing which makes us unmysterious because alike — destroy the wonder of her ignorance and her simplicity.

The second time I met her she was unmooring the tarry boat they had at the end of the field. I had left my grander to Mr. Sherlock. When she saw me she turned swiftly and said I must do it. Suspecting something, I would not, whereupon she began to push me and I to resist. It was a narrow path between the trees and the river-edge (a right-of-way all along by the river) and as somebody came walking by she had to step forward into the boat; when I drew back I saw the great hole in her stocking. She was furious with me for seeing it, and as we rowed down the river we quarrelled lightly. The next time after that, for perversity she just wore no stockings at all and as she stepped saucily into the boat the water, radiant under the drooping sycamores, shone cool on the muscles of her legs.

'Was the hole in the stocking a threat or a promise?' I said; and again we quarrelled as we rowed.

With such little notes we built up our song, until one spring, at the time of the gales that come with the equinox, the moon full and racing and the winds tearing through the creepers about the house, I dared ask her to show me the woods she so often boasted of; secret woods, she said, not known to city-folk like me. But she would not and she would not, because they were her secret woods, and she again said how lovely they were and what you found in them, and I pointed over the valley to those trees and those trees and along the hills to those trees, and each time she just scoffed and said her wood was a secret wood. To be sure, and she smiled her quizzical smile, if I happened to be there some evening when she happened to be going to it she could hardly stop me from following her, but as for promising ... So I happened to be there and she happened to be going to it and she led me over the hillbrow, past the little graveyard that crowns it, and by winding roads into a little pine-wood from whose opening at the far side other valleys opened wide and distant away up into Ireland, off under the wild blowing dusk of the evening and the risen moon that had maddened the tides. Unacknowledged though it all was, we had made our first secret tryst.

Finally the day came, late that summer — it was my last year at school — when Christy Tinsley and my grandfather and I went out to the Sherlocks one morning to gather mushrooms, and in the heat of the high noon the old man went in and left us and her brother Tom resting in the shade of a chestnut in the centre of the vast field by the house. I strolled away idly and Christy followed after me, and when I returned she was lying on her back, half asleep, her heavy hair like rust in the grass, one white hand outstretched, fingering her brother's curls where he lay beside her.

'Christy's gone after more mushrooms,' I said to Tom. 'Persistent as usual.'

He looked at the basket, and went zigzagging away. In the hot drowse of the noontide the cattle were all under the hedges, heaving their flanks. Overhead the tree hummed loudly with bees or bluebottles. I lay down again and her arm, upright from the elbow just as when her brother lifted it, sank slowly until the fingers touched my hair. They wound into it and lay still. I looked at her. She seemed to be asleep, but I touched the hollow of her white arm inside the elbow and I said, 'Elsie'. She murmured, 'Yes, Tom', and began to play with my hair. Again I stroked her arm and said her name and again she said a sleepy 'Yes, Tom', but I saw her lips quivering, and she was gazing up at the deeps of greenery quite fresh-eyed. I said, 'I'm fond of you, Elsie'. She said, 'I'm fond of you'. Then she turned her head and cried, 'Oh, it's you, Corney!' Blushing, she jumped up and ran through the grass. Then she looked back and laughed. That blush is what I mean by the 'wonder of her ignorance' — there would have been no blush if she had been a cold coquette: and yet she had wanted to tell me she loved me, and she saw to it that she did.

It annoyed me, sometimes. When we were friends and I thought it time she came out of herself she still remained — I do believe she remained as long as I knew her — looking out at me through the lattices. Even that night in her secret wood — as she appalled me long after by confessing — while I held one hand, the other, in her pocket, clutched her rosary-bead for protection. It made me feel, too, that I must be very careful with her. I once lent her a novel that contained one page that was a bit too passionate. I had to mark that page and tell her to skip it. And when I took back the book and said:

'Did you read that page?'

'Oh, no, Corney,' she assured me. 'I wouldn't when you said not to.'

That was the sort of girl she was. So, then, feeling she might be imagining worse things, I gave it back to her and bade her read it.

'What did you think?' I asked.

She just laughed. Her innocence was extraordinary.

There were two other places where we used to meet, and one was when, with Christy and my grander, we tore after the warring factions who turned the city into a bedlam at every political meeting. For, however much her father grumbled and disapproved, she loved to watch the stones flying, and the stub-legged police crashing their batons on flesh and bone, and women screaming and the tar-barrels sending their black smoke into the sky. She and I were mad Parnellites in those days and when we shouted his name as we swayed back and forth in the mêlée, we felt every shout as a blow for the old cause; it was a triumph for us if we saw old Phil, my grander, up on the wagonette, his badge in his coat, his stick waving down to the surging sea of faces, and behind him in his place the pale face and the burning eyes of The Chief. The other place I met her, and the only place I was certain to have her to myself, was when she and I walked home of mornings from early mass. For I had found that she came in along the fields every fine morning, and though it was a long walk for me, as often as I could I took to going there too. Her church was up in the polite suburban backroad of Sundays Well where on one side were high gardens sloping uphill to meet their houses, and on the other were polished doorways whose low gardens sloped to the river-brim. Between those river-houses we would catch little views of the city far below us, diminished to a town, divided by the river that was dwindled to a stream, and the roofs falling downhill or rising in leaf on leaf to those other hills by Lehenagh I knew so well. When the silent suburban road petered out and we came down to the first bridge over the Lee where I must go my way back around into the flat of the city, we would be awkward over our leave-taking, shy with unacknowledged affection, and part in the end so secretively that we would not even turn to see one another going away. It was one of the few advantages of our kind of house that I could do such things. Vicky did tease me with questions about this sudden piety, or my grander would say something like, 'Well, there's some good in everything, it seems — even religion'. But my father and mother said nothing and noticed nothing.

It was on these morning walks, when the city was not yet quite awake and the fields were yet dew-misted and a fog slept over the river, that — as if it were the time to catch secrets — I began to see how much Elsie was really fashioned by her parents as I by mine, made part and parcel of them, almost without a will.

I wanted her to come with me on a certain night up to the Hoares. (In the way lovers have we were always trying to exchange our worlds like that. She had taken

me to her wood. I had brought her to see the timber-
yard and the Bishop's Marsh. She had shown me her
private nooks on the river. I now wanted her to see the
city at night from Lehenagh and to talk to Tomeen
and Dan Jo.)

She leaned her full bosom over the river-wall and
scraped dust into the water below.

'I know it's all nonsense,' she cried, 'but I'm not
supposed to stay out after dark.'

'You would be with me and my mother and my da.'

'Yes, but there would be all sorts of people there.'

'Bad people?' I teased.

She scratched at my hand and then she sighed and
puckered her brows and threw her arm wide over the
river.

'I know it's silly. But you have no *idea*, Corney.
I'm not allowed to go *anywhere*. It's *sickening*!'

She always spoke with immense emphasis — no *idea*
— *anywhere* — *sickening*, and her nose and lips made the
most comical movements. 'Don't you see,' she
laughed, 'that I'm the Queen of Sheba. I'm made of
gold. I'm a pound of butter in the sun. My daddy is a
water-bailiff and he has watching on the brain. He
thinks I'm a salmon and all Cork is trying to poach
me.'

'Like an egg? Not merely the golden goose, but the
golden egg as well.'

I pulled her golden curls. 'Corney!' She slapped
me and looked warningly behind her at the sleeping

white cottages and the one or two villa houses whose blinds were still drawn. One window creaked up and a girl's hands came out under the sallow blind and the woodwork to lift it farther.

'Come, Elsie. You came with me to the wood. Your daddy needn't know.'

We strolled on idly. As usual we slowed up as we neared the bridge.

'No, Corney,' she insisted. 'You don't realize what it is to be born into a good family.'

I let the implication go. She went on:

'Take my brother Tom that's in Maynooth to be a priest. He used to get up when he was at school, at three o'clock every morning and kneel down in his room and pray. That was before poor mammy, God rest her, died, and she used lie awake worrying over him. When he was stopped praying he wouldn't go back into bed but lie on the bare boards. She used steal in and find him asleep there and draw the blanket over him, terrified for fear he would wake and know that she knew. It was terribly cruel on his health. And twice a week, hail, rain or snow, poor mammy herself used go in to her confraternities in town. I don't believe she ever committed a mortal sin in her life.'

'That's two saints,' I teased, 'in the one family, and you make three.'

She was cross at that, so I hastened on with:

'Elsie, for goodness sake, you'll be going into a convent next. You're almost in one as it is, in that

81

house of yours, cut off from everything. I don't like you when you're being saintly. I prefer you when you don't wear any stockings.'

But my joking only offended her more, so she walked on quickly. As we leaned over the bridge parapet she threw out her hands, palm upwards.

'It isn't going to melodeon dances keeps a person from being a saint. I'm not even . . .'

'Look here, Elsie, there's no such thing as a saint nowadays. There's only people who want to be in the world and people who want to be out of it. Take my father, for instance.'

Instinctively she condemned him by starting to defend him before I had said a word; but I went on:

'He's a builder. He's a very pious man. He's at eleven o'clock mass every morning. He's always giving us good advice. He's miserable with piety. Yet he extended a church at Togher last year and now there's a crack down the gable from the finial to the damp-course. Bad materials, that's all it is. Now, I don't blame him — it's all business, but what I mean to say is it's all very well for Blessed Bernadette or Saint Francis. They weren't in business. What I want to see canonized is a jobbing builder!'

She sighed.

'I often *thought* of that. I wish there wasn't *any* business at all in the world. I'm glad my daddy isn't in *business*.'

'If it wasn't for the poachers breaking the law he

wouldn't make any living. Even he makes profits out of the sins of others,' I laughed.

'Oh, money, money, money. It's *all* money. I *hate* it.'

'Well, you don't want to get out of the world, do you?'

'I do *not*. But look at the old women in the Kerry hills; *they're* in the world and yet I'm sure they're *all* saints. Look,' she raced on, 'at my uncle in Dripsey. When he was young he used walk in there along the hills to the Butter Market,' her arm flung up to the hill behind and beyond us, 'all along the Pike Road with the butter on his back to sell and out again in the evening with a half sack of flour or meal. I have a great *gra* for him and he is one of the best-living men you could meet, never a word of complaint, and he had a hard, hard life with his sons growing. I won't let you say a word against him.'

'I was never out there,' I admitted. 'We're real townies.'

She had made me lonely, talking like that. She made me feel she had many friends and relatives who loved her and whom she loved. I took her hand and patted it and whether there were any windows watching or not, I lifted it and kissed it.

'You're coming with me to the dance,' I ordered.

'I'm, not. Anyway it's the Feast of Saint Anne. She's been very useful to us. I said a *novena* to her for Tom's examination and he passed it at the head of his class.'

'Oh, botheration to Saint Anne. Do you want me or Saint Anne? Or is it a case of "Saint Anne, Saint Anne, get me a man?" And that you want us both?'

Acerb when driven to it, she said:

'You have a good opinion of yourself, haven't you?'

'I wish *you* had of yourself. If I asked you to a party to meet three priests, or something, you'd come all right. That would be an *honour*! Eh?'

'Not on the Feast of Saint Anne.'

'Oh, to hell with Saint Anne!'

She whirled from me. She pulled her old brown hat, one of her father's felt cast-offs, down on the side of her curls, cocked up her chin, and strode her martial stride along the last bit of pavement out to her fields. We did not talk for a month after.

As I crossed moodily over the bridge I saw old Condoorum come limping down to the river in his soiled bawneen with his long shovel on his shoulder to begin a day's digging for sand and gravel in the river-bed. A few gulls swept down around his black hat and then settled snugly into the river. As I looked down at him, walking indifferently into the shallow water, and dragging the chain of his sand-boat — a stooped vulture — I began for the first time to question the old miser's friendship with my grandfather. So, now, when that dirty affair between those two old men comes grinding back out of the past, like his chain along the beach, to break again everything that seemed so simple and easy, my father's ambitions, my mother's vanities, the unfortunate Virginia, and my own boy-hood — so cruelly that I hate even in memory to see it break once more — I see him like a lanky bird of prey. He comes out in the dim hour before dawn to catch the little things of the fields; and with him, always, there is a small white figure in the distance floating away out of sight under the trees. From that on between the little round figure in the distance and the angular old man below (as between her world and my people's, and between her world and the Hoares's) there was a perpetual challenge. Even as my love for her and hers for me was not a surrender but a war.

III

His real name was not Condoorum but Lucey, though as to why Condoorum, all anybody ever knew was that his own tribe invented the name as they invented names for every one of themselves and all the neighbours about. So, they had christened themselves many times over until they were the Dins, because Condoorum was a Denis or a Din Lucey: the Trojans, because they worked so hard: the Muds, because they made their money raising sand from the river-bed: and many other names whose origin, like Condoorum, was as misty as the faint ridge of untranslatable names that rise lowpeaked in the distance beyond the earlier reedy and invisible windings of the river by which they lived.

When we knew them they were not so utterly poor as when they first came down from the hills, down out of a wild windswept corner of the Musheraghs called Fornocht, meaning stark-naked. Old Mr. Sherlock told us that when he first knew them their mother was often seen in her bare feet, browned by sun and rain, carrying on her back great sacks of mash from the brewery to feed the pigs: or bags of spent hops for the strawberry-beds whose fruit scented the hillock behind their cottage. They were so poor, he said, that they were of the class of paupers about whom people, mystified that they can live at all, say that they must have secret hoards and be as rich as Croesus.

If old Condoorum did actually in time make money, it was his growing litter that made it. For if he was the Triton of the Lee they were his cherubs and went with him to the river from early mist to the silences of dusk. Even in my time you could see the last of them floating with him in his flat-bottomed boat out to the shallows, where between them they worked the long-handled shovel from dawn to dark like a machine; when he had shifted a load behind his cabin the cartload was at once carted into the city to some builder. We bought all his sand and gravel from the time my grander began to know him.

By that time he had put every man Jack of his sons to a trade, until he had a bricklayer, a joiner, a carpenter and a mason, and the rest on their way to be stone-cutters, plasterers, cabinet-makers, a slater or a painter according to their talent and his need. He had two girls: they remained what they brutally called pot-wallopers, to the end.

Slowly he began to rise out of his poverty, though he was all the time as grey of face and hair as an old water-rat, so dirty and miserable in his soiled bawneen and his patch-layered trousers and his unshaven face that you might in pity offer him a penny. He would have taken it, and he would have thanked you with an extraordinarily gentle smile. My grander said the man was a hero, he worked so manfully for his family. In all the time I knew him I saw only one soft touch in him — he was very fond of birds and he would bring scraps of food down to the river for the gulls to swoop at: you often saw a line of them on his gunwale when he worked on the river. As for his clan, they would skin a flea for the hide of it in the way of business, but it was, as we say, 'given up to them' that no poor man ever passed their cottage without getting a good meal or an old coat, given with an outrageous amount of up-braiding that anyone should be so neglectful of himself as to go hungry or cold.

My grander met him quite accidentally through Arthur John Coppinger, and from that date Condoorum began to borrow money from my father in order to start building on his own account, and later, in secret, went into partnership with my grandfather.

It was all such a small kind of thing at first that you could hardly call it building and my father called it patching. But within four or five years of his first meeting with my grandfather he was already clear of all his debts to us and was making a new income of his own. This was when my father was being pushed by my mother into church-building, to the rage of my grander, and there would be nightly arguments about the policy of the firm and the wisdom of my grander's old-fashioned ways and the cunning of Condoorum who was in his turn following them out.

I would sit between them in front of the fire, holding hands with my 'simple' brother, Robert, who stared gob-open into the flames, his head jigging in a Saint Vitus's dance: in the dining-room we could hear Maurice and Michael and Barty and Vicky murmuring over their school-lessons. I would look eagerly from father to grandfather, for I was to go into the office when I was seventeen and I took all their discussions very seriously. Besides these were nights when we were truly a family, just like the Sherlocks.

'Well,' my da would say, sucking hollow-cheeked at the tip of his very long-stemmed pipe, 'it's all right to begin small. But you must extend! That's the idea — extend!' Taking out his pipe to point meticulously at his father.

'Of course, John!' my mother would agree, as she threaded a needle under the lamp or looked around it to glare at my grander.

'Little by little makes big,' the grander would counter heavily, crossly. 'Small money accumulates. But to pour money into a big building-scheme, it's, it's . . .' He threw his hands up and puffed with his lips. 'Mind you,' he cried, 'you might get it back! You might. But it's gone until you do get it back. With a small scheme your money is always there drawing interest.'

'Sha!' from my father's nose. 'Sha! What if you get it back and doubled?'

'If? If?' beating the armchair.

'Didn't you, father, the first day you put a couple of quid into a pigsty, have to risk all you had? If I get this contract from Canon Whitley for the new Blarney church — no talking outside about this, Corney: four walls around us and all to that — on my tender of two thousand pounds. . . .'

'I've known men,' implored the old man, ruffling his hair with both hands and gasping out with shut eyes as if he were choking, 'to tender for County Council schemes and the day they got that tender they could have resold it at ten per cent, and before the job was done, what with sites, and labour, and clauses in the contract ... My God, boy, have sense! Have sense! Look at this man Condoorum, now. . . .'

The voice with which my mother says, 'Oh, John!' to my father, and leans back in her armchair into the dusk, is not to be described. My da leans forward patiently:

'Now, father,' he says, 'let me tell you a story. When you sent me as a young lad to Cork I was great friends with two men still alive — Tim Callaghan, the walker in Grant's, and Georgie Philpot, who was the only boy in Brother Burke's Trades School could beat me at the high jump.'

In surprise I asked:

'Were *you* good at the high jump, da?'

'The best out,' my grander would say. 'He won them decanters there behind yeh — damn the bit ever went into them' (this with a glance at my mother), 'at the Drapers' Sports when he was sixteen.'

'I did, so. I wasn't bad at all — if I kept it up. But I had to work too hard. But anyway, myself and Tim and Georgie used go every morning at seven o'clock out the Lee Road to that well, it's there yet, under the graveyard by Sherlock's. I used bring the cup. It was one you brought from Skibbereen, father. We'd drink a cup of cold water each, and we'd walk back, smart and steady, to eight mass in Saint Francis's. Now,' pipe-stem stabbing, 'that was the favourite subject between us: how so many men never realize that they must always and always keep on extending their business if they want to rise in the world.

'Well, what happened? Only myself followed out the wise course. Tim stayed on and on in Grant's until he became a walker. He never got a step farther for all his walkin'; he was out for security, if you please! What happened Georgie? He made a grave mistake — he *began* by extending. He had high notions, do you see, like the mountaineering goat. He launched out into a big shop of his own before he was one half ready for it. And, would you believe it, I seen him the other day outside the Victoria Hotel on the gutther, with a little handtruck, and his shirt out through his elbows, and he cadging from the English travellers to be let drive their baskets of samples from shop to shop for a few bob. He saw me, and he turned away from me. And I didn't pretend to see him. The poor divil wouldn't like it, do you see? No, I say and I say it again, begin small and then extend. 'Of course', dusting the ash from his pants, 'Georgie was always a bit too fond of the drop.'

'Ach! Sure! Your friend Callaghan — I know him well — a poor oinseach without a bit of go in him —

he's no example for anyone. But look at Condoorum, now, piling it up and piling it up. I *know* it. I *talk* to him . . .'

'For God's sake, father, leave Condoorum out of it! If it wasn't for that ould miser's sand and gravel I wouldn't come in a donkey's bray of him.'

'Yes,' I interposed. 'Our firm is in a strong position, grandfather!'

'We're living in a substantial house,' nods my da to him.

'The district might be better,' said I to him, 'but it's as well not to make too much ostentation, do you see?'

'We're making the finest connections,' says my mother. 'People like Mr. Coppinger, Chairman of the County Council, Canon Whitley. . . .'

'But, man, man, man, man, it's a question of £ *s. d.* This man Condoorum, do you realize it, has made, I compute, lemme see, gimme that paper . . .'

Scribbling with the wet butt of a carpenter's pencil follows here, while my mother raises her eyebrows around the lamp at my da and my da's lean fingers wave it all away. He goes on talking to me as if it was all settled long ago:

'Corney, my son, I'm looking to you, now, when you grow up, for to continue my policy.'

'I'll consider it very carefully,' I would promise him.

'My God Almighty,' the old man shouts while my mother tut-tuts over her sewing at the expression,

'Do you realize it that at three per cent, a conservative estimate, this man has already made five thousand pounds of a capital sum. Five . . .'

Then the final word — always the final word, from my da, restrained until the very end of his patience:

'Father, let's make clean money.'

The moustaches fly back over my grander's ears, his fingers dash their knuckles through his beard, he mutters, cries, 'Cod, man, bloody cod', and my da quietly goes on with his ancient joke:

'Cod's ways aren't our ways. Neither are Condoorum's. You know I met the canon to-day in Patrick Street? He thinks he can get permission from the bishop to start building soon.' And so on, while my grander leans back re-totting the figures on the paper and paying no attention to these grand plans, and probably doing other sums about the scheme he had privately started with Condoorum and that was to have given us all such a grand surprise one of those days.

It did. From the books which are the history of our rise and fall it is all made clear now. He had borrowed four hundred pounds from the bank (not his own bank) which he easily could without saying a word to my da, the firm being still in his name, 'Philip Crone and Sons'. With the better part of this secret loan he bought a plot of land not far from our own house. He then egged on Condoorum to borrow another four hundred from my da, and to go partners in building four small houses there. The whole thing was fantastically unbusinesslike, for no partnership agreement was drawn up; but these jobbing builders, for one thing, had rule-of-thumb minds, and hated lawyers, and, for another, Condoorum held the money, knew my grander was doing all this in a secret way, and above all, had something at the back of his own mind that only came out afterwards. They were too clever by half, the pair of them.

At first all went to plan and the four houses began to rise in the small square which still stands and bears a stone plaque inset with our name and date: but as soon as my da found that Condoorum was building, as he said, 'up to his own cheek', he flew into a furious rage and at once demanded back his four hundred pounds. Condoorum might have been able to do it, and, perhaps, borrowed the money elsewhere, if in his mean way he had not bought a long-desired slum tenement and started to re-build it, callously leaving my grander with four unfinished houses on his hands and a secret debt of four hundred pounds to the bank. All he did was to implore my grander to make my father hold his hand: and then he calmly went on with his slum-house. The four houses, he knew, would await his pleasure; and there was quick money in slums.

For a year the four wretched houses remained unfinished, and they gave great pleasure to my father who passed them daily and referred to them nightly, saying:

'Well, there's Condoorum for yeh, with his piling it

up and piling it up, aw? Piling up interest to me, the foolah!'

By the end of that year I had taken over the books from my grandfather, and so was in the secret; knowing that four hundred pounds of our money was piling it up and piling it up' with the bank, I would look across at him. He would say, weakly, with a glance of appeal at me:

'I don't see us getting that church from Canon Whitley, yet?' — and start doing sums on his cuff.

IV

THAT was the way of things when, at the beginning of April and well into the season of Lent, my mother's sister Virginia returned on a visit to Cork. She had married wealth in London, and was now Mrs. Virginia de Wolfe. She came with trunks and trunks of clothes, astonishing us by her grand ways and gracious manner, a handsome and mature woman, dark as a grape in bloom. My mother, when she kissed her in the hall, declared that she had never realized how lovely she was. When they had gone upstairs my father murmured to himself, 'most refined' and began to ask us who would be good (not, I noticed, 'good enough') to meet her. To my sister Vicky she was a goddess. My brothers were afraid of her. She swept me off my feet. My grander tried hard to be cold and not look at her — but he couldn't: she so held him that not for a year did he dare make his bitter joke about de Wolfe and the sheep. When he made it he was sorry, for my da, as usual, stole it from him and played on it with talk of black sheep and bald rams and about my grander being the real wolf, and himself being the boy in the story until nothing but a bitter quarrel would end it.

She was so kind as well as lovely that it is no wonder she impressed my grander, whom, in turn, she liked from the first. It was because she liked him, I think, that she found out all his ways, his ways of staying up late; and rising at dawn to kill the slugs in the bit of a back-garden; or walk alone before breakfast out beyond the Lough of Cork into the fields. She felt the knot that was hidden inside him — what she called to 'the damp of the grave in his bones'. So, discovering at once that I rose for early mass, she began to rise at the hour when from her elbow in bed she saw the sun hit the convent spire and light the green fields across the city, with the angelus tinkling to wake the nuns. And she actually brought him, the 'heathen', with myself and Elsie to Lenten mass every single morning.

I did not know, then, whether to be glad or angry that she broke in on those morning walks with Elsie. She was most pious and went to the altar frequently, and this so pleased me that the surge of emotion, almost an incipient vomit, used to make me hide my face in my palms to see her come up the aisle, her hands tipped and her lashes on her cheeks. The other few worshippers used to look at her, too, in a kindly and edified admiration, as they well might, for with her dark eyes, her warm skin, and, lovely aberration of beauty, her fair-flaxen hair in coils under her hat, she had the colouring of a viola or pansy.

And yet, like Elsie, she was not a perfect beauty. Her nose was a cocked nose, as if the modeller had tipped it with his thumb. Her smile, though it was a curve of delight about her fine teeth and vanished delicately, like Elsie's smile, into her cheek, was created too often and too firmly. It suggested not motherliness, as Elsie's did, but the strongminded kindness of a Medusa. But she had one great attraction — the height of her body and its movements, smooth as if she walked on water. To her finger-tips she had that flowing quality, and when she sat and drew her dress over her shoes, to the mere tips, all in one gesture, it was like the sinking of a wave.

Not only did she take the old man out of himself but she helped to fit him back into himself again, arranging his great long attic until it was as pretty as a schoolgirl's den, green paint on the woodwork, cream curtains, maroon rugs, and talking with him for hours, there, late into the night. And for others she loved to arrange things — pouring dresses on my mother who took them with a kind of terror of delight at putting so much grandeur on her back. My da responded by buying a little curricle with two ponies, and there were visits to the Hoares, and out to Canon Whitley at Blarney, and even a picnic on a fine spring day under the budding trees along the valley of the Lee; and then, at home, high-teas to which the 'quality' came — a painter-and-decorator with the rainbow on his wrist, a jeweller with a horseshoe pin in his cravat, grocers with the teadust in their cracked nails, a hosier, purblind from the shirt-festooned dusk of his shop, and the usual stray Franciscan or Dominican priest. (Seculars, being more worldly and more free, always came to dinner.) My mother and father were delighted, feeling they were 'in the swim' at last. My grander, for good reasons of his own, held his peace. The rest of us found it luxuriously pleasant to watch from afar and feed on the scraps like the servants of Dives.

It is odd that my shrewd father did not find it all too pleasant. No doubt when he built his first row of houses and by courtesy of my grander fixed his tablet on the wall *Erected by John Crone, Builder*, he felt that he had thereby lifted his name and family to the rank of respectable public citizenship, and that it was only natural for him to find, by degrees, relatives of the same rank eager to own him. It did not occur to him that to rise in his own adopted town was one thing, a little toy city, but for Virgie Flynn out of an unprosperous side-street tavern in Cork, a poor man's daughter, to marry into elegance in a real city, was another pair of shoes.

The Sherlocks were not taken in; they would not accept what they did not undersand, and Elsie disliked Virginia from the first day. Even the Condoorums saw nothing in it all but a joke, calling her Poll Grand. The Hoares, Tomeen and Dan Jo, were alone in accepting her — as what, I do not know — but they did it with great glee. Dan Jo had her out in his trap every third day. Tomeen quarrelled with his son over her. They had her to races all over Munster. It edged on a scandal when the polite Mrs. Hoare was driven to say to my da, 'She's almost a legend, isn't she?' But we never seemed to notice anything: not even when she suddenly got tired of going to mass and could hardly be got out of bed on Sundays: nor when she tired of the fast during the Lent: not even when she stopped teaching my mother 'refinement' and my mother began instead to teach her the comfort of her own slothful ways, the pleasures of punch, the ease of going around in your petticoat until four in the afternoon; not even when Virginia improved on this by dressing up as dusk fell, to go off with my mother and a crony or two dining and wining in the hotels instead of preparing dinner for us at home. Only afterwards do people notice things like that and then talk as if they noticed them all the time — how she would be so fondling to every man who came into the house, arranging a cushion for him, asking him if he felt the draught, solicitous as a mother. We took it all for graciousness.

One day I was alone with her up on the moor above the Sherlocks's, chewing her expensive sweets, and later, as her talk made me feel childish, filling my pipe:

'I suppose, Corney,' she smiled, 'when you grow up . . .'

'I am grown up.'

'. . . you'll want to go to London or big cities like that?'

'Maybe. I don't know, now.'

'All this place is very lovely. But it's very quiet. Is it going to be dull for you?'

'Not at all. I don't see why anyone ever leaves Cork. Look!' I cried, 'Isn't it lovely?'

She looked where my pipe followed the river meandering between low fields to the hills. There had been much rain the last two days and everything was bright and the dark hills were so sodden you felt you could squeeze them like a sponge. The birds were chirruping.

'Yes; it's nice; it is.' She sighed.

'I wouldn't give all the city of London for that valley,' I cried, 'those pines — the cows — that little white houseen below with its shoulder stuck into the hill. Oh, Aunt V. — it's the loveliest place in the world. Why did you ever leave it?'

She drew my hand down and stroked it.

'I hope you will think so always. London is a . . . a drab place.'

'Of course it is,' I puffed with content. 'It's a very material city. You know — getting and spending we lay waste our powers. The world is too much with us, late and soon. Dear God, the very houses seem asleep.'

I was looking at the farmhouses in the far beds of trees. She looked at them. The weir was loud with rainwater.

'Why are men always gambling?' she asked drowsily.

I explained that it was for the excitement, of course.

'I see,' she smiled. 'I hadn't understood that before.'

'Ah, yes, that's what it is,' I assured her. (Women are very dull about these affairs, I thought to myself.)

I leaned back and she let me lay my head on her lap so that I saw the perpendicular horizons, and the colours were ten times more brilliant, the trees all sideways and the river climbing side by side with the sky. The raincarriers, heavy wine-bags, climbed up from her knees.

'You should never marry a gambling woman, Corney,' she said after a time.

'You mean, it would be expensive?' I said.

As if she were talking to herself she went on:

'You see, men take what they win, and they take what they lose, just as it comes. When you marry, your wife will have to take what you win, and take what you lose, just the same — as if she didn't mind either. But the woman that likes a gamble — she won't be content to do that. Would you,' she went on, 'Corney, would you, if you married a woman who was that kind of woman, would you take what she won, like that, and take what she lost, like that?'

I thought she was a little excited but I did not notice it in time.

'Fair is fair,' I mumbled and hummed a tune.

Coldly she lifted my head. Quite angrily she cried out.

'No, you would not. None of you would do it. You're all the same. You wouldn't, you wouldn't, you wouldn't!'

On the turn of the wrist, while I gasped at her fury, she laughed out loud, got up and said,

'Come home, boy. Put your pipe in your pocket or your daddy will smack you.'

And off she billowed down the path, leaving me to follow like a pet dog. On the road below us my grander was walking with Mr. Murphy-MacCarthy, a buyer in one of the big city drapery houses. I saw the buyer look at her intently. He was a large imposing old man, well known for a great church-goer, and in his firm said to be the arch-spy on the employees. As I watched them all sullenly, he said,

'Mrs. de Wolfe, may I speak with you for a moment?'

They moved away and I sat with my grander on the low wall, morosely flinging moss down into the lag-field.

'What does he want her for?' I asked, and I felt as if I had fallen down a dark hole.

'Walk on,' he said, and then after a while: 'I didn't know she knew him?' And after another while, looking back, 'Tell her we're going on'.

I went back and they were in deep conversation, even in argument, for he was smacking his palm with his kid gloves, and I caught the words 'How much do you want?' — spoken by which of them (so much does the mind become tricked by its own disturbance) I could not tell when I tried to remember after.

When she saw me she turned crossly on me, then smiled her firm smile, and said sweetly to Murphy-MacCarthy, who was very red in the face:

'I think that will be all to-day, thank you.'

She turned back with me, taking my arm, and saying,

'We were talking of the Condoorum houses?'

'What houses?'

'It's all right, Corney. I know all about it. Your grandfather has confessed it all to me.'

Then she told me she was trying to get Murphy-MacCarthy to advance money for the houses so that my grander could finish them on his own. But I did not believe her, nor when she said that was what made her talk to me about gambling. (She was deceiving me doubly, as I found out a week later — she did not know I handled the books of the firm — when her name cropped up in connection with the title-deeds of the houses: they had been transferred to her by the bank, and the loan to my grander was marked 'closed'.) I did not press her, for the moment. As soon as I saw my grander had been confiding in her, my mind filled with old random suspicions. I was reminded of his son, Melchisidek Crone. I profited by her wish to placate me by asking bluntly if she knew him.

'I know about him,' she said, looking ahead at my grander's back. 'I know your uncle Mel. But your grandfather doesn't like talking about his son.'

She was worried by the question.

'He ran off with an actress, didn't he?'

'I believe so.'

'She used do Ophelia in the play-tent, usedn't she?'

'Yes.'

'Tell me, Auntie V. Was my grander soft on her?'

She looked ahead at the old man's back. She stopped me.

'What do you want to know, Corney dear?'

'I want to know. I just want to know. But don't tell me if you don't want to.'

'And then you will know just the same? Well, let's leave it like that, Corney dear.'

She smiled her lovely smile. Then it suddenly vanished and she kept looking at me, and as suddenly I was not a boy but a man, and turned away from those heavy tired eyes of her. It was one of those horrible moments of life that everybody knows and hates to remember for very shame. Still I persisted, to have my will of her, and to over-ride that sense of shame — as if my persistence would not afterwards add to the blush of memory:

'I know that way, already,' I said. 'Did he quarrel with his son over her? That's the point.'

I tried to hold up my head and be defiant: but she just looked down into my very heart so that the worm in it curled as she said gently — refusing to betray the old man:

'Why, of course, he quarrelled with Mel over her, didn't you know that, Corney dear? The boy had to go away.'

For a while I glared at her: then I gave it up. In silence we came up with my grander. He waved his stick over the valley and began to say what a grand day it was, thank God, and how the rain with God's help would bring a great harvest.

A MONTH later my mother gave a special party in honour of Virginia — our last party. My grander said it would have been the last in any case because she was long since grown dissatisfied and weary and had shown him letters from her husband begging her to return to London.

At first during the dinner my da seemed to be very pleased with her and with himself. He had got Canon Whitley to come, and Mrs. Hoare, and Virginia was gentle and charming to the canon who was on her right; and she was a great success in a different way on her left with little Mr. Foran, of Humbert and Foran, a firm of solicitors who had been very useful to us in the past. She kept attending to the canon like a hostess, filling his glass in spite of the hairy hand that tried to cover its rim, and watching every need of my grander who sat opposite, his dicky crackling, his face shining and his cravat in a ring as big as a bangle.

'Ah, come now, Canon,' she protested to her right, 'and why wouldn't I be attentive to you all! Sure, he *is* my father, I might say, now that myself and my sister have no daddy of our own. Poor daddy died when I was a little girl,' she sighed, and though it was not true (like many dramatic fibs of hers) we let it go. 'I had to go out very young to make a career of my own.'

'Oh, dear me!' commiserated the priest, not knowing that this, also, was a fib.

'It was so hard to leave Cork,' she went on, and she picked a fleck of dust from his sleeve and rubbed the place with her little forefinger. 'It's so quiet and lovely. I'd live here for ever.'

'Well, now, then, Mrs. de Wolfe,' murmured the canon. 'It ought to be easy enough to manage that. There are many openings in this city for keen business-men. What did you say your husband was, eh?'

She turned hurriedly from little Foran and said, 'A solicitor.'

'Good profession,' smiled little Foran at her. 'The oldest in the world.'

Here the reel began to wind in the fish — my grander talking of politics.

'It's the most go-ahead city in the United Kingdom,' he leaned to the canon to say. 'Spreading on all sides. Why, there's no one knows the size of Cork. Trade flourishing. Ship-building, house-building, tanneries. And if there's a decline here and there in a thing or two — when we get Home Rule everything will rise like the Phoenix from its ashes.'

'An imaginary bird,' murmured little Foran to Virginia.

The old priest merely scratched the hairy bits under his eyes and rubbed the backs of his fingers; but it was enough for my grander who cried out, as he took his fifth glass of Burgundy from Virginia:

'You're not going to tell me,' sweeping his moustaches over his ears, 'you doubt the coming of Home Rule?'

'It's always coming,' said Foran. He took the almonds from Virginia with a leer and prodded again at my grander: 'And should I ask what's the latest from the Westminster seat of war? Or should I ask what's the news from the nest of the Skibbereen Phoenix?' (Referring to my grander's part in the Phoenix Clubs so long ago.)

'Don't,' said the canon. 'The country is distracted.'

'So I hear,' went on Foran acidly. 'Mr. Parnell is finding some very pleasant distractions, too, behind the bivouacs.'

(*Sotto voce* he whispered wickedly to Virginia, 'As the schoolboy said, "The brave general received his *hors de combat*".')

'Would you say,' intervened my da, who like everybody else in Ireland at this time knew well what was being hinted at, 'would you say that Mr. Parnell is, you know, well, I mean, given to conviviality?'

It was like a man who plasters one kind of dirt over another on a mud house to make it look better. My grandfather rose in his seat like the Resurrection of Lazarus.

'I never, as a personal matter, saw that man touch more than one glass of wine, and I've seen him repeatedly down in the Victoria Hotel, at dinners and banquets. It's a libel. I even know the wine. Moselle.

One glass of Moselle. And then, mind you, then only when somebody would insist on giving him a present of a bottle. He gave Ireland every blessed penny . . .'

My mother pulled him down, and while the two chaffered irritably Foran whispered across to him.

'As you might say, they both took any given amount.' To the company he insisted, by now cross in his liquor: 'I didn't say it was wine. And he can't sing. So it must be the other thing, eh?'

'Well,' said the canon in that slow mumbling voice of caution which is a characteristic of all Irish priests, 'I never, I can truly say, put absolute trust in Parnell.'

'Nor I,' agreed my da eagerly. 'I often said that to yourself, Canon.'

'He did,' agreed my mother. 'He did, indeed, Canon!'

'You undershtand,' said the priest in his heavy West Cork brogue, 'he isn't one of our class. And he isn't one of our persuasion. I mane no offence, Mr. Foran . . .'

'Where could the offence be?' asked Foran in bland surprise, while Virginia winked at him.

'And that means a great deal! O'Connell, now, was different. You understand, in his case, Ireland always knew *where she was*. But in Parnell's case . . .'

Foran shot in:

'Nobody knows where she is, or who she is?'

Whereat he leaned back and rubbed his hands in glee. Virginia — while the table bowed its head —

laughed. Encouraged by this, Foran pressed towards her.

'Where is he when he isn't there? That's it. Isn't that it, Mrs. de Wolfe?'

Chidden by the cold looks of her sister and my da she turned on him.

'Why ask me?'

'Oh!' perked Foran, unabashed. 'Handsome is who handsome knows.'

There was a roaring from the end of the table — Arthur John Coppinger. He was there because he was the guardian of my friend, Christy Tinsley, ever since the death of his father. He was as restless as if his chair were a horse, the typical fire-eater. Besides him was his wife, a woman so big that we called them The Lion and the Mouse.

'What's all this about?' he cried, and he cried it up to us about five times. It was an old trick of his at the County Council: it gave him time to rope in every listener before he began. Really the pair should have been called the Fox and the Goose.

'But I know what it's all about,' he barked. 'It's an underhand sort of defamation of Mr. Parnell's moral character, isn't that precisely what it is, Mister Foran?'

Foran said one word — once.

'Maybe.'

'Oh, for goodness' sake,' implored my da. 'Let's not discuss it.'

'Ha, ha!' cried Arthur John, and he wagged his

pink jelly-fingers. 'What I say is — hunt the rat from his hole and squash him, — no thanks, ma'am, no more wine — *squash* him. Mister Foran suggests that some moral law is being broken, isn't that it, Mister Foran?'

'Well, we have a guardian of morals here amongst us . . .'

'And of reputations, too, sir, while I'm here. The question is put. What — has — Mr. Parnell — done'

The glasses jingled at each blow on the table.

'Now,' pleaded the canon in his loose, easy-going way, 'wouldn't it be betther to let sleeping dogs lie?'

'Lie?' asked Foran gently.

Virginia was by this a trifle red, as if somebody had pinched her under her eyes, and one eyebrow was arched and the other was bent over an almost closed lid. She turned on Foran, and then on all of us. In her rising and falling accent, up and down for un-needed emphasis, she sang at us, very near to her temper.

'You're all saying nothing,' she protested, 'and you're all suggesting a great deal. And far worse things by not talking out. I admire Mr. Parnell. I do.'

Ten 'quite rights' from Coppinger in ten seconds.

'I don't care what Mr. Parnell does. I admire him. I do.'

Three slow 'Now, nows' from the canon, and his heavy hand decapitated each 'now, now' as it came. In a different voice ten more 'Now, nows' rattled in protest from the repeating rifle down the table. A ponderous big gun finished the battle with a deep boom:

'Listen!' said the canon, who, as by withdrawal from the mêlée, was a heap of flabby pillows deep in his armchair.

'This talk. Is getting. Very. Common. I hear it, in every house, I visit. Now, such talk, so far, is only the smirching, you understand, of a *private* character. That's bad. But it could be worse. I say, Talk dies. And I say, Let it die.'

'But if it's more than talk?' from Foran, who was now quite serious.

'Time enough, when we know that, to talk again.'

The company was patently relieved, and my mother rose with her professional smile to take us into the sitting-room. But Foran was not satisfied.

'I do know,' he said very solemnly.

'What d'ye know?' growled my grander as if to a dog.

'I know that Parnell's private life is becoming a public matter. Friends of mine in the know, legal friends, in London who don't exaggerate, tell me that there is a suit filed in the Divorce Court.'

He gestured with grace to the canon, across Virginia whose anger made her lovely, and he spoke with feeling.

'I'm sorry, Canon Whitley, but I am not talking scandal, and you may as well hear it here as in the paper to-morrow or after.'

'Well, I don't care,' cried Virginia, and she leaped up.

The canon's eyebrows leaped, too, and his lower lip curled down. My da rose and in a voice that concealed nothing suggested that we move into the sitting-room. I and Vicky and Christy Tinsley and young Coppinger were left behind; for as the last of the group went in my da hastily closed the doors on us, like Gabriel on the unbaptized: as he did so we heard the canon say solemnly to Virginia, and saw my da's eyes nearly roll up under his hair:

'It's a very serious matter, Mrs. de Wolfe,' and she saying back to him, in the words of my grander:

'It's just bloody cod!'

When my mother, coming back for her reticule, opened the doors, Virginia stood like a statue in the window, tall as the window, backed by the glow from the limestone walls of the cathedral and the green of the churchyard grass-slope; she was saying, a liqueur-glass in her hand,

'We must stand true to our leader. We must stand by him.'

'Up to a point,' from the double-bass of the canon.

She kicked the whirl of frill with her heel and with a lifted glass she cried,

'He's a gentleman. London is a gay place. Gentlemen . . .'

'Play a nice little game of twenty-five,' gushed my mother at us, with her hands dancing, and her smile working, and we staring past her until she banged the doors, her smile suddenly gone and her face like an exploded balloon.

We tried to play Spoiled Five when the table was cleared, with Vicky winking and I itching to get into that sitting-room. Then as the argument inside grew louder and louder a ring buzzed at the hall-door and I ran to answer it. In the sitting-room I saw Virginia swaying before the maid who offered coffee. Her arms were extended. She was thrilling a song — not learned in Milan:

Have you ever seen a feather,
A tiny little feather,
　　No matter whether white or pink or pale?
Have you ever seen a tiny little,
Underneath the weather,
Little feather on a tether
　　On a tom-cat's tail?

During that pom-pom-pom of the swing of the ditty, my grander was arguing crossly with the canon who by now had the face of a murderer:

'And then London is different. A man of the world like him. Blokes like him have to knock around a bit.'

'Yes,' from Virginia.

'No,' from the canon.

As I ran on I thought they were like bees hitting their heads over a carcase. It was Murphy-MacCarthy muffled up at the door. He had his trap to take Canon Whitley to the station. My mother made him come in for a drink. I held the pony who jingled his bit, and as it was Maytime the window was open. On the red blind the figures passed, gigantic. Children were playing below the cathedral close. Dusk was fallen, and dark clouds behind the three steeples. I led out the reins and sat on the sill, back to the window, watching the clouds above the steeple tops.

My mother was smothering them with jokes about monks who made good drink for bad priests to drink it. Coppinger and Foran were hard at it:

'What happens, what happens, what happens? Get a London regiment into Cork barracks and what happens?'

'Tell me.'

'Vice follows every army, vice follows every army. It's history, history, history.'

'Now, said Foran, 'here's a man knows London well.'

'Knows it too well?' (Virginia).

'I know it very well.' (MacCarthy.)

'Bet you do. Bit of a dog yourself, if the truth was known.' (Virginia.)

Pom-pom-pom-pom!
When the tom-cat meets his lady on the tiles ...

'Yes, I know London very well. And its ways are not our ways. Mrs. de Wolfe knows that too.'

'What the devil do you mean?'

'Now, now, now, now, now ...'

'*Pom-pom-pom-pom.*'

'Ah, look, Virginia!' implores my da, that's not a nice song.'

'My God, can't I even sing a song, John? And what does this old lad mean anyway?'

The County Council roar came out over many voices.

'It's all a matter of values, values, values, a point of view, the way you look at it, travelled people are different, different, what's wrong with us we're not different like that, we're too narrow, do y'see that, Mrs. Wolfe, d'y'see, d'y'see, d'y'see, see? Point of view?'

The canon boomed again:

'Listen!'

I lifted the red blind and peeped in. The canon's face was as red as his stock.

'Just listen!'

Virginia stormed at them, at bay.

'Listen to what? Listen to who? Point of view? Button my shoe? What the devil are you all up to? I sing a little song . . .'

'Ah, now,' my da's hands were like a Jew. 'It's not a nice song.'

A piping voice came from the Lion by my ear; all in the typical flat Cork accent, all *dis* and *dat* like a negro whine.

'Maybe Mrs. de Wolfe, you don't know deh world. Dere are wimmen like dat.'

'Like what?'

'*You* know.'

'*I* know?'

'Yeh *know*.'

'Know *what*?'

'About *dem*.'

Virginia ran her hand through her golden hair.

'Wouldn't yeh pity 'em, Canon?' said the Lion with the voice of a mouse.

'Shut up, Mary,' said the Mouse with the voice of a lion, and my head bobbing and the blind bobbing while I tried to see them all.

'Such. Women. Cannot. Be. Defended.'

'But what,' screamed Virginia, frilled and whisking, 'is everybody talking about?'

'Dem,' piped the Lion.

'Mr. Parnell,' explained Foran with a grin.

'Why don't people ask for proof? My God, why don't people ask for *proof*? Proof, proof, proof?'

'Well, ask Murphy-MacCarthy, he's back from London.'

My mother had a bottle of Benedictine in one hand and a flagon of Chartreuse in the other. My da kept rubbing back his lock. Jelly-fingers waved his handkerchief in my grander's face and babbled of 'proof'.

Over the scream of the fiddle-and-piccolo babel went the deep thump-thump of:

'Well. I. Am. Going. Home.'

Virginia's voice rose:

'. . . fat lot any of you know about it, anyway . . . a gentleman . . . as for this shirt-and-stocking-buyer . . .'

The entire company was moving towards the door saying awkward excuses and farewells. My da was everywhere. He said to everybody in turn, 'Excuse me'. He bobbed like a gander here and there.

'How can ye say such awful things?' my grander wailed.

'Without *proof*!'

The red and black drum bumped out his last four dull thumps. 'Good. Night. Missus. Crone.' With this promise of a diversion he produced a silence.

'It's unhappily true,' said Murphy-MacCarthy sadly to my grander. 'The man is a moral delinquent.'

'Proof!' said Coppinger, turning on his exit.

'A moral outcast.'

'The Fenians won't stand for it. They stand by Parnell,' growled my grandfather.

'The *people* will not,' said the buyer.

Virginia pointed with her long white arm.

'You are the kind of man who loves to tear men like Mr. Parnell. He is a man ten times your size. You hate men like Parnell.'

'We have our standards, Mrs. . . . er . . .'

He faced Virginia. She had one eye closed and one eye open and over the open eye the arched back of a threatening eyebrow.

'That,' he said with majesty, 'is what you will never understand!' and he turned to the canon to lead him away.

Then, while my father held her arm, she held the

buyer's arm and in four words she told him what she thought of him. As the last word came I let go the tassel of the blind. The reel snapped it up so that in the clap of sound I don't know whether that word was slug, or bug, or mug, or thug, or what it was. But it finished everything. I was half in through the window and the pony was blowing at my backside as Murphy-MacCarthy spoke and with a kick of my heel I got the animal's nose. He galloped down the street and I let him gallop. The old buyer turned at the door and rent her.

'I know one of your names,' he said with scorn, as if he were telling a salesman what he thought of his cheek in trying to sell him Sacred Heart badges at a mere thirty-three and-a-third per cent off in the gross. 'One of your *many* names.'

My mother burst into tears. The Lioness by my side hid her face. The folding-doors were opening and the three youngsters stared out. My grander looked as if he would strike old Murphy-MacCarthy who was now absently looking around at the canon to see whether he had really said something as awful as he was beginning to think he had. What would have happened next I do not know of there had not, at this moment, been a sudden new excitement. For as I stared I felt myself torn out of the window from behind and I saw the vulture-face of old Condoorum twisted with fury. He thrust his long body through the window and just as Virginia opened her mouth he shouted in:

'Crone, yeh thief! Where's the title-deeds of me

lovely houses? Phil Crone, yeh limb of Satan! Where's the deeds of me lovely houses?'

'Go away,' says my father, as white as a sheet.

My grander tried to push Condoorum away, but as they tried to push him out he boldly scrambled over the sill into the room. There he stood and faced my da.

'I won't,' he shouted. 'I've been knocking for the last hour and nobody would let me in. I'm in now and in I stay.' He turned to the company. He saw Foran. 'There's the man,' he sobbed, 'has the deeds of me land and houses. There's the divil has 'em whipped. There's the robber. And you too,' to my da! 'Ye're all thieves. Give 'em back to me. I'll cut yer tripes out if ye don't give 'em back to me.'

'Go out!' says my da.

'I won't!' says Condoorum.

'Excuse *me*, everybody,' wailed my da to the ceiling, as if he was asking God to let this chalice pass over him, while Condoorum kept on lashing himself into his rage, telling everyone he had been 'robbed'.

'I think it's all my fault,' said Virginia, but nobody heeded her, only my da. By now he realized that some of his money was in danger and at once he became master of the room. He spoke, cold and hard, to my grander. The crowd stopped to listen.

'Have you been having dealings with Din Lucey here?'

'Has he what?' wailed Condoorum. 'Isn't he afther selling me out? The dirty grabber's trick . . .'

'Silence!' from my da.

'And what about it?' demanded my grander of his son. 'It was a good investment. I borrowed,' he explained, 'four hundred pounds off the bank to finance his terrace below.'

'You borrowed . . .' my da wilted.

'And,' defied my grandfather, looking at Condoorum 'if that chapejack there hadn't tied us up with his bloody boghouses of tenements, things I'd be ashamed to own . . . Why the misfortune,' he cried at Condoorum, 'should I go on paying the interest when you wouldn't build the bloody houses?'

'I see,' mocked my da, grasping the whole thing in a second. 'Be silent,' he snapped at Condoorum who was bursting to shame us. 'And now the deeds are in the hands of Mr. Foran here of Humbert and Foran?'

My grander looked at him in astonishment. He looked at Virginia. He looked at Foran.

'I sold them to Mr. Foran,' she said sullenly. 'I needed the money.'

' 'Tis thrickery,' howled Condoorum, flinging his black round hat into the centre of the carpet and talking to it as if the hat were the evident proof of the trickery. 'My darling houses in the hands of a little estate agent. The Crown bum. The felon-setther. Me sweet little houses,' he wept, holding out his empty hands to the lot of us. 'My dotes of houses. My . . .'

'*Your* houses?' cries my grander.

'Yes! *My* houses. Didn't I put labour into 'em. Didn't I put my shweat into 'em. Didn't I borrow four hundred pounds from your son there for to build 'em? Didn't I let you hold the deeds and leases of 'em? Didn't I trust yeh with 'em?' — giving his hat a fierce kick into the corner of the room.

'And what the blazes do you think I could borrow four hundred pounds on? Is it on your kips of jakes of bits of tenements? It was *my* money went into them.'

'You sold me to Foran behind my back.'

'I did not. I gave them to this girl here,' indicating Virginia. 'It was the best investment I ever made. I wanted her to always have a bit of money of her own. I knew that poor girl's story six weeks ago.'

'And she,' concluded my da quietly but savagely, 'sold them at a profit to Mr. Foran.'

'And the upshot of it all,' cries Condoorum, 'is that my threasures of villas are in the hands of an estate-agent that would get blood out of a stone. My dotes of . . .'

Out of all patience my da roared at him.

'Why can't you finish the rotten houses?'

'How can I? Where'd I get the money and I up to my neck with my city contractions? He'll seize them houses. O, vo, vo! But I'll bankrupt ye. I'll pay ye back no four hundred pounds. Is it to sell my tenement I'm working at . . .'

'You'll pay me . . .' my da was insisting when Virginia spoke to Condoorum.

'I,' she said proudly, 'will pay the interest for you. And you can finish the houses in your own time.'

Out shot the calloused hand.

'Give me the money now.'

She opened her purse and from it she pulled a lump of notes. Silver, keys, gewgaws, fell to the floor. She thrust the roll into Condoorum's hand.

'Now, get out! We have no more to do with you.'

As they parted, to let him out, Foran smilingly halted him.

'The deeds are at my office, Mr. Lucey. Any day you like, you know ... we can sign *our* partnership agreement?'

He went, and the guests went. Murphy-Mac-Carthy had to travel the quays to find his pony, and while the canon waited in the street the group gathered about him to talk. My da sent Barty and Vicky off with Christy and then he went himself off down the quays after Condoorum. The room was empty but for my grander and Virginia. They sat side by side on the settee, while I, gob-open at the window, watched them.

'You'll be treated terribly when I go,' she said.

'Oh, I'm jake. I'm me daza. Don't think of me. But what about you? My poor girleen, what'll you do?'

'I'm going to look after you,' she said.

'I can't let you go back to London,' he said.

'Wherever I am I'll look after you.'

My mother came on them through the folding-doors

facing direct at me, and she threw down on the floor all the coloured silks and satins she ever got from Virginia. Then with a great sob she ran from the room. Poor Virginia looking at them began to cry, too. I turned away because my grander took her hand and kissed it, and I was amazed to see the night behind me and the stars in the sky.

I walked out the roads where the hucksters' windows glowed and the lane-brats howled in the fans of light thrown across the dust. Out of all that had happened I thought most of what I had seen last and in addled wonderment I kept up and up the hill. A relic of March wind in May made the sound of seas in my ears, and the west was all cold and yellow. I was astonished at the lightness of the sky over it, but when I looked up the dome was blue. To the east, I thought, it will be a still deeper blue. But when I looked across the city, the risen moon was there in a ring of mist, the man's face in shadow. Leaning under a gas-lamp that leaped and fell under the wind I thought: 'Life is like that. Here am I, and there is my da, and then, there is my grandfather — something that nobody at all expects.' And I left it so, as, tear it to and fro as I may, I have left it always, unsolved in the end.

Virginia went away. My da, who was an obstinate man, got the deeds from Foran and bought out Condoorum, but there was so much hugger-mugger that by the time the four houses were built we lost a shoal of money over it. As to the canon's church, eventually he gave the contract, and our firm was never paid for it in full in his lifetime: for years my da was, instead, helping to run church carnivals and concerts to pay himself, and sometimes when he would look at the books and see the ancient debt he would turn the page sourly, saying:

'And when it comes to renovating it they'll give the job to someone else.'

It was the only church he ever built, for my mother gave up the struggle, and thereafter it was the same old march, heel-and-toe, with rum in the kitchen, and my da in the parlour at his 'seventy-six and nine . . . eighty-five . . . eighty-five and nine . . .' — and, upstairs in the attic, Lear in the house of Regan, warming his hands over the green-globed lamp on the floor, and the frost on the slates and Cork asleep, and he thinking and thinking, God alone knows what. He never touched the business from that day on. As if his pride were killed, he made over the business to his son.

I do not know whether there is any connection, but Vicky astonished us all by suddenly becoming very pious — with great horned beads and big prayer-books, and devotions to this saint and that saint, and much abstemiousness, and she went around with a face like a Magdalene. We disliked her for it, but she bore our mockery with such an air of resignation that we finally left her alone. My father was always chiding us and encouraging her, and he was delighted when she entered a convent — though it cost him dear at a time when he could ill afford it. A year later, she left the convent and went to London to become an actress. By then there was only myself and Robert left at home, for Maurice had gone to Canada, and Barty and Michael to an engineering firm in Manchester. Maurice never came back: he wrote once only to us in a ten-page letter that the end of the world was due on December 31st, in the year 1900.

VI

I CAN understand Vicky's 'going in the nuns'. That summer I began again to go to mass every morning and it was nice to meet Elsie Sherlock there and be asked to her house just as before. They were charitable Christian people and unlike the rest of our acquaintances they said, simply and openly, that 'it was a pity about Mrs. de Wolfe'. They were more kind than ever to me, so that between evenings there and mornings when I saw Elsie at mass, her face like a calm sea, her eyes deep and childlike, her dress so simple, I sank back soon into my old content.

Morning after morning, when I saw her kneel among the communicants waiting for the communion, I, who knelt behind her, wanted to stroke her ankle in her shoe. Her curls under her father's old hat became the curls of all the women in the world: her waist was the waist of a statue: she was losing her identity for me already, merged into myself. But that is the misfortune of my nature, that all things end by becoming me until, now, nothing exists that is not me.

But that merging was imperceptible. It was happening, as these things happen to everybody, so slowly that it was, if you can understand me, happening too fast to be observed. It was like a sunset in the clouds. You look at it for a second, the colour of all the death-colours of life moulding impalpability into shapes that

can never be ordered by human thought because they
do not last long enough. As long as you look you hold
in your mind those palaces of delight that, while you
look away and back, are all gone and all come again;
and yet had you not removed your eyes you could not
have told that there had been a new birth. I felt, after
Virginia went away, that I had a new knowledge and
that I held it. I felt I could soon begin to crumble the
world between my fingers and examine it. Whereas,
before she left us, I was already gone under my horizon
and did not know it.

Take those nights when, after she went, I used to lie
with Elsie in our secret woods above her house, looking out over Ireland, knee into knee, and all about us
other woods creeping over other heat-fogged hills,
demesne after demesne covering valley after valley.
I noticed that she would lie, quite still, in my arms,
so that I said one night, 'You are like a fallen tree'.
As I said it the first pine-pollen fell on us under the
night-wind, and she closed her eyes and smiled. I said,
'You are the tree that the wind blows'. I felt under her
sleeve to her shoulder and thinking that I did not move
farther to my desire only because my desire did not
want it, I said, in pride, 'I am the wind, Elsie'. Yet
she did not say one word, and I knew that she thought
of herself, rather, as the shorn lamb for whom the wind
is tempered by God. When I said another time,
looking slyly into the crevasse of her bosom, 'It's not
usual for the snow to be in the valleys, Elsie' — she

just looked into my eyes and said nothing. Well, it was a good defence. Whatever she would be, it was I who must make her. The truth was that we were both unfashioned, played on by some secret wind we never heard.

And yet, in spite of all that, and for all that, I know that this was the free time of my life — fluid, wayward, unplanning, careless of reason or result. It is all the real freedom we have before, in time, we become stamped by our own hands — *Done*.

VII

ONE evening I was lying in the garden near the stream, pretending to myself that I was studying a book on Building Construction, when my grander came out through the rosery. The bony hand took out his watch by its hairy chain. He used to tell me as a child that it was a mouse's tail; it was really the hair of his dead wife woven into a strand.

'I've finished washing the plates,' says he. 'Robert or God can dry them.' (Robert was my simple brother.) 'What about coming to the devotions? It would be a nice stroll across to the Dominicans.'

The face of the gold hunter snapped to.

'Ach, I might as well, I suppose.'

We were going more from habit or as a political gesture than anything else; because if people like the Sherlocks said Parnell was an adulterer we had to show that Parnellites could be Catholics too. Only people like Christy Tinsley took no part in all that righteousness that came after the divorce case; the Fenians despised Parnell and the politicians too much to bother their heads about his reputation or their own.

When we came to the chapel of the Dominicans across the quays, the red sign of the Opera House plumbed the high tide among the fishing-boats. It was a soft night offering rain, and the little lay brother was out on the steps taking a look up and down at the bridges. His back rounded, his hand screwed sideward from birth, his gob full of speech as a monkey.

'Grand salubrity in the atmosphere,' he chattered. 'We have a poor house to-night, with the Opera in competition with us.'

He cracked out his double laugh, the breaking of a nut.

'Will it rain at all?' asked my elder.

'Yeh, what rain? We're dead from praying for a drop of wet all the summer. But did we get it? Not if we prayed ourselves sick. What I say is, what a fool God 'ud be to send us rain when He knows we'd jump off our knees at the first shower. What a fool He is! Hehe!'

'It's a way of looking at it,' said I, for I found him a most entertaining study. 'Pay the doctor when you're well, eh?'

'God,' winked the lay brother, 'is a fly boy. He knows us down to a T. I'm sure He do be always laughing at us. But we have no sense. I'll tell ye a good one, now.' He gathered us into his arms and whispered wickedly. 'It's all about Father Fallon. I'm telling no tales when I say he's a bit tight on the money-bags. Being the bursar, I suppose he have to. Well, he have a nephew that's a limb of the divil for every wild kind of andrewmartins. Up in Dublin he lives. He have his wife and his little family plagued out. O, a proper divil! Anyhow, me bucko fell sick there last month and he nearly hopped it. It was a matter of days for him to go upstairs — or downstairs, hehe! — or where-ever he was booked for. Well, Father Fallon had us all praying for him that he might repent and die in the state of grace.'

He could hardly restrain himself — he clutched us to him like two children, peering around him.

'Yerrah, we prayed and we prayed until we had holes beat into our breasts, and be the hokey didn't the boyo repent all right? But didn't he recover too? He repented and he got well and he said it was a miracle and the hand of God. Didn't he travel down from Dublin this very day and walk into Father Fallon and thank him and thank the community — such eloquence — and such piety — 'twas . . . 'twas . . . 'twas edification itself. Father Fallon had us deaf boasting about it. But then what does the boyo do? He asks Father Fallon for the lend of the loan of twenty quid for to go to London and get a job and turn over a new leaf. Ho! Ho! Ho! Twenty quid!'

He squinted as he laughed. He banged his two thighs with his long hands.

'Twenty quid! Out of his own pocket! The Community is charmed with it. That'll cure him of his avariciousness for a bit. Oh, God is a fly boy. Two birds at the one stone. A fly boy!'

'Yes', said I. 'He is. But maybe He's more fly than you think. It's on *you* it will fall. See how tight the bursar will be on you from this on.'

The monkey face grew dark and sorrowful.

'Be the holus. I never thought of it. O dear, O dear! O Jericho! It's true! Counting the candles he'll be. I do light a fire with one now and again. Counting the matches. Picking up the butt-ends of tapers. O glory to the Most High, I never thought of it.'

'God is a fly boy,' I teased.

'My heavens, may be he's at them candles this minute . . .'

Gathering his white skirts, he ran, leaping, and looking back, while we laughed at his sad face and he waved his hands in the air, warding off brimstone. A minute later we heard him tolling the bell over our heads.

Despite its handful of worshippers and the lighted candles on the altar the chapel seemed chill and empty. Light drains slowly from the cup of the sky, and the square skylights in the flat roof were still orange with daylight. It was all the more empty and bare when a little wind soughed down a ventilator. And when, later, the chant of the rosary done, the incense broke blue against windows as leaden now as the leads that bound them, and the humpbacked monk brought candles (butt-ends amongst them) all blowing in arrow-shape for the Benediction and the voices rose to the line of triumph:

> Et antiquum documentum
> Novo cedat ritui . . .

— even then, the beginning and the end of the power of the Church, all seemed blanched and bleak. It was as if the worshippers were too few, and became mindful of their fewness, became mindful, too, of the sorrow that always in Ireland fills into the plain-chant at that point as if the ancient glory of the Word were to us become, in time, as weak as the glory it displaced.

Old Phil cannot have felt any of this sorrow (or this glory) for what he bellowed in my ear was a revel of sounds without sense, or at most a word or two picked from his neighbours or from old memories of the chapel by the sea in Skibbereen:

> Boo boo bum bum hocumentum
> Bo bo aisy riwlcheweee.
> Hasty hehe hoho humhum
> O salutaris Hostia . . .

We were an edifying pair for all that, even if I, too, like most Irish Catholics, sang with more pleasure in the music than the meaning, of which I only understood, then, the vaguest sense. We were the last two to leave and it was the ticking of the sacristy clock that drove me out — it was so lonesome, and I wanted to go out to the Sherlocks. Presently the old man came up the nave, curling his bones of fingers around his buttons, dull cloth buttons on his black serge cutaway. He touched the font with the dignity of a Moses calling the rock to flow water, and he placed his hat on his head like a Quixote who might at any moment call Ho! for his horse.

The little monk was outside. He had news for us.

As he locked the great carved door he told us— Parnell
was dead. 'May the sod lie soft on him,' he said. 'I
said to Father Burke, "Lave us have prayers for his
soul". But he said, "It's a matter for the Superior.
God pity us all".'

We looked at the red lights of the theatre. The tide
was its looking-glass. There was no sign of rain, for
the little clouds were all gone wandering lambs over
the masts of the ships.

'Would you mind opening that door, brother?' asks
my grander.

'Did you forget something?'

The key turned and the monk set his behind to the
door to slew it in. My grander went in, set his five
fingers in the font, blessed himself, and knelt among
the dirty mortuary cards of the hall. We two drew
apart and from time to time looked in. We talked of
Parnell and the theatre and the Italian sky above the
old Athenaeum. He did not come out. When he rose
he leaned against the font and cried, and when we
tried to get him out Father Burke came.

'An old Fenian', I whispered. 'Don't cross him.
It's Parnell.'

The priest tried to pat him on the back but he drew
his stick over his shoulder like a falchion. The priest
went away, shrugging. Over and over as I moved him
along the quays he said, and I had no heart to tease the
'heathen' who said it:

'Dead and not one prayer for his soul. The Leader

of the Irish people! And not one little prayer for his soul.'

Along the quays where the shawled women sat and gossiped you would think nothing had happened at all; but as the word went around we passed one or two groups talking of him. Then, as we rounded up the hill to Sunday's Well, we heard behind us near the chapel the slow, deep boom of the band. We could see the tattered green epaulettes and the dark facings. It was his own band, the Parnell Guards. They passed over the North Gate playing the 'Dead March from Saul'. The great drummer lashed with his sticks on his drum: the side-drums trembled.

Like heavy feet that clank into a tomb the notes fell on the chill autumn air. There was no link, no movement from one sound to another. They hung in the brain like dead leaves. The dirge locked the mind as the tawny fog locked the embrace of river and sea. We watched them pass across the bridge, the sound growing fainter as they moved slowly out of view.

Me. Me. Fah . . . Me. Ray. Doh. Te . . .

The sounds died along the street and with a sigh we turned away. A flight of crows lifted our eyes. Night was still far off. Far behind the empty bridge the unsmoking city had barely begun to twinkle.

(It was the end of our piety. All the bitterness of the miserable years after Parnell soured us both — made us full of hatred and contempt. Less and less often we went into the city for the faction fights and the tar-barrels and the speeches. My grander returned to the pubs and the old meeting-rooms where he met his friends who had known the old days and would talk to him of their glories as captive Jews might talk of Israel. In that way when I had not Elsie I became a bird alone, a heron without a mate in an expanse of grass.)

That night I went out to the bridgehead. There I met her and she drew me into the Condoorum cabin for a gossip. We were met by Mabel-in-the-stable-the-lousy-rat (their name for the eldest girl) and she hailed us with her usual half-quizzical flattery. She wore pince-nez for grandeur and her face was smooth, her mouth young with red smiles, her lank hair like elephant ears beside her cheeks.

'Well!' she cried, with her two hands extended in a Sacred-Heart supplication. 'Glory, Honour, and Praise be to the Most High, and isn't this a grand visit. And isn't it grand and salubrious you are both looking.' Expanding in her wonderment she poured out her full, slow river of talk. 'Is it a lie, for me, Miss Sherlock? Or can I call you Elsie? Sure I knew you since I used to have to put a rubber apron on me to take you on my lap. And look *at* him. And he smooth, groomed, and placid. And look *at* me and me with my ponthers and my paraphernalia on me in the presence of two aristo-crats. Ye're noble. My dear children, be seated. I do forget my etiquette.'

With joy she laughed wide at her own jokes, and

nobody could say whether she was laughing at herself—
she was her own impresario — or at us who were her
audience and victims. We sat among the dusty cabbage,
the lettuce, and potatoes. The clanking of the band was
beating in my mind.

'Parnell is dead,' I said quietly.

'God help us, he is. The poor man. And I suppose
we'll have more elections now and more ri-ra and
broken heads. Look at the dust of that chair. Let me
give it a whisk of my apron. Sure I love to have ye and
I'm not prevaricating. I do have all the swanks of
Sunday's Well in here and they do be fobbed up and
folled up and I declare to my God they're not a patch
on either of ye. I tell you, you'd think they were the
wives of some foreign Rajah Khan or some sooty
bastard from remote regions they have so much paint
and trash and muck on their gobs like ladies in a raree-
show. I declare to you the two Miss Simpkinses came
in to me here to-day and they had tay-hats on them
would fill a kitchen. I thought every turn they gave
would knock my lamp. To see the likes of them tip-
toing through the tulips in my restricted quarters and
they keeping the light behind them — as if I didn't
know them since I was that height with their two flat
feet' — lifting her own to show her father's boots on
them — 'that I'd know in a coalhole and they the sort
that has hair on the chest and wouldn't tear in the
pluckin'.'

While she bent with laughter at her wit, Condoorum

came in with two spades. He waited until she was finished.

'Are ye walking or are ye waiting?' he asked drily.

'We just dropped in', said Elsie cheerfully.

'Is it true', I asked him, 'that Parnell is gone?'

'Is that a fact?' he asked without interest. 'Oh dear! We must all go some time.'

Elsie came over by me, looking fondly at me, because she saw I was broody, and at the same time Donal, the ex-soldier, drew up outside in a common country-cart. Beside him was a pretty fair-haired girl, a regular English miss. He was the foolish one of that family. He had joined the soldiers when he was a mere child at school and became a drummer-boy because he could play the piccolo. He once lent me a book on farming: it was marked in ancient gall-black, yellow with the absorbed ink, *War Department*, *Military Prison*, *Rangoon* and he had scribbled all over it with pencil. As if he was in chains below decks he had written incessantly, *Roll on Malta*, or *Roll on the 3rd of July*, and in one place, under a woodcut of a pig, he had the verse:

> I curse the day I took the shilling
> And joined the Royal Munsters.
> I curse the day I said I was willing
> To fight with the Bloody Munsters.

And underneath that, again, *Donal Lucey*, 12457, *Third Batt. Pte.*, *R.M. Fusiliers. Roll on Malta.*

'Here's our coadjutors', said Mabel-in-the-stable,

and then she whispered, with the same note of mockery, elusive as smoke, that Donal had met the English 'one' on a pilgrimage to Lourdes. There was a joke, there, somewhere, that tickled her. But I hardly heard her. I was at the door looking at the river and Elsie touching my hand.

'It's sad,' she said gently, and I replied:

'For God's sake come out of this.'

'My dear,' says Mabel, and she patted me on the back, 'aren't we going to our farm? Why don't ye come with us?'

'All aboard!' cries Donal. Elsie, on the impulse, pushed me into the cart and for want of better to do I went. Condoorum sniffed. Mabel locked the door. We jolted off.

Their farm proved to be a market-garden tucked away on the waste ground near the Bishop's Marsh, behind an old tin shed — the *Blarney Railway* terminus. It was fenced with rusted sheets of iron, bedstead ends, railway-sleepers thick with slugs — typical Condoorum makeshifts. But there were tidy rows of furrows, green-topped with lettuce or celery, or dun with withered potato-stalks. They were making potato-pits in pyramid-shape against the winter.

The fall of dusk, kind to the field-plot, exposed the decay of the houses around it. Rising out of the river was a discarded iron-works, ironically called The Hive, with every pane of glass in its iron-bound and Roman-arched windows shattered by hooligans' stones. ('Boys!

Who'll hit them windas across the river? Aw?') Its tall chimney was moss-greened: lonely on a pedestal over the coping stood the iron lion, his tail rampant. Farther down-river was the giant dunce's hat of the glass factory, also abandoned: its storehouses beneath leaned into the tide. In a place where you might expect a gasworks to smell, or turbines to hum through the night, a rat went plop into the river and two lane-girls, the first attendant virgins on the night, roved the deserted quays.

And it was right it should all be dead, when he was who might have brought it all to life; fitting that along those quays the eye could trace ruin upon ruin. By the humped bridge of the iron-works (my grander and I had rumbled over it years ago on our way to the dissecting-room of the University) I could see an inset terrace where, once on a time, at least, the servants of fashionable people had gossiped over Cork tripe and Cork beer. Now, washing hung from a rope thrust out into V-shape by a sweeping brush, and when a woman sent a hiss of ashes into the tide I knew they were cleaning the grates for the night. Often, when we used pass it by, we saw by the glow of those basement grates old crones fumbling over their tea on wall-papered tables, children combed into the ashes.

Elsie tipped my hand again and smiled.

'Cheer up, Corney,' she said.

'Do you see that terrace?' I pointed. 'Lighted under the eaves. There was a suicide there once, or a murder,

I forget which. The courthouse is just behind it. My grander took me to the trial and we saw the razor held up and the man leaning out of the dock to look at it. It must have been a murder. His counsel took off his gown then and held it up in the court. "Gentlemen of the jury," he said, "I should be unfaithful to this gown I wear, to this badge of an honoured and an honourable profession, in the attainment of which I burned the midnight oil, if I did not strain every nerve to prevent this unfortunate man from being separated for all eternity from the bosom of his wife and family".'

'Did he?' asked Elsie, impressed.

'He did, and my grander said that the judge cocked a queer eye down at him, as much as to say, "Here, this bloody bloke is going a bit too far!"'

Elsie laughed, and thinking I was beginning to forget, ran from me over the plots.

Faintly, but suddenly, I heard again the slow 'Dead March', and as a faint wind of memory it came and went . . . Fah fah soh . . . They were circling the city in their misery, unable to return home; to be silent; to think. What a place to have come, and what a night, where topers were said to come down the river, in agony of thirst, and in a boat open their gobs under the refuse pipes of the brewery, eager for even the dregs of malt. Again it was wafted to us:

Me. Me. Fah. . .

'Why,' I stormed at Mabel, whose bottom lumbered

before me among the celery-beds, 'did you bring us here? You said it was your *farm*!'

'My darling boy, my dear Cornelius,' she halted suddenly on the tiny path, immense, while I bumped into her rump. 'Isn't it grand and glorious to see the land promulgating the food of life? I tell you, Corney,' going on and stopping again as if she liked these collisions in her rear, 'it's a lesson to anyone. There's one half of Cork thinks cabbages grows on trees and the other half eating things out of menageries of tin cans that I'd not touch if I was on a coral island for fear I'd get a pimple in my stomach would arrange out with my toes to the sky.'

She turned, her moon-face hanging over me.

'It's lovely,' she swept her hand over the entangled rust of iron and root, and looked at me over her pince-nez. 'Sure, my boy, it's like Paris!'

Elsie, delighted with the oddness of it, came leaping over the yellowing celery-tops. I pointed to the convent by my house. Its red and white stone, limestone, sandstone, lifted a gabled bulk thick with dusk against the foggy fort beyond.

'That's where you went to school, isn't it?' I said, pleased to think the childish babble I heard there had been, in part, her babble.

Straws of smoke from the lighted cabins rose against the bastions and a last touch of filtered sun, gone underground a moment after, caught the crucifix on the gable-peak. At the same moment a bell intoned a frail summons, slender as the motes of cabin-smoke. Her hand went out to point to it.

'They're going to prayers,' she said. 'They'll go to sleep, then. It's hard in the bright evenings.'

Her hand sank with the sinking ray and her look was a note of love, well struck, but when I touched her fingers she snatched them away.

'Elsie, come out the road. Come with me, Elsie. The woods over Dunscombes. Before the last dark.'

'Puh!' And ran — she always seemed to be running from me like that. Her curls swayed. Her leg, swelling over the ankle into muscle, was a peasant's leg. I followed.

The English miss was saying to Condoorum:

'Oh, yes. Pa wouldn't leave his garden even for the boat-race. We live at Mortlake-on-Thames. There was everyone on the tow-path, running and shouting, you know, but not pa. He just digs on and on and on. 'E's a wonder, is pa.'

'Ha!' From Condoorum, in approval.

Donal, called Tiger at home, leaned on his spade and bit his earthed nails — wherefore Tiger.

'God above, there's nothing like it here, Corney. I know the Regatta of course is me daza and all to that. But,' gnawing viciously in his wonder at them, 'them English is a marvellous race. Only two boats they has in a regatta and all over in wan minute. And thousands at it. Think how cheap that is!'

Down at the river's edge, away from them, the town

crept near with its closed shops and the night silence; violet houses, slated against southern rain, falling across the sinking tide. The old little tram rumbled by under lights yellowed with age. When she said Thames, she said Tems — probably as the Saxon chronicler Alfred said it, and when she said London it was a boom of guns. But Cork-on-the-Lee, the hiss of a jakes, when you said it many times like the Litany in the churches that say Prayfrusprayfrusprayfrus ... But supposing one said, The town of Urshensk on the navigable river Zusha does a regular trade in hemp and oils; the Cathedral of Saint Nicholas contains a miraculous image reputed to ... The metallic bell across the flats called the dark nuns to curl into their beds, into a dreamless sleep, or like the saint who dreamed of butterflies and sunlight, to dream of their country cabins, the rank turf like dung on fire, the old dog across the hearth, the rick, the sister or brother in the byre, never to be seen again. Another rat prop-propped into the water, an immense rat. Suppose one said, The town of Cork on the navigable river Lee does an immense trade in distilling, glass, iron-smelting. It returns two members to Parliament. Would that be better? The bell, falling away, replied with the name, *Parnell*.

So the faint far boom of the lament went heavy-treading through the streets, and its boom was the boom of London, and its beat was the beat of the slowing heart. But London spoke a strange unvirginal name —

her form tall as the window where she stood, her arm white as the dusk, her body gleaming, a round knee, a rising flank, milk-cream . . .

Breathless I rejoined them. They had earthed their spuds.

'Elsie, you're coming with me.'

'We're off,' said Mabel.

'Elsie, before the dark. In the woods. With me.'

'Indeed, no. Is it miss a grand jaunt up Fair Hill?'

'We're going in our chariot, my dear Cornelius. We must plant the winter cabbage in our second farm.'

'Elsie! Elsie!'

But they put the plants on their laps and they drove in their tumbril through the deserted city. People had crept indoors. The bell was silent — the iron tongue. There was distant cheering as if the anti-Parnellites were making a cruel triumph. But, to plant our tuppence-worths of greens, we must form our own procession, along the poor quays where the mothers leaned over the walls and showed their fatted calves. We climbed steeply towards Shandon on our tour of Cork, and Elsie's nose wrinkled with delight at another of Mabel's stories.

Shandon rose up over a narrow street where shops jutted canopies of wood over the pavement. By a narrow lane we at last came to a still higher hill and so stood over the city. Below us she was threaded by channels, about us she was girt by praying spires, beyond, as to our hands, the small houses shoulder to shoulder, dimity-screened and dim, made steps-and-stairs of the hill. We passed an old woman dozing on a chair by her door, for the autumn evening was still and warm, and at another door a woman who stood with a hand on her son's shoulder and looked in content down into the bowl of smoke. Up and up, and the penny-leaves crammed the crevices of the walls, and behind us the higher we went the more horizons of green crested the smoky valley. Beyond all those steep pents of horizon must be, I thought, the milk of the sea and its invisible line waiting to crown this island city, until, sea-bounded, she floated like a raft.

We climbed up higher still over the brow, and there away and away a new land of hedges, nameless baronies and townlands and the nearer litany that I knew and intoned to Elsie as they lowered the threads of roots into the earth and the hurlers shouted in the field and the cows dribbled by us on the scarlet road:

'Elsie, the woods of Ardrum, and that forest road, it's a tonsure across them, and Saint Anne's woods, and the Curragh woods, and Blarney woods.'

'Eoh,' said the English one, 'I *would* like a Lager.'

'We don't do that at all here,' comforted Elsie, paying no heed to me and easy as her own blood. 'Do we, Donal?'

For all his unlineal softness, there was a wink in his roving eye.

'Gor, no. The wimmen in Ireland does dat behind the door. "Come you in here, now," ' he imitated the

country-women's furtive voices, ' "and we'll have it all
by ourselves away from the min." '

His laugh was at himself, like Mabel's—and at his girl.

'But, 'aven't you got any saloon bars? Tea-
gardens and tables, and sun-shades?'

'Jez, no,' and he said something about concrete yards
and drains.

'Elsie, won't you walk home with me?'

I said it beggar-like, tipping her bare arm still
fawned by summer. It was round, warm, soft, her
jacket lying across it. The wind curved her skirt between her limbs.

'Elsie!'

Her attention seemed to be all on Donal, charmed
by him, but she turned to ask Mabel what time it was
and Mabel looked at the pub and nodded at it: the
doors were closed. At once Elsie turned for home,
crying out that she would be slaughtered. Waving
backwards, I ran after her, and after us Mabel shouted
that it is hard to keep computation of the flight of time.
We took a short cut down over the fields, with Elsie
apparently too startled to listen to my talk; until in a
cleft of the hills the harbour opened up to us and she
stopped and smiled at me.

'I forgot. Daddy is out to-night after the poachers.
I needn't hurry.'

At once I took her waist, knowing by her smile that
she had fibbed to Mabel so as to be with me in secret.
I again stroked the down of her arm. She looked at the

winding lochs of the lower Lee and talked of her father's work. He would lie, to-night, off the banks with the Conservatory men and there wouldn't be a sound but the mud whispering; not a star, the mere tip of a moon, and they would wait and be ready to dash out for the fishermen trawling with illegal nets after salmon out of season.

'And watching is in season, for it will be no use when the moon gets bigger.'

With intelligence she spoke of the old Game Laws that let a man be hanged for stealing a salmon, and permitted man-traps. When she explained with her fingers and my fingers how fish are caught in the meshes of the nets I wanted to turn it to foolishness and love-making, but she talked on and I allowed her to wrap me with that talk of simple things back into an envelope of time and the world and common life that I had, all the evening, in my loneliness, been trying to deride.

All but the edges of the day were now folded underneath the earth, and the planets had begun to shine, and we on the hill road above her house saw the river wind with light and remembered rather than saw the land about it. We crossed the little moor and on the pathway among the furze we halted in the last afterglow. The wind in the pines was indistinguishable from the weir in the wind. To our right was the old graveyard, now hardly used, and as she talked of that the sense of being warmed by people, of warming them, that lovely sense of crowds that you lose as you grow old, came over me again like a hot breath.

'The graveyard, so near? Aren't you afraid?'

Pressing her waist.

'Afraid? I'm terrified when I'm alone. But,' she romanced, 'when I was a kid I used play among the stones. That was when old Daddy Sullivan lived in the lodge. He had a great view of the valley of the Lee but he saw it across gravestones. He was like a grey mouse who used to come out' — she humped herself and made a funny face — 'in the evening foraging for kindling. It was all old coffin-wood he used, thrown up by new burials. He used say there were people in it since the Famine days. They made grand fires — all green flames.'

'You're an awful little liar, Elsie,' I teased, and smacked her behind.

'Indeed, I'm not,' she said, swaying down jauntily before me. 'I saw hair sticking to the wood one time.'

I let her go on, unsuspecting. The moon-edge came out, delicate as a shell, and the fish of the river turned its belly. Then, as she was a little way from me I moaned out — 'O-o-oh!' She gave a little scream and turning ran back into my arms. I laughed, but when I felt the little ribs of her corset through her light frock I held her tightly and nodded to the woods.

'Elsie?'

'No, no,' she said, as in one shuddering word.

'With me, Elsie?' in a rising note of pained surprise.

The wind was a cold wraith down the hill and the clouds mere thinned ghosts flying before it.

'With *me*, Elsie?'

She watched me coaxing her. We would be alone, we and the smell of the waterfall and of the dead leaves rising out of the dark road under its canopy of trees. But if I left her, I coaxed, I would see not the glow of the moon through the trees, but, alone in my room, the altar-lamp leaping under the wind.

'Darling Elsie!'

'But all Cork' she protested weakly, 'and the little nuns in their beds.'

I drew her, smiling that smile of fear that only lovers know, into the woods, and we heard nothing but the sough of the pines, a sea-shell moaning, and once two boys ran by on the road below, talking aloud to keep their courage up. Once there we loved fiercely, and in spite of that fear that never left her, she loved that I should love her, and that I should make her love me, more than all she better loved before we met — by my hands that were colder than her body. She would, even then, I think, have loved me to the uttermost if I had not loved her too much and been too frightened by her eagerness to blow on the secret fire she had exposed.

We parted without speaking, and when her door had written and unwritten its line of light on the fields, I turned homeward. The alders moulted with a crackle like stone, and in the city every step was an echo. From my room I looked and looked over the roofs. The sky was clear but the moon was ringed by a mighty spectrum, and within that coloured circle, spread wide as the world, there was a movement of cloudfloes elsewhere invisible. The planets were faint pricks. There would be rain.

Then I thought of the dead man, and how pale his face would be, and I said into the passing floes of mist:

'I'll say to Christy, when next we argue about religion: "Christy, beauty is all there is. It's the end. It's the only perfect thing there is. It is the perfection of the moon, Christy, a harmony thrust on an imperfect world. Everything comes from it — all our beliefs and faiths — all our dreams of a perfect world hereafter. So that if there were a square moon, Christy, you'd be talking about the corners of Heaven. All life! Everything! In the perfect moon!"'

But I was simple . . . Tingling with love, sated, her flesh my flesh, her love mine, mine hers, I did not know there would be a time when, for so much wanting her my very bowels would groan like millstones that grind air.

For a week after we met daily, because she was about to go away on a visit to her brother the priest in London and we knew we could not meet, then, for a month. Even between those meetings I wrote to her, searching translations of the Latin authors for a quotation to flatter her, or writing quatrains of my own. She would reply, teasingly, with a pious leaflet, or fondly, with a long humorous letter about her brothers and sisters. Once Propertius brought back a mother-of-pearl rosary beads and, as it shimmered, I prayed on it for us both.

VIII

LATE one night towards the end of that week the
rain woke me and my window-blind blowing in. I
heard my grandfather stirring upstairs and then he
was knocking at my door.

'Come up, Corney.'

I followed him and found Christy Tinsley before me.
He gave me a queer hard look, as if he were weighing
me up. Up to this I knew him for a rather soft fellow
with a weakness for drinking and smoking in club-
rooms where he was distinguished from dozens like
him only by his silence. But to-night his greenish
eyes were like crystals, the cornea protuberant and
transparent, and with that down-looking trick of his it
gave him a look like his father, intent, suspicious. Of
the elfish smile that people liked in him there was no
sign. Burying his chin in his throat he said deeply:

'Corney, I'm in a bit of a mess. I've been hiding here
for four days. In this room. I'm afraid there's a peeler
dead somewhere.'

I looked around. There were signs of cooking — a
saucepan, a tea-strainer and the like. We sat around the
lamp, as usual, with the rain walloping the slates.

He was a member of the Republican Brotherhood,
he told me.

'Have been for two years or more. You know we

stood in with the politicians — until, you know . . . We thought it was our chance — the Land troubles. The gun and dynamite is the thing to talk to the English with. Parnell got us when he said, "The only way to talk to an Englishman is with your hand on his throat. Or a knife".'

(That was the Phoenix Park murders he was talking about.)

'But he sold us,' he went on and he said that more than once, bitterly. 'Threw us aside for a woman', or 'A woman told him to do it and he did it'. And the like.

I turned to my grander. He shook his head and I remembered they had been there for four days and nights (that would be since the night Parnell died), arguing and arguing until they were addled.

'God almighty,' cried Christy, while we shushed him into a lower voice, 'all Ireland knows it. She was having her child by him. Were we fools, I ask you? But if he could stop, we couldn't. Our men are in gaol for him. Hundreds of them.'

'Ssh!'

He named them. He listed them from Portland to Peterhead. Philip Carney, Tom Kelly, Mortimer Hogan, James Mulquain, Dick Cassidy . . . As if they were his family he was naming. They were going mad in prison, eating ground glass, beaten, half-starved. His eyes glinted as he described it.

'Didn't you know? Didn't you know?'

'Be quiet, Christy.'

'And he didn't give a damn about them. They could rot there for all he cared. Or half Ireland cared either. So long as he had his kissing and his love-making. And now he's gone, will anyone at all care, only squabbling over his bones? What, "know"? Of course they know. But — there's thousands in gaol, and all forgotten already. Men in for cattle-driving, cattle-houghing, evictions. And they're bad enough but they'll be out in two or three years. But Collins in Peterhead, Tom Clarke in Dartmoor — they'll stay there for ten, fifteen, twenty years, over the end of the century.'

'I was wrong,' moaned my grander, 'ever to trust him.'

They were on edge, the two of them cooped up there for days, talking, talking.

'What's happened, then?' I asked.

'I say we *couldn't* stop when he stopped. The night he died,' he said sullenly, 'we did something.'

'We?'

'I was in it.'

'In what?'

''Twas a barracks.'

The rain beat the roofs. He went on. With a few shotguns they let fly at a police barracks that night — Elsie and I had been looking down at the harbour loch at the lights of the village where they did it.

'Did ye kill somebody?'

'No. We didn't want to. But on the way home the side-car ran into a policeman who was cycling without a lamp. We knocked him flat and he was badly hurt. His skull. We took him up and brought him to the hospital in Cork — we couldn't let him die there, could we?'

I shook my head sadly.

'Of course not,' he agreed. 'We left him on the steps of the North Infirmary and rang the bell and came away. We met Canty and Stoney Sullivan,' mentioning two medical students we knew, 'coming up the hill.'

'I see. "Will you tell me, Mr. Tinsley",' I went on, imitating the voice of a prosecuting counsel, ' "what exactly you were doing when these two young men met you? The Court would like to know what you were doing at midnight down the Carrigtwohill Road when you ran into this policeman? The man remembers seeing shotguns with you. Perhaps you would like us to believe that you were shooting duck on the river?" I suppose,' I went on, 'that's your idea — the peeler saw you all right, skull or no skull?'

'We don't know for certain. He was conscious. That's why we're lying low. If he dies, and God send he does, we're all right. But Phil here tells me they've been watching my lodgings ever since, and Arthur John has been here twice since wanting to know where I've gone to.'

'Ah! "Your guardian, Mr. Tinsley, seems to have no idea, et cetera". You're in a mess, all right.'

Grander was clearly helpless. He kept fiddling with the wick-winder of the lamp. The wind had the flame leaping. He was hopeless, exhausted. We began to argue and kept at it for an hour, but Christy was short-tempered and the old man was stupid and savage and we got nowhere. It all depended on, 'If the peeler dies', and we said that 'if' over and over again.

'When, precisely, did you pick up the policeman?'

'Half-past eleven, I told you that six times, damn it!'

I was in the wood then with Elsie. And the Condoorums knew I went home with her after ten, so I couldn't say I was with Christy — unless Elsie would swear falsely that we met him on the way. . . .

'Where were you, grander?'

'Galvin's pub. And we were talking for an hour outside it.'

I gave it up. We were each at a window looking at the cold rain. The old man stared at us miserably. Christy must do what a hundred like him had done before him, fly the country until we found out what the police really knew; and if the peeler lived, he must fly farther and end his days in America or the colonies.

'I'm afraid there's no more to be done,' I sighed, and I went away, but when I was in my room and was again hearing the sudden rise of the storm I realized that the pair of them, between them, hadn't as much sense as would get a fly out of a cup. So I stole upstairs again, past the sleeping doors. Grander was talking to him about Virginia de Wolfe and saying he could stay with her in London. (We never even thought of his calling on my brothers, Maurice or Michael; they were already lost to us, divided by their own ambitions and their own lives.)

'Are you sure,' I said bitterly, hearing this talk of Virginia, 'that you wouldn't like him to stay in a police-station? A woman that's known to every policeman in London. A common . . .'

'Stop.'

'I once heard,' I taunted, 'of two dynamitards who wanted to blow up London Bridge and they asked the detectives who were following them to show them the way. Look here, Christy, have you any money?'

'A few shillings.'

'And you?'

The old man just sank his head.

'Then for Christ's sake will you tell me how he's going to get to London?'

Once more we quarrelled. In the end we decided miserably that he must cycle out to Bandon to a cousin of his father's and wait there until we got the money to send him out of the country. In spite of his weariness I made him get up and set out on foot before morning. He went, and as the dawn crushed between two rain-clouds we watched him go up past the cathedral, the rain lashing his bowed head.

Three hours later the police-detectives were knocking at the door. Never was my da more true to his nickname — Christ-on-the-Cross. It was the last blow for him when they searched the house, and up and down he cursed the two of them while they warned him to respect the law. Then he turned on me.

'And, boy,' he roared, 'if you have hand, act, or part,' and he running his claws through his hair, 'or if that fool of a father of mine had . . . This bloody business. . .'

'Don't be swearing, father,' I said.

'Christ . . . O God, look down on me!' He sank, in his shirt and trousers, on the plush chair in the topsy-turvy dining-room and he wept with vexation. I went off, as if to mass, but really to borrow some money for Christy before they got on his track. I got it from Elsie — she gave up her holiday to let me have it, and went with it to Bandon and we were driven in by his uncle to Blarney and so away to Dublin on the train. There I saw him off in the boat. But when I got back to Cork my da just put his black sombrero on his head and bade me come with him to the police. They had been looking for me while I was away.

'Take the boy,' he said to the foxy-bazz of a police-man who met him in the guard-room. 'If he has done harm let him be punished. If he's innocent, ye'll pay dear for it.'

And so, just as when he used to chastise me as a child, he handed me over and left without a word. They had arrested me, I realized, in order to lure Christy into the open. He came back and was arrested and as the peeler lived and saw even more than they had feared, they also got every man who was out that night. I was released on heavy bail, but when the trial came, that Christmas,

I had to stand in the dock beside the others, and Elsie and the Condoorums had to give evidence to free me.

All Cork, as they say, was at the trial, my da and Elsie's father and the Condoorum tribe and my grander and Arthur John Coppinger. The Crown went as far back as old Arty Tinsley's record, to show that Christy came of a bad stock. Everything came out, even to the way in which Tinsley was nearly sold to the cut-'em-ups; my grander's career in Skibbereen forty years before; and how I was in the woods at midnight with Elsie Sherlock — unknown to her father, who told her afterwards that she had publicly disgraced herself, had made herself cheap, ought to be sent to the priest, had disgraced her brother in Maynooth, and he forbade her ever to see or speak with any of us again. He promised the judge he would see to that.

I was acquitted on Elsie's evidence and the Condoorums'. With four others Christy was sentenced to fifteen years in gaol, commuted to ten years because they were all mere boys. He was taken from Cork Gaol on Christmas Eve morning over to Millbank in London. I was at the station, where I saw him hustled from the Black Maria into the train with everyone staring at him. He waved a handcuffed hand to me. Then the detectives ordered me to leave the platform.

I spent that day tramping the bitter streets and the sodden fields, without a soul to talk to or a door to knock at. I sent a letter by special messenger to Elsie, but she returned it and I swore I would never write to

her again, think of her, speak to her. I hated her
cowardice. I hated the way she let her family crucify
her, bully her with gentleness, shape her whole life by
a look or a sigh. By lonely wandering and brooding I
increased in bitterness. My contempt spread to so
many people, that I felt what had happened to me was an
image of the far worse that had happened to Christy,
to his friends, to the Fenians, to the Land Leaguers, to
Parnell.

That was the only Christmas that saw no letter or
present pass between us. I did go into the city to buy
something for her — to be sent with some small message
that would touch her with a sense of my magnanimity.
I met her, possibly on the same sort of errand, and we
stood on one foot and looked away at the traffic.

'Good night, Miss Sherlock,' I said.

And she said, 'Hello, Corney'.

'I suppose,' I said, 'all the Holy Family will be together out the Lee by now?'

'What do you mean?'

'Father Arty and the embryo from Maynooth and
the nuns.'

'Tom is home,' she said coldly. 'Sister Eustacia is
in the Poor Clares. They do not come out. My other
sister is in Tipperary — in the Presentation nuns. It is
an enclosed order.'

'Well,' I quoted, 'it's a good order. Let them be
locked up so that they may make fools of themselves
only in their own House. As Shakespeare says.'

She gave me one look and she said:

'Corney' (with a sigh), 'you can be an awful *idiot* sometimes.'

And off she went, while I congratulated myself that I had got under her skin. Then I set off swiftly round and round the crowded streets. I saw several people I knew. I met only one who spoke to me — Arthur John, and he said, 'Merry Christmas', as if he was saying, 'You poor sinner'.

Late on Christmas night I stood on the high hill over the frosted and moonlit roofs of Gilabbey and whispered down at the city ... and then, off again, round and round the lanes, all lit, all loud, and not until the small hours did I return home, exhausted and shivering, glad to see the light in my grandfather's gable-window high against the night clouds. I stole up to him and we comforted ourselves, each at his own loss, over a bottle of whisky stolen from the larder. In the end I went into bed beside him. He talked of Christy and Christy's father, remembering, self-blaming, self-excusing. He talked me asleep.

It was a bad year for me. In spite of myself I could not keep from trying to see her, even though when we met we would quarrel again; and we did quarrel when we did meet. By the end of that winter I had spoken to her only a few times, and then by accident that I tried to arrange so that neither of us should feel we were meeting deliberately: though, in secret, I thought sometimes that she connived with me and walked after dusk where of old we used to walk after dusk. When we met then we were like electric magnets that might keep an obstacle suspended between them, so that if we could only desire less it would fall and we could touch. These were the nights I had not foreseen, and as I lay abed staring out at the skies, smoking endlessly, my imaginings became more daring and passionate. I used try to interpose other things between us; wandering and drinking with my grander, and he hinting his sympathy and trying to plot for me; I would even turn to praying when the asp hurt cruelly; or I read of all the unfortunate lovers of the world such as Aucassin, and the Knight in Chaucer, and Troilus in Boccaccio, and Vittoria that Michael Angelo loved until he was seventy, and Beatrice who was a child like Elsie, and it was an ease to read, between those barren meetings:

The thridde, ferthe, fifte, sixte day,
After tho dayes ten of which I tolde,
Betwixen hope and drede his herte lay,
Yet somwhat trustinge on her hestes oldë.
But whan he saugh she nolde hir terme holdë
He can now seen non other remedye
But for to shape him sonë for to dyë . . .

'But for to shape him sonë for to dyë.' That helped to keep what I called my 'last beauty' unsullied, a bitter-sweet.

We met one hard spring night, when I was trembling

for her affection as a drunkard trembles for drink too long kept from him, and I told her of the way things were at home. In pity she held my hand.

It was the only night we came close together.

'The house is like a bloody dishcloth, Elsie,' I said. 'My grander hasn't left his room for days, now. Robert is the maid, with an apron round his waist. The old lady too — she's gone to the devil. No wonder the others are all running from us. It's well for Vicky — in a convent.'

'Yes.'

'I suppose you'll soon go into one?' I said.

'Do I look it?'

Then, as girls do, she began to prove me to see what kind of love I had for her.

'That night,' she said, shyly. 'After the wood.'

'Which night?' I insisted: for I would not be ashamed of it. She lowered her head over my lapels, fiddling with them.

'*That* night. When Parnell died.'

'Oh, that night? Yes?'

'It changed everything. We were just friends up to then. Comrades. Then it got serious.'

I was silent, or rather, silenced by her.

'Don't you feel it that way?' she asked.

I laughed and said, 'No', though it was true; for I knew that if I admitted it my lyric would change somehow, and even as she looked at me now doubtfully, I thought: 'So we have come to it? At last? Out of the lazy days when there was nothing to do but play with one another? Out of the kissing in wintry corners? Into the heat of the day? All our grasshopper days gone for ever?'

Seeing that I was saddened by the thought, she was satisfied, and changed quickly like a shrewd wife.

'Isn't that godly?' She threw her arm over the elms below, all swaying as if they were seaweed that moved in an invisible sea. Perversely I said:

'It's lovely, anyway.'

'Is that all, Corney?' Still probing. 'Just lovely.' And then, 'You haven't been to mass for months and months'. 'Isn't it enough for it to be lovely? It takes away all the ugliness of life to look at it. Isn't that enough?'

She looked at the far-off clouds, dissatisfied. I insisted:

'Of course it's enough. Down there in the fields — things prowling on each other's trail; the buds pitted already by insects; cold in the new nests. It's all there, Elsie, the cruel and the lovely in one.'

'It's not merely a world of brutes,' she said, almost sullenly.

'Except that you and I are aware of it, the only difference between us and that tree ...'

'You once said,' she stabbed, 'that I was a fallen tree. It's not complimentary. I'm stupid. Was that it?'

'Elsie! Look! The night in the wood, you say you cried when you went in home. You were full of sad thoughts. If I go questioning that rippled river there . . .'

'It couldn't even tell you that much.'

'It couldn't. It doesn't think about itself.'

'Then why think about it?' she appealed.

'I don't. I just say it's lovely. You want to drag God into it. My child, it all just is. That's all.'

She protested passionately.

'God made it in all wisdom. You and me, and the woods. You don't need to know more than that.'

I smiled:

'Yes. He made it. I can know nothing? That's true. Then I may as well live like the birds of the air?'

Half-gaily, half-angrily, she mocked me.

'Have *sense*, boy! You know there *is* a meaning. You can't know what the meaning *is*? It's a mystery. For God's sake, let it alone.'

'And how,' I cried back, 'do I know even that but from what I see? There is the work of God — the foxes, the weasels, the storms, the ferrets, the dying trees, that flood. We learn from it that life just lives by itself. It's there, there, and nothing else but there. Then live like it, without a thought.'

'Without a thought?' she puzzled.

'As you said: "Don't think about it." '

She tousled her hair while I laughed at her sullen discomfiture.

'You're too clever for me. I can't argue. You have a soul. You forget that.'

'Ha? The fields and the trees taught you that, did they? No, no!' I cried, weary of this talk with such loveliness all round us. 'That is all we need to know — the river's darkness, the upturned elms, seaweeds swaying . . .'

'My brother Tom,' she said absently, 'calls seaweeds algae.'

She kissed me that day, tenderly and sadly, while the choked sky weighed us down and the hills wore white cloud cloaks over their shoulders and the little birds sang as if to tell us to stop for God's sake and let them go to sleep. The rain kept us under the trees, and the water ran down our necks. She said, almost pleadingly:

'Of course *I*'m a Christian.' And then, 'Corney, will you go to mass to-morrow?'

When we left she had her little fist tight about a scapular, and she drew me under an ivy and with a pin from under her skirt she pinned it to my braces: it was cream and brown, the Tertiary of Saint Francis, and wrinkled from her clutching fist.

'You're a saint, Elsie!'

She said, with passion:

'If you only *knew*!'

She left me, promising to pray for me, looking fondly yet timidly into my two eyes. I left her, priding in my own intelligence, and in the satisfaction that comes on a man when he is gradually moulding another mind to his own image and desire. But, as if she had become afraid of me when she went over our talk in her mind, she did not come that way for weeks and weeks, and I was once more trailing the roads, saying aloud:

> The thridde, ferthe, fifte, sixte day
> After tho dayes ten of which I tolde,
> Betwixen hope and drede his herte lay . . .
> . . . whan he saugh she nolde her terme holdë . . .

And so, again, to that acrid sea of Despair that swims in the heart between the hills of Anger and Desire.

Not until the end of the summer when my grandfather had scraped enough money, and I had filched
enough from the cashbox, did we visit Christy in Millbank. We were the only two who ever went to him,
and that was the only time we went; his guardian,
Arthur John, wrote to him sometimes but he never saw
him from the day of his arrest. My grander's Parnellism was blown hot and cold by that visit so that I had
to laugh at his sudden changes of feeling. He had
never lost his veneration for the Chief. A coat that he
once held up before the flying stones and bottles during
Parnell's last visit to Cork he would never wear again,
and it hung behind his door, honoured as a sudarium,
brushed and tended. Still, there was Christy, his old
friend's son, in gaol, without a relative to think of him,
without a friend to visit him; and he was only one of
many others who had fought when their blood was up
and were never thought of after the storm.

But when we saw Mr. Redmond in the House of
Commons and he shook hands with us, the old flame
leaped up again because he was the only one of the
Party who ever visited these prisoners or tried to inter-
cede for them with the British: the others scratched
and squabbled and forgot.

We met him in the Inner Lobby, in his finely cut

clothes, with his dignified jowls and his firmly-curved nose, and he told us that he might, if he only had a united Party behind him, get something done. But even as he spoke to us, there across the wide pavement was the crooked head of Healy with the grey hairs through his squat beard, peering over at us as he scratched the small of his back under his coat and stretched himself after long sitting in the House.

'Oh, Jasus,' my grander growled, 'look at that black bastard Healy. The man that sent poor Parnell to his grave.'

And he fingered his stick and his beard bristled as if he was going to run across and strike down the man who hated his dead leader. And when we left Redmond and were sitting alone in the Strangers' Gallery and saw the broken benches of the divided Party he bowed his head on his stick and cried like a child.

'Parnell, me poor man!' he kept saying into his hands. 'They kilt yeh. 'Twas here they kilt yeh dead.'

I had to take him out, still snivelling, past the staring attendants and the policemen, out into the London streets, along the Embankment, and he beating his ferrule on the ground and sobbing at me:

'The grandest wan of 'em all, Corney. And be Jasus, they kilt him. The lousy Irish — they turned on him and rent him.'

'Think of Christy, grander. He deceived Christy. He betrayed him and his likes for a woman.'

It only made him worse. He leaned over the quay-wall and he waved his stick and he looked with glazed eyes down into the water.

'No, no, no. He didn't. The grandest man of 'em all. 'Twas the bloody English done it. They put that woman in his way. They . . . they . . . Oh!'

He straightened up and he looked east at Westminster and west at Millbank, and he began to shout at the passing hawkers and clerks:

'Ye bloody English. Ye hoor's bastards. Ye bloody Saxons. The Fenians are right. He was too soft with ye. Too soft and gentle. O God, this day if I was only a young man again, I'd tache ye.'

And so on and on while I pulled at him and besought him and dragged him away from a Cockney drayman who had halted his horse and was listening in a growing anger. I got him into a pub and I had to get him out of it again because he began to get maudlin there over his malt, with:

'Poor Ireland. Down and out. Divided and bruk. O Vo! Vo!' And, singing in his liquor:

> 'O harp of my country,
>   In darkness I found thee,
>   The cold chain of silence
>   Hath hung o'er thee long . . .'

Where the barges flowed gently but swiftly by, and in an old curio shop the figureheads of ancient English ships breasted out to the traffic, we turned aside for our visit to the gaol. After long waiting, during which the old man's spirits sank to a dry ebb, we saw Christy.

He was broken. His bright eyes were dark and his finger scratched idly and helplessly on the table as he talked in snatches. Like fools we talked of the Lee Fields and of the Sherlocks, and he said Yes, and Ah, and he looked at each of us in between like a sick child that looks up at you without strength as much as to say, 'Do something'. We told him Redmond would get him out, and that we were trying everything we knew. But when the warder ordered him away he looked foolishly at him like a man who understood nothing of what was said. The prison doctor said Christy had been violent and had tried to eat ground glass.

Sitting on a bench up in Hampstead we looked down at the smoke of the great city and we listened to a newly-released prisoner tell us of life in the gaol and about how Christy had begun by beating at the cell-doors and how he had been caught passing a note to a fellow-prisoner — they were not allowed to speak with one another — and how he had been searched, in the shame of nakedness, and punished. They were hardly allowed to sleep. At regular intervals all through the night the warders would open the door, look in, and then, deliberately (I could not believe this) bang the door with an iron crash. They were so near the heart of London, there, they could hear the bells chime the hours and quarters, and they would doze or lie awake hearing them. Several men had gone insane and more surely would, and though in that, again, we could not believe him, it was true. Years after they gave a banquet in Cork to two released Fenians and, the morning after, one went up to the madhouse. Another man, after fifteen and a half years as a convict, told us that he had been in a gaol with Irishmen right and left of him in the one corridor, and at the end he was alone in that row of cells.

We went back to Redmond and pestered him. We hung around and waylaid other members. At last I actually saw my grander go sidling up to 'the traitor', Healy, and talk humbly to him. They were all sorry for Christy. But they could or would do nothing for us.

So, in time, we began to forget Christy because we could not help him and we began to open our eyes to the London about us; for, God forgive us, we had our own lives to live.

You know, the human heart is a dark pit, and sometimes a soiled and dirty pit, and there are selfishnesses in it that we see only when those selfish desires have been satisfied. Did I come there to see Christy? Or did I choose the time because I knew that Elsie was there, that autumn, on holiday with her brother? Our few meetings had been like sips hardly tasted, so that when I knew she was being in London I swore I would meet her where nobody could spy on us, and she might be kind to me and we would make love as of old.

I met her in the street and because her brother was

giving a retreat to some convent of nuns outside London she had the day free. I wanted to see the docks Dickens wrote about in *The Old Curiosity Shop* and so we went in a horse-bus (that was not half slow enough for me) down to Tower Hill and London Bridge. I don't remember much of what we saw, and anyway we took the wrong side of the river after Tower Hill. I know there was the transparent skeleton of a gas-cylinder, low in its bed because the summer was still there — late August — and the spire of what looked like an abandoned church stood up among the masts, white with the pigeon-droppings, black with soot. There were millions of red and yellow chimneypots, and here and there a dark tree strove up through some slim crevasse to the sun and air. On Tower Hill I went into a little tobacconist's shop where the man talked to me with pleasure at having somebody to talk to. He was a fat man in his shirt sleeves, and very old, and because I bought some of his brands of snuff for my grander I can still recall what he said:

'I 'ad a shop in the City at one time. I sold great quantities of snuff. I always sold Candle Brown to the Bank people. But the Laundrymen took Wilson's Mixture. On a Monday morning, if you get my meaning, I'd sell as much as three pounds of it. The printers 'ad their own snuff — they took Morton's Mixture. A dark brown. They sometimes took Prince's too. But 'ere? Oh, it's only bloomin' Irish coalies 'ere. All baccy and clay-pipes!'

It was Morton's Mixture I bought for old Phil — printers being as near as I could get to builders. From him we walked on and on, between the high warehouse walls, dodging the drays, past the dock-gates that were dappled with the shadows of Virginia creepers and little trees. Through those gates we heard and saw old-fashioned dry docks, and the great new docks, and at every point masts stuck up behind houses and streets. She talking of Cork and its little quays and comparing the two cities in every way, or I talking of Quilp and Mrs. Quilp and looking idly for the Dragon Wharf, we walked on and on and in and out, over bridges, past little cottages with their courtyards, and warehouses dusty with their own stores, from Wapping into Shadwell, and Shadwell into Limehouse, careless that we were in the most evil spot in all London. And so out to the vast marsh that was, then, probably the most lonely spot in all England — the Isle of Dogs and the long, lone London Wall.

It was hot. The rank grass about the windmills did not stir. It was as if the little breathing ripple over the Thames could not curl down into this land that was lower than the water. There did not seem to be a soul in those levee-hidden meadows as we stood and looked first over the land and then over the wide water at ship following ship up or down, and our minds dilating with the image of a world's trade and the vastness of an empire of which this was the very heart and centre. I said:

'I feel, Elsie, that what you once said is true. We are like two pebbles in a load of gravel as big as the world. Grains of sand in a Condoorum nightmare.'

The silence and the solitude, unbroken here by the faint, far hum of London, stole over us like a cloud. Like it, we stole to meet it, crept into the meadows away from the brown sails and the white sails and the oars that seemed to tickle the Thames. Yet, even now, though her skin was warm in the sun and my hands were unafraid, we refrained from last love. For I still held that vast image of power and wealth, and beside it there rose the image of a prison far up the Thames.

We lay there and we kissed thought away, until hunger and the long shadows woke us and we rose and went back along the Wall to where we knew a ferry would cross us to the Greenwich side: there, she told me, the South Eastern and Chatham Railway would bring us back to town. Still we did not hurry because her brother was away, and his housekeeper on holiday — that was why she came to him at that time — and the evening was magnificent to every point of the compass: sheaf-strawed, gold-prickled to the west, a cold, perfect outline of blue to the south, with a greenly watered silk taut in the sky behind it: then a reflected wild-fire clambered into the clusters of whiteness in the east; and, where all light was gone, in the north, a coldness as before the Deluge, or as if somebody suddenly put out every light in a bright shop window. Turning from mystery to mystery, finding dogs' heads and strange shapes in the red eastern cloud-world, finding in the north, after that blinding colour among the cloud-worlds, the mere ghost of life, and again around to the chaste blue of dawn, and the blinding corn-chaff of the sunset, around and around, again and again, hardly moving a foot ahead, until the darkness drew us into silence and a solemn mood. In that mood we walked to where an old man sat, sucking a broken clay in the prow of a ferry-boat that had already begun to lose its shape and colour in the fading of the day.

He was not crossing for another quarter of an hour, so we sat in the stern and waited, and heard the squeak of tackle from some boat on the river or the lapping of its wake. He was a talkative Irishman and very intelligent, and when he talked of London Wall, its vast length, its history, how felons hung in chains along its bank in sermon to homing sailors, that too began to grow in the mind until it was not a wall but a thing made up in the imagination. The lights began to spring up and a faint fog crept from the estuary.

'Time would make even a penny smooth', he said, 'and soften its touch. Age cannot wither nor custom stale, as Shakespeare says.' His pipe glowed under his nose. 'This ferry, now, is old. Old? Hum! Let me see. How old would yerself be, lad?'

'Twenty-five,' I said, though I was much less.

'I'm near as long pulling them oars. And there was men at the oars in this same spot since Queen Elizabeth. Many a man crossed the water here and left no sign;

and many a man that left many a sign more lasting than water. Daniel O'Connell crossed this ferry. For, as you know, there's a great number of our people in this part of the world.'

'How did you know we were Irish?' cried Elsie in delight.

He laughed and began to unship his oars.

'And what's more ye're from the South, and I'm no water-rat if ye're not from the County of Cork itself.'

'We're from the city.'

'Ye're not?'

'But we are. Aren't we, Corney?'

He paused. He looked sharply at us. His hair was grey but his brows were thick black. He would have been sombre if he had not a soft kindly mouth, wide above his narrow chin. Even before he spoke I was looking at him, just as curiously, for I felt something coming.

'Would you ever have heard,' he asked slowly and cautiously, 'of a builder there named Philip Crone?'

I might have staved him off if it had not been for Elsie.

'Sure,' she cried, all excitement, 'that's his name. 'He's a Crone. His grandfather — isn't your grand-daddy named Philip, Corney?'

'Mother of Dod,' he said shoving his lighted pipe into his pocket, 'and are you Philip Crone's grandson? The son of John Crone?'

He peered.

'By Cripes, I can see your ould grandfather's tough phiz in ye. I was wondering where did I see ye before.'

'You knew him?' I asked.

Two men approached and entered the boat. They greeted him and said, 'Jim isn't coming'; so he pushed off. From time to time, he said a few more euphemistic oaths under his breath and then he turned to us in the prow and said:

'Would you like to meet yer Uncle Mel, lad? You never saw him. I know that.'

Again Elsie intervened.

'Of course he would. Wouldn't you, Corney?'

He pulled on and when the two men got out he said, 'Stay where you are. I'll run you back to Wappin'. You can get a horse-bus there. I live in Wappin',' he explained.

While I thanked him weakly, and Elsie thanked him heartily, he ran up a tawny sail that caught the light evening wind, and with one look to see if the wind was true south, and would bowl us up the reach he took the helm and sat between us. The ripple gurgled by under the planks. He talked little, because there were many lights of shipping taking the tide to watch and avoid. Gradually the great dome of the naval college dropped down like a sinking balloon and we could see only the lights of London and its vast pall glowing overhead like a thundercloud. He asked many questions. How old was my father? How many brothers and sisters had I? Was my grander in good health? He was in London! By the hokey! He hadn't remarried, had he, the ould divil?

'How did you know,' asked Elsie, 'that Corney is like his granddaddy?'

'I often and often seen the ould lad. I lived for a time in Cork, ye know.'

'And where does my uncle Mel live?'

'In Wappin', and he'll be right glad to see yeh. And his wife too.'

I didn't dare ask if she was the Ophelia of the play, but I asked his own name.

'Timsy Curran, then. Look, there's the Black Eagle wharf, away there by the lights of that schooner. No, that's a barque. There! After the Famine people came from the quays of Cork to that place at a pound a head. By the tens of thousands they came. D'y' see that stairs — that's where Blood landed — the man that stole the Crown jewels. You know the parish priest here is from Bantry? A nate man. There's the tip of the gable of th'ould assembly rooms, there between the two warehouses. The old Gordon Lodge. Sure, the Masons are the best of people — 'tis they have the schools building for us, and the Catholic church. Your Uncle Mel is in the Lodge.'

'You know him well?' I asked.

'Well? He married my sister, Julia. Sure isn't that the whole story? He ran away with her. It left his da cracked — your grandfather. The ould lad was gone about her. But she wasn't the first woman he was gone about. Nor I suppose the last!'

He apologized at once for that.

'You don't mind me saying it, I hope?'

Elsie looked at me. I looked at them both.

'I . . . I was wondering,' I said. 'I mean about my . . . my grander.'

'Never mind. I was a bit loose-mouthed. But if you didn't know, my lad, you might as well know it. Say nothing upstairs. They've forgotten and forgiven. As I say always, time would make even a penny smooth.'

We climbed to the wharf: a house had been built far out on it, over the water: it looked like a tavern. We entered a small kitchen from whose side-windows we saw the crescent moon over the river. There was a pungent, hungry smell of frying onions.

'Julia,' cried the boatman, and we saw her in a corner, turned suddenly from some task, fair-haired, round and soft — the mature enlargement of the mottled tinplate photograph of Ophelia I had seen fifteen years ago in the attic of the Red House. 'A nephew of Mel's. Corney Crone, if you please. And the lady's name?'

I told them.

With a lump of beefsteak in her fist she turned eagerly to us.

''Tis Virginia sent you?'

'No, no,' said Elsie.

'Your da?' to me.

'No, no,' I said.

181

'Not ould Phil Crone?' — to both of us.

'No, no. We just met Timsy by accident.'

'Glory be!' she cried. 'Well, ye're very welcome company. Mel! Mel!' She went to a door with a round window like a porthole set into it, and called him. 'Mel!'

He came in, wiping a pewter tankard (for it was a pub). His name, Mel, because the Irish is *meal* had always suggested honey to me, and I had thought of him as large and red and merry. He was small, watery, with my grandfather's hard eyes; he was bearded, too, but there was no grey in his beard. He had the look of a man who had been through hard times. When his wife said, 'This is Corney Crone, your nephew,' he opened his eyes very wide and contracted the muscles around them — for like all my family he was shortsighted and I know I have that same trick of frowning and peering.

'Corney!' Down went the tankard and out came the hand. 'You're welcome, lad.'

'He met Timsy at the ferry, I think,' said Julia. 'They never knew we were here.'

They clustered about us, eager to examine us, and they badgered us with questions about Cork and the family. Mel was a bit cold, but that was his manner — we're not a warm family at best — and it was plain that our visit gave him real pleasure, as if he hated being cut off from his people and my coming was a link with them. Even so, the visit might have been a failure if it had not been for Elsie. She loved them and their house from the start — it was all, she told me after, so Quilpish, so bizarre, so tumbledown — and because they saw she loved them they were delighted with her; and with so much goodheartedness about me I found myself thawing until I was winking at Elsie who by now had a big glass of sherry in her fist, and gossiping with Julia who had thrown another lump of steak into the middle of the onions, and giving Mel every scrap of news from the family that I could think would interest him. The kindly Timsy left us to attend to the tavern and we sat around the tea-table gossiping for hours. In the end Mel leaned back and said:

'Begod, it's like being back in Cork again. Ah, he wasn't a bad ould fellow. Only like all of us,' he leaned apologetically to Elsie, 'weak in the carnalities. And too proud. Proud as Lucifer.' Glaring at me, but as if with sympathy for the old man: 'Hard, too. You don't know it, of course, Corney. You're too young. But we had a hard life of it growing up with him in Cork. No wonder your father is ambitious. I could see it in him and we growing side by side. He wanted to get away, you know, from all that hard life — from the hand-to-mouth existence. So did I — and that's why I just, simply, in one word, ran away. But John, so you tell me, stood his ground and made his own life? You know,' nodding all round, 'I admire him for it.'

'You're grand and cosy here, now,' encouraged Elsie, looking around at the red fire in the little range and the pictures of ships and the oars in one corner where Timsy left them, and, enviously, at the porthole-door where we could hear glasses clinking and voices gabbling in the bar. Mel looked at his wife.

'Aye! 'Tisn't bad. But we had hard times, all right, Julia, my old soldier. Didn't we, girl?'

She patted his hand, and raised her teacup.

'Through thick and through thin, my lad,' she cried, and I felt Mel did well to marry a girl of such spirit.

I was loth to stir. I wanted him to go on talking about my grandfather and our family. But it was late. We went out through the taproom where, what between smoke and the dim light of the lamp, and the faces of the coalies dark with coaldust — ringed about the eyes even after much washing — we heard more than we saw; though what we heard was clear enough, a flood of sound straight from Ireland, Kerry and Clare and the soft *affetuoso* of Limerick, and the rising Cork accent, and the Tipperary voices, long-drawn out, as if everything was said in faint wonderment. They were all appealing suddenly to Julia for a song, and willingly, even with an air of bravado, she cleared a space and dragged Mel with her. It was clear that she was the real force behind that marriage:

'Come, Mel, boy! In here with me and give them the ould touch. "The Exile's Return".'

They interchanged most lines of the ballad, sometimes sharing a line, sometimes calling on the coalies who roared the refrain out of the human dusk their bodies made around us. She had a good contralto and she let it go:

Julia: It was midnight when Barney stood foreninst his home.
Mel: That he often had dreamt of since first he did roam,
Julia: But now that he saw it by the light of the moon,
Mel: All that was left was — Come lads!
All: — an ould ivied ruin.
Julia: He took off his hat and he stood by the door,
Mel: And looked at the tree that grew out of the floor.
Julia: If that is my fate, says he may it be soon
Mel: To lie under the sod of — Now! —
All: — the ould ivied ruin.

They went on for maybe ten verses at that, with the tankards swaying and always the hoarse voices coming in with a shout, half sorrow, half rage, at the words, 'the ould ivied ruin'.

Julia: He stood by the hearthstone that long was gone cold,
Mel: While the teardrops of sorrow from his two cheeks they rolled,
Julia: To think of how often in a New York saloon,
Mel: He'd dreamt of returning to —
All: — The ould ivied ruin.

There were cries from time to time from the dark mass — 'Good man, Mel!' or 'Ah, God help us, then', or 'The devil he did', or a silence for several verses when the pathos of the thing moved them too much, or thoughts of the 'ould land' they might never see again; but at the last verse they took the song to themselves and the taproom roared with it.

> By the soul of my fathers I swear I'll not rest
> 'Til I come back to Ireland and fight with the best.
> Come back to ould Ireland both sudden and soon,
> And build up again — the Ould Ivied Ruin.

That did not satisfy them, either: they saw the chances of a merry night, and being already warm with heat and the drink they called for more songs. Whereupon Elsie, a little merry herself from the sherry and the heat, stood out and sang them a song about Cork and its drisheens and the emigrant boat at Passage and Cork Harbour Lights, with a chorus that they took up readily, cheering her every time, it so pleased them:

> So good-bye and good-bye,
> And good-bye and good-bye,
> And my eyes *are* dry,
> To the cocks *and* the geese
> *And* the dogs *and* their fleas,
> *And* the fish up on top of Shandon Steeple . . .

Laughing, she escaped their black paws and their cries of, 'A darlint girl', — 'My tush of a girl' — out with Timsy and myself to the door where we said a last good-bye to Julia and my uncle Mel. Then the three of us were zigzagging up the narrow streets, a laughing group, delighted with ourselves and the grand night we had, and I shouting to Timsy,

'My God, Timsy, and to think her brother's a priest and she with two more in Maynooth and God knows how many nuns.'

'When the cat is out,' she laughed, and her hat in her hand and her curls to the cold air, 'every dog to his day.'

'So good-bye and good-bye,' sang Timsy, 'and good-bye and good-bye, and my eyes *are* dry . . . My Father, where'd you get her? Are you going to marry her?'

'Of course I am,' I cried.

'If I have you,' she said saucily.

'And good-bye and good-bye, to the fish on Shandon Steeple.'

I knew he would be singing it for days.

'The fish would swim off in to a cloud if he heard of it,' I teased her.

'And what would Canon Whitley say?' she teased back.

'Oh, good-bye and good-bye,' maundered Timsy, and we joined him as we strolled into the road, arm in arm,

And good-bye and good-bye
And my eyes *are* dry,
To the cocks *and* the geese
And the dogs *and* their fleas,
And the fish up on top of Shandon Steeple.

We only sobered down when we came where the flares hissed over the fruit-barrows and old-clothes stalls, where there were rabbis in skull-caps and big-breasted Jewesses that would rouse any man, they were so warm-skinned, so soft, so luxuriant, making Elsie, fine girl though she was, look like a staring fish. In a dream we left Timsy at the bus. His last words were to 'give his love to good old Shandon Steeple', and we could know by his lips that he was singing the refrain as he waved. We jogged through the dark City and into the bright West End where there were other beautiful women and another kind of gay life, and so north through poorer districts, past the Italian quarter, to her house. It was well after eleven o'clock.

There in the poor house of a London priest the Ordo lay open at one end of the table (his desk) to mark the feasts and guide him through his breviary and his missal; and at the other end of the table (his dining-room) away from the pens and inks, was his table-cloth, worn thin and holed from innumerable washings and ironings. The fire was still alight, with the glow through the ashes to remind me of the glow of light through the clouds that afternoon, and as we sat on a sofa before it and poked it up and added a few lumps, we talked over and over everything that had happened during the day.

With my arms about her I said, at last,

'Must I go now, Elsie?'

But she turned back to Mel and his wife and how

happy they were in their queer little house and how he did well when he ran away from Cork with her, and again how happy they surely were, and she put her arms around my neck and said, 'You must go', and I held her and kissed her and said, 'Send me away', and yet delayed to recall that lighted tavern and how nicely we two could live and love in it — the moon, the *hoot-hoot* from the river at night, the lonely Wall far behind.

I did not go and she did not send me from her, though even then I had to plead and plead for my desire. She made me turn away my head and from under the lace fringe of the bedroom blind I saw the moon from where I lay. Then she stamped out the candle with one blow of her hand and I saw her shape for only a second. The street was silent. We were silent. Then her passion blazed.

The next thing I saw was the grey dawn under the brown laced fringe, and there were the houses, windows, roofs, staring at me sullenly as, at the end of a long trial, a judge might stare at a murderer.

When I was in the street everything had that same corpse-like look. The sun might be risen somewhere off beyond the Thames, over the lowlands of Flanders, but it was not risen here. Without it the houses were blind men. The air was still as a wakehouse candle. My feet made dull sounds as if I walked on the bottom of a dead sea. I could think of one thing only — how she had trembled when I loved her, and that she had not said a word the whole night long, not even when I

had left her, saying we would meet in Ireland, except
to nod and smile faintly. From blank to blank of
thought I wandered on. There was a gasworks, a row
of empty warehouses — or they seemed empty in that
submarine dimness before dawn — there were bridges,
a canal with a sleeping barge, a maternity hospital with
a light or two. I was walking faster and faster now, as
if something were following me and I wanted to shake
it off. Then I grew angry with her; saying she had not
trembled in the fields below the Wall, and that all
women must be like that, wanting love, but wanting it
to be taken, not wanting the blame or pain of it. But it
made no matter, and the echoes of my feet followed me
just the same. It was a relief to see a man driving a
dray, and then more drays rumbled over the cobbles
and more men. That was what I wanted — to be taken
out of my burning brain and mingled again into men
and life and the warmth of crowds. But I saw a man
who was like Timsy Curran and I hurried away down
a side street not to see him again. Somewhere I stopped
for a long time looking between bars at a smooth grass-
lawn, it might have been Gray's Inn, the dew pointing
it all over with a mist. (I feel too ashamed to confess
even now how or why I passed on from all that dreamless and tender purity of grass and flowers.) Then there
were the drops shining on the cabbages of Covent
Garden where I drank a mug of coffee among the
carters, envying them their busy work: and, when I had
left them, there came, a long time after, the clank of the

bell in Millbank Gaol, and the scaffoldings of the new Catholic cathedral. The altar-bell tinkled as I passed beyond the porch and came to the bustle of Victoria, and our hotel.

My grander was at breakfast. Casually he asked me where I had been, and I told him I spent the night with friends in Wapping.

'I met Virginia, last night,' he said. 'We had a long talk.'

His eyes wandered away to the window and were lost in the sun-greyness outside it. I too held my cup in my palms and was lost in the growing dazzle of the street.

'Do you know what I found out?' he said. 'She sold them houses of Condoorums to give the money to your uncle Mel. They bought a pub in Wapping with it.'

I was surprised at the mention of Mel, and the kindliness of his voice.

'Ah, some women are very good,' he said. 'They can be divils. They can be angels. But, when they're good they're too good for us entirely.'

He put down his cup and he looked at me and I looked at him and he smiled. Then he winked. I stared at him so coldly that he took to a furious stirring of his tea, but at once he pulled himself together and he glared at me.

'What do you mean?' he challenged.

'What do *you* mean?' said I.

'Where is this you said you were last night?' he

asked up in the top of his head, challenging me again.

'With Julia Crone,' I said savagely. 'Down in Wapping.'

He took his cup in his palms and looked out the window, and he smiled slowly.

'That's odd,' he said, 'for I was there late last night with Virginia. They took a great liking to you.' Then, wickedly he added: 'Both.'

His glance was followed by a grin that said, as plain as plain, 'We're a pair'. There was nothing for it but to surrender into a watery smile. The next minute he was talking about the house in Wapping and how he was going there to end his days in peace. We took the night-boat for Ireland. We were both morose, but we were polite and kind to each other all the way and I did not even glare at him when his last words to me going down the gangway in Cork were:

'Corney, me boy! Home sweet home! And two comrades in distress.'

As if his world could ever have had anything in common with mine. . . .

PART THREE

THE DESERT

Railway stations, ever since that time, have become a favourite refuge of mine, and I can recommend them to people of troubled minds as a sedative. There is nothing so easeful as to sit far down the platform of one of those empty factories that never seem entirely free of the moisture of steam and always smell of it. You feel even the heat that produced that smell as a ghost of heat, and see the world beyond the bright arched opening as a still-born life, and you hear of that life only dim clankings and bangings, distant as the echoes of the upper-world in the halls of the dead. What little movement goes on under the murky roof is seen through a wan light, dim of necessity, sifted by the soot and steam, and so, like the air, never pure. Life rushes in and rushes out at the pitch of excitement, breaking all moodiness for an hour. The calm between is restful as a grave. Very few people have observed this.

It was while exploring solitariness in this way that I met, by accident, Marion and Stella. I was standing one night out beyond the arch of the Great Southern station on the shore of the last straggling platform, beyond the advertisements for ink, or soap, or Venice (there is a great charm of irony in the inconsequence of these faded appeals) and I was looking over the cold inland lake of steel, when suddenly I was reminded of a place still more remote — the vast shore that stretches for miles away from our little seaside town of Youghal, a strand so long-strewn that I think nobody but myself can ever have walked to its end. I found a train already waiting on a side-platform.

There were hardly ten people in it, and by the time we had travelled down through the thirty-mile valley that stretches from Cork to the coast between rich uplands, red on the heights, limestone on the level, there were hardly six people in the six carriages. There is much to be said for that form of escape. From the solitariness of my empty coach I reversed the position of the idlers in the stations through which we passed, and as little village after little village floated by, and empty stations deep-buried in the sunset-translucent greenery of land in the finest heart, and we came to the marshes of Youghal, with its roar of a vasty shore, and its tiny terminus, I enjoyed myself thoroughly as a kind of Inspector of Isolations.

Of these, the last was the most perfect, for it was late, not merely of season (the first week of September) but of hour, and there was not a soul on the old concrete promenade, cracked and pitted by many flying storms, and sand-strewn by the autumn wind, while of the score or so of villas that lined it, every third one was boarded up. And when, after an hour's walking I looked back, all I could see, far away, was the little merry-go-round that had begun to steam out its mechanical tune, and the few flares to attract what idle pennies were left in the villas. The ebbed tide, seductive as a woman, whispered far out from the shore, and when at my feet its faint wavelets, mere bubbles of ripples, died in phosphorescence on the sand, so tenuous that they could exist only as light, I murmured to myself with pleasure: 'The tigress is only pretending to sleep — waving her tail.'

But then, as I stood there, I realized suddenly that in those dead years in which I lived, the years after Parnell, the shore of Ireland was empty, too, and would remain empty for a long time, and that I was merely one of many left stranded after the storm. I began, fevered by that thought, to walk on and on and I did not stop until blackness was about me, broken only by the lighthouse sweep across the crumpled skin of the sea, and the long pale line of distant foam. For it was the first bit of wisdom that I ever really held firm in my hand. It made me realize what life can do to men, stamping them out like tin cans. When I thought of it I felt so indifferent to myself, so freed of my conscience that I wanted to rush home to my grandfather, to write it to Elsie . . . Immediately I thought of my grander I stopped. I realized that life does not entirely stamp men with a dead hand: he had been in that trough before, and it had not killed him — since he came back from London, inside a bare few days, he was become again, incorrigibly, one of the fiercest and most conscientious Parnellites in the city, an all-night committee man, a three-newspaper man, a speechifier, a tender of graves. Life, apparently, was a challenge. That is a great thought.

Back on the promenade and still pondering, I saw a familiar figure in a greatcoat approach, and I saw that we must meet on the long empty pavement unless either of us turned back. It was old Mr. Sherlock, and I had not seen him or spoken to him for over a year — not since the trial. As I recognized him my belly went weak as with hunger. He saw me; hesitated, stopped. We shook hands.

'How are yeh, Corney, boy?' he said, kindly enough. 'Elsie writes to me that ye met by chance in London.'

I admitted it. He turned sideways and tapped the seawall and looked at me.

'Well,' he said, 'you know we all like you, and all to that . . . and I suppose, as they say, bygones can be bygones. And we all live and learn.' He went on breezily. 'We'd like to have you out the Lee Fields some night, Corney. You won't give us the cold shoulder, now, I hope. Will you? Of course, to be quite honest with you . . .'

'I know what you mean,' I cried roughly: if I had not been rough I should have been afraid of him.

'What *do* I mean, then?' he faced me in his smiling way, and he eyed me gently under his brows as I in my sullen way eyed him under mine.

'You mean you feel you ought to see me, and forgive me, like a Christian, but you wish to God that you didn't have to, and you're sorry you met me, isn't that the truth of it.'

'Now, now, Corney. Easy on. Don't be so hard on yourself, lad. And don't be so stiff. Look at the thing from my point of view, Corney. I'm the father of a family. And I have a daughter. And I'm very fond of that daughter . . .'

I was no longer afraid of him. He was become a mumbling old man, with a daughter and a family, muttering and whining and sighing about his duty as a Catholic father. I could have said it all for him, out of my own da's mouth, all except what he did not know about Elsie and myself — all that he might know only too soon.

'She's a very good girl, mind you. Only a bit flighty. Flighty. But even so, she's the best daughter any man ever had, as good as gold. But you know that, Corney, and I needn't tell it to you, and you know I know it. Of course it's no credit to me. It was all her poor mother's upbringing, God be good to her. She brought them all up like a little Holy Family.' He smiled into the wandering light in content at the image of Nazareth. 'It's no wonder,' he said in pride, 'that there's two of them priests and two of them nuns. I do my best, too, I suppose, in a way. I might be a bit strict and old-fashioned, but of course, don't ye know, I suppose she'll be marrying one of these days.'

That, I saw, was what he had really wanted to say, and having said it he hurried on with:

'Isn't it grand weather, though, thanks be to God, only a bit hard. Yerrah, sure, you ought to come down and see us some night. Father Tom will be home next week and we expect the Jesuit in the end of the month or early October. He's giving a retreat in the cathedral,' he said, with an innocent vanity.

I stared at him, pityingly. Come and eat their cream-crackers and sip their milk? And hear the two priests giving out edification? And Elsie across the room thinking of her secret sin.

'Ah, but it's too cold for bathing, though. Do ye know, I went in there for a bit of a dip this morning and I couldn't get the circulation back into my legs for half an hour. I was rubbing and rubbing. There's a very cold wind here sometimes from the south-east — it's very exposed, don't ye know. But 'tis grand. 'Tis grand. God bless it. The salt water is good for yeh and they say there's iodine in it when the seaweed begins to burst. Are you down?'

'Down' meant 'down for holidays'.

'No, I just ran down for the evening.'

'Oah? Very nice, too. We're all down. We always come in September. It's cheaper. Elsie will be coming back with Father Arty — did ye hear he's transferred at last? A curacy in the diocese. I'm sure Elsie would like to see you. We're staying up in Williamstown.'

On that we parted. I was angry because he had broken my mood, dragged me out of my cave of self, filled me with pictures of Elsie and fears for her. As I walked onward, three children with balloons came by, chattering about the merries. I was saddened by them, too, because our family had never taken a house there on the beach or played all together on the summer sands.

Stubbornly, I went back to my wide shore the following night, free to do it because my da was off to a confraternity meeting in the Priory: my grander was in his committee rooms: Robert was washing dishes or doing some other job that should have been done by the maids we could no longer pay: my mother was out a-gossiping. This time I went an hour earlier so that I should find the tide at an even farther remove, and the stars stuck even farther out in the wet sand. The merry-go-round was not yet twinkling, and as I passed along the grass-tufted road before the villas a visitor or two lounged in the tiny gardens watching a group of children playing cricket on the shore. There was one bather in the sea, far out as a seal. Ahead of me on the empty shore a few cattle lay on the beach. But to revisit a scene and not be able to recapture its mood is a sad affair, and by the time I came to the sand-flanked cattle I had halted before the suspiring wavelets many times, and been answered only by a heave of discontent.

It was then that I met Stella — how, is of small matter now: all I will say is that when we met I was in a very disturbed state of mind, and there is no reason why I should tell more. My first impression of her was that

she was a very kind woman and we were soon talking.
I was trying to take in her slim figure, as of a boy,
without hips or bosom, her flaxen hair, her large blue
eyes, and her mouth that quivered like sheet-lightning.
The fading light was so kind to her hair that I could not
say by how much she was older than me. A visitor, I
thought, because her voice and dress looked foreign.
In her fist she held a bundle of painter's brushes.

'I was painting,' she said, 'and I stayed too long.
The light is gone now. I hadn't noticed it,' she added
petulantly as she looked around at the sky. Then, as if
to get an excuse for not leaving me yet, she said, 'Would
you like to see my picture?'

We walked over to it. It was a bold picture of the
shore and the sea, done in soft colours, and though I
knew nothing about painting the sureness of the strokes
impressed me.

'You know Youghal?' she asked, as we looked at it.
'You live here?'

'No.'

'But you know the place. Is that like?'

I looked around at the shore and the distant greyness
of the promenade beyond which the merries were now
oscillating with their lights and their pretty tune. I
murmured that I knew nothing about painting.

'Never mind that. I know all about that. But the
place, has it caught the spirit of the place?' Her eagerness was flattering. She persisted: 'Is there something
you miss in it?'

'It's the place without a doubt. Only, those merries, and the yellow lights. They're such a contrast with the loneliness of the beach. They're part of the place for me.'

She looked where I looked.

'Ah! The roundabouts. And the lights. I see. You want a typical picture. One that catches the essential spirit of the place, not a *bit* of the place. Well, I wanted to know. That's very shrewd of you.'

She spoke with apparent sincerity. She cocked her little head on one side and looked at the picture, held arm's length away. I looked too, and then I suddenly saw that she was not looking at the picture but at me out of the corner of her eye. She smiled again, a wide smile that ran parallel with her chin, almost to her ears, and she puckered her brows under her fringe of hair. Then she cried, 'You're quite right', and with one sudden sweep of her arm she shied the picture out into the marshes.

She laughed as she picked up her easel.

'I didn't like it. I stayed too long. But I have a picture I did farther out on the shore and looking towards the prom. Would you like to see it?'

I said politely that I would, though I did not think she meant it, and I was chagrined when she said:

'Well, please carry my easel and I'll show it to you.'

She ran up the dunes and vanished behind them: she was entirely at her ease and when she came to a criss-cross stile she clambered over with a complete indifference to my presence that was an entirely new experience. She did not seem to mind that she looked ungainly as she pulled her long skirt over her knee to kneel on the top rung, though there was something of the figurehead of a ship about her as she stood for a moment on the stile and looked around her at the marches and the sea. There she stretched her arms wide, suddenly, and laughed back at me as if she were going to dive into the earth. Young girls, I know, have that boldness of gesture, and in their unawareness of their own bodies they are captivating; though they soon become aware of them when they notice our admiration, and then they leave their innocent cave of self and become uninteresting. Because she was far from being a young girl her gaiety and her innocent freedom of movement, her birdlike poise of head, her catlike stretching of the limbs, were a revelation. Unconsciously, no doubt, I must have compared her with Virginia's deliberate grace of the courtesan, and Elsie's self-conscious shyness that was born of her religion: for are not all our impressions comparisons, and does not what we think in the end depend on what we have experienced in the beginning?

Behind the stile I saw what looked like a fisherman's or a herd's cottage.

'My house.'

'Do you live there?'

'Only for the last few weeks. I was painting in the town, back there, and got tired of it. So I came here.'

She meant the business-end of Youghal, a mile or more beyond the promenade. It would be a good place for a painter, I thought, and said so. It had many deserted wharves (for Youghal was once a city of importance) and was full of mighty, but now empty and decaying, warehouses, all standing up like bulwarks to the sea and wind.

'No, I didn't paint those. I painted the boats. I came three hundred miles to paint an old boat or two. Things I could find on any English beach. It sounds foolish.'

As she was turning the big key inside the porch of the cottage, a simple whitewashed building with a red corrugated-iron roof, pent so high there must have been thatch under it, she said:

'Though I'm not really English. My mother was Irish and my father was born in India. I was educated in Belgium and I have lived almost as much in Paris as in London, so there you are.'

There was nobody in the cottage: she explained that her friend was in town buying food, saying it so casually that she clearly did not think it mattered much to anybody if she chose to live there by herself. Her pictures were all about the walls, and they made the place gay with colour; a fire smouldered on the open hearth. Making me sit down and rest, she took a canvas from the window-recess and handed it to me without a word. It was the long view back towards the roundabouts — one bold sweep of grey sand, with dark hummocks for the dunes, and a rich blue for the marshgrass, and half the canvas was the multi-coloured sea powdered out to the horizon: then to the left she had a wavering smudge of green for the old line of the promenade, and a few blobs of ochre picked out the lights. Used as I was to the nice smooth pictures at home I thought it 'queer'.

'It reminds me,' I offered, thinking of a picture I had seen in a London window, 'but of course I know nothing at all . . .'

'It reminds you? Yes? A picture or a place?'

'I'm not sure,' I temporized. 'It was a French picture.'

'You *must* remember! Where was it? What was it? Who was it?' And in the most casual way she laid an arm around my shoulder to look with me at her canvas.

'In London, in a window. A beach like that, with a fat woman and a girl, and a parasol. Maybe it was a bad picture?'

'Please no,' she laughed at my blushes. 'Not a bad picture.'

'No, it was a good picture because there were only three altogether and they were standing on red velvet. The others were women dancing, fat women in short skirts.'

'You don't mean Degas?' she cried. 'Not Degas?'

'Yes, yes. That's right. I remember now.'

She stood back and took the canvas from me.

'But you must be the only person in the whole of this country who has ever heard of Degas. The greatest living painter. And you know him.'

'Well, I forgot even his name. I really only looked at the window because the picture reminded me of Youghal.' She stared at me so long that I put out my hand for her canvas and tried to mutter something about it, but to my relief she put it aside, saying gently, looking gently out of her blue eyes:

'No. You have said the perfect thing. I have reminded you of Degas. You must have some tea. By the way, it will do you good.'

As she said that I noticed she had a pleasant lisp. She made me stay, and as she laid the table, in silence, or went out for water across the field, I heard the faint windy moan of the sea, and a tree over the house that rustled and swished across the tin roof. Her frocks, all pink or scarlet, hanging on the door of the other room, moved a little in the wind. Through the deep-set window I could see the dark night-hills, and the marshes below them were another sea. It was the clank of her water-pail that woke me. She still did not speak as she made the tea (as if she were thinking some thought out of her own world), and all the time I heard only the boozing-and-the-woozing of the falling and receding waves and the soft rustle overhead. When she lit the lamp she again looked at me in its light, and again her look was free as a child's, clear as clear water, so open and pure that it rejected, as a glass rejects a barb, the

slightest familiar thought. Then we sate and ate, and
as she cupped her cup in her hands and looked at the
picture in the window her eyes were lit faintly, at regular intervals, by the circling sweep of the lighthouse.
It had a weird effect because her pupils dilated and contracted every time the light came and went. I had seen
her bag in a corner, with the label of a Paris hotel
stuck on it, and I mentioned Paris to hear her talk of it.
For the first time I heard it spoken of with casual
intimacy — Nadar's in the Boulevard des Capucines,
the Guerbois in the Batignolles, the Zone, names of
streets in Montmartre, but all with that air of affection
that makes absent places and people seem perfect, and
in between she would expand her lips into a smile as
if to share the delight of her recollection. I had no such
words to utter, for London meant Wapping, and Wapping now meant Elsie, and Elsie meant that sepulchral
dawn under the blind, and the rest that I should only
dare to invoke when Time, as the ferryman said, had
made even that penny smooth.

Now, she was speaking not of places but people.

'They said to me, You are making a mistake in
keeping to portraits. You want more poetry in your
work — paint landscape for a while. But I can't do it.
I went to the town to paint boats, but there were children in one boat so I had to paint them. Even to-day
I had to put in the cows. Something alive, even cows,
I must have. They were all painting people in Paris,
all for Chardin and Greuze and Millet and Courbet.

They were right and my friends were wrong. Literature is gone the same way, and they are right, too.'

The light, coming and going over her face, had an extraordinary mesmeric effect, and the leaves on the roof beat incessantly like a fan. The names she spoke were enough, in themselves, to evoke a whole life and world till then undreamed of.

'I love Degas, that's why I can't paint dead things. A dead strand, a dead sea . . .? No!'

'But the sea and the shore are lovely,' I protested.

'The children I painted last week, and the old fishermen, were more lovely.'

She handed it to me: before I saw it I said:

'But children are always lovely, and old men often are.'

(I was thinking of the cherubs in Raphael's Transfiguration, which we had at home. Afterwards she sent me a copy of Ghirlandajo's Old Man with Grandchild, the man with the whelks and lumps on his nose and the child trustfully looking at him. I loved it, but I don't think I could ever have loved her picture of the two children in a boat.) When she saw me looking with puzzlement at her picture her mouth wavered like water under wind.

'I had to keep my distance, I admit. They were hardly clean. But they were lovely.'

'Were they?' I asked.

She took it from me roughly and scurried to a corner where there was a pile of canvases. A wide belt held her waist, in the fashion of the times, her sleeves billowed from shoulder to elbow. With her hair in ringlets on her brow and her bare round arm she was one curve and billow. She planted several canvases before me, all excitement: they were of old fishermen and idlers down the quays, rough people done in a brutal kind of way. Her finger roved swiftly here and there, and she was between instructing and arguing, between eagerness and politeness, but more as if we were two students in a garret than two strangers. That, too, disturbed me afterwards when I tried to recall how I had felt.

'There's a spark of soul in everybody. A music. And, my dear child, I have seen it, heard it. Even in those old topers.'

'I prefer the sand and the shore,' I said obstinately.

'Yes, yes. It's lovely, but so are my old men.'

'Lovely?'

'Yes. Lovely.'

I looked my disbelief.

'Isn't he like that?' she pointed at a picture.

'Of course he is,' I agreed. 'The old toper. You can see him. His crafty eyes. His red nose. But not *lovely*. And if you like lovely things as I do — why paint these common people? Not when I can have the sand and the shore and the wide sea.'

She stamped her foot and dragged away her paintings.

'But the sand and the sea can tell you nothing.'

I leaped at the sentence. I explained to her all that

I would have explained to Elsie. She leaned back on the table and listened for a little while. Then, condescendingly, even acidly, she said:

'My poor boy, all that is of interest to you only because you are a man. Because you are alive. All that nonsense about birds eating snails and snails eating leaves. If you were dead what interest would it be to you? Why on earth do you want to watch a slug when you can watch people? Can a slug hate? Can a slug love? Can a slug talk?'

'I wonder,' I said, 'can a slug love?'

That must have impressed her for she gathered her work together in dismay, and so as not to embarrass her I went to the window where the beam of light swept the crumpled wetness of the sea. The dark line of the horizon was still darker than the clouds it severed from east to west, for the day clung yet to the fringes of the sky. An old man, perched high on the sand-dunes, stood gigantic against the ocean, and the tireless sweep cut for a slow second into his clothes and face, leaving him indecipherable in the sudden dark. She was at my side. With a passion of trembling she gripped my arm.

'That bundle of rags there!' she gasped. 'That lump of rock! I can almost see the lichen on him.'

I had decided already that she was not pretty, but the sweep of light and the light of excitement in her gave her face an intense vigour. The rock lumbered heavily out of sight, peering for something — maybe his cows. She fell silent again, and then she said:

'I must meet my friend. Will you come?'

She wore no hat. When she threw a cloak of chequered plaid over her shoulders and turned up the wide collar her fair head was like a stamen coming out of a flower. On the sand she said:

'You haven't told me your name.'

'Cornelius Crone.'

'Mine is Stella Taylor.'

I jerked towards the breakers. I was trying not to be impressed by that vision of the old man.

'How lovely!' I said.

She halted and blazed at me.

'Only because you and I are walking by it.'

'Do you mean,' I cried, 'that you or I can make it lovely?'

'You or I can make it anything we like. My old sailors are lovely to me. They're just drunken louts to you.'

'But which are they?' I demanded so loud that it was almost a shout, and I stopped until she spoke. 'Which *are* they? Actually.'

She laughed with a merry patience, with an air of tolerant wisdom that cut into me.

'Oh, Cornelius, you have no sense. Is this the Search for the Absolute?'

I found myself asking her for advice — Stella had that quality that she made you reveal yourself — there was nothing of the east wind about her. I talked about last night and my ponderings on the shore.

'And, do you know,' she laughed, 'that I was at the roundabouts last night winning shillings while you drooled over the sea?'

I continued to talk — about Parnell, and Christy, and the Fenians, and my grandfather, and — as a cat pushes away a ball of wool and teases it towards its paw again — I moved obliquely to and from Elsie. We were, by now, on the promenade. The turn of the tide beat heavily on the sand, and the arc of light circled remorselessly. There were no stars in the sky, but a ship, far out, had a cargo of them. She leaned over the wall and looked over the darkness. I listened to the syrupy tune of the merries, and did not notice her silence until I saw that she was weeping silently.

'Please don't mind me,' she cried. 'Keep looking at the sea.'

I looked at it, standing very stiff. And I was just thinking how kind she was to weep for me, when she said — rising and sighing and taking my arm:

'Your poor grandfather!' She sighed deeply. 'And your poor friend, Christy Tinsley. What a life they have made for themselves.'

'But they didn't,' I protested crossly. 'It wasn't his doing. I mean to say, politics . . .'

'This is a sad country.'

'It's your people who made it sad,' I cried. 'You English.'

'No,' she said, drawing me to walk on, 'I don't think I could live here. It's all wrong. You all remind me of flies a bold boy would put under a glass, all beating against it. Even my old men down the quays — they talked to me like that. And, then, poor Parnell. No, no! Come to the roundabouts.'

'But, good God, do you want us to be slaves for ever and ever?'

'There are some prisons you can never break. You Irish don't know, and you never will know, the ones you can break and the ones you can't break. I believe you don't want to know. You remind me of Dante's people in Hell who "lived wilfully in sadness"! Come to the roundabouts.'

I thumped the sea-wall.

'But which can we break?'

'I don't know,' she cried. 'But I do know that you, Cornelius, don't and never will know, because your mind is a core on core of prisons. It's an onion of them. Come to the roundabouts.'

She changed her tune and said kindly:

'I shouldn't say that. You may change. You are young.'

She hustled me along until I stopped her once more.

'But about those sailors in the picture. You didn't answer me.'

'They're alive. That's all I know or care. How much money have you?'

'I have a few shillings.'

'I have much more than that. We'll have great fun

at the roundabouts. Marion will be there waiting for me.'

'But the sailors . . .'

She stopped dead and took me by the two arms.

'What's short for Cornelius?'

'Corney.'

'Corney, look at me.'

I looked at her racing mouth that was straining not to break into laughter, at her large blue eyes, at her flaxen hair. She was really attractive, I thought, and smiled at her eagerness.

'That's better,' she said and hurried on.

'What's better?'

We came to the merries. There the wooden horses raced around with staring eyes, and an old bookie I knew well from seeing him in Cork, one Billy Cunningham, bawled through leaping fingers, 'Wawawawawaw, Rollenbowlemin', and an old woman I knew screamed over the 'Anchor, Star, and Crown'; and other figures all of whom were familiar to me in the same way, and to whom, for Cork is a small place, I was probably just as familiar. People live in such towns, rubbing shoulders, until the shoulders become like the stone that lollers polish with their backsides, not merely familiar, but, as the alchemists say, their 'familiars'.

We tried the horses first, and when we passed the tiny statuettes that tip with their hands and move their heads left-right, right-left, she pointed at them with delight, and moved her head and hand in imitation.

'Aren't they funny?' I shouted over the music.

She saw a dirty urchin watching us and every time we passed she halloed to him and he began to hallo to us, shouting out, 'Come on the queer wan', or 'Come on the wan without deh hat', or, to me, 'Come on Needle Nose' — as if we were in a steeplechase. She shouted down to him, 'Get me a stick, jockey', so he got a rope and he flogged the rump of her horse as it passed. When I saw old Sherlock watching us curiously from the crowd I at once began to cry out with her at the ragged boy, and when, after all my pennies were gone, I had shared all her last pennies for this and that, and I had said good-bye, it was that scene that remained in my mind all the way home in the carriage — the small boy, her glowing face, old Sherlock looking oddly at the pair of us. With them I saw the granite figure of the cow-herd on the dunes, and the searchlight carving him into sudden detail for one moment of vision. Those stood out of a tangle of other things — Paris, the Batignolles; old sailors down the quays; Stella crying for my grander, Stella laughing; Chardin, Greuze; 'The sea would mean nothing to you if you were dead'. The gaslight flickered in the ceiling. The lights of the little stations flickered in the wind. A new world went shimmering through my brain with the fields that shimmered below the train, and as a child gropes for a sun-ray on a wall, feelers went out from me to catch the elusive light of her life and mind.

But the estuary came, and a vaster darkness where a

red eye and a green eye chugged down the river-loch to Passage. And in that darkness of the night, that great stretch of water, empty but for the chugging boat; with a few lights of houses away and away across it, and the other multiplied lights of the city that would soon come twinkling ahead when the loch narrowed to a city-river between trees and walls, I thought I saw — and in that cold night-air through the carriage window and that smell of water as if the sea itself were rotting — something more like an autumn evening than an autumn night in the gradual withdrawal from me of the quietude of my day. In another mood, of love or ambition, it could have meant so much that was removed from strife, so much that would have lifted the heart to the stars — but just touched with Stella on another world that was already slipping away, even as the day slips away, wandering after something that always eluded me, fearful of absolute loneliness, despair, isolation, like this one lost star in the sky, like that boat stranded on the mud, this house lost in a mountain-valley, a sheep in a great night field — I felt like a lover without his love when everybody is passing by in laughter. I felt only the hollow silence of the night. And sure enough, as the loch diminished and the docks came in view, and we passed high above the first city-road, there were the lovers arm in arm, happy in their forgetting.

For the third time I went back, this time to meet Stella again and her friend Marion, in search of Wisdom at all costs. But life plays many tricks on us, and I did not go until one night had intervened—the cashbox was empty—and not until I had spent that night out by the Sherlock house. Knowing they were all in Youghal I was able to wander at ease by the weir and around their deep-set house, and because it was a warm September, as so often happens in Ireland, the night was soft and kindly and I was able to sit for a long time by the river-bank, looking at the shuttered windows of the house and hearing the tinkle of the water over the stones, or touching the chill water with my fingers. When it grew colder I found that the hot air lingered on the hill fields and I stood there among the haycocks, burned brown in the fresh green of the after-grass. There, too, I began to brood on Elsie, noticing, with a sense of a time coming to an end, the thinness of the air, so different to what they call the *heafth*, or thickness, of the summertime, its choke of smells and buzz of invisible noise. In that memory of vanished joys came the memory of all others — of Elsie's golden hair, her kiss, even those trembling limbs, and I began to plan how when she came back that empty house would be waiting for us. It would enclose us. We would be more bold. We would be dear to each other. Unless, perhaps, and I could see them shining in the gloom behind the shuttered windows, the heavy furniture — a wardrobe full of other people's clothes, a table with someone's hat on it, the photographs of the priestly brothers — would make it all so personal to her family, so dusty and old, so thumbed by other lives, that there

would, even in that darkness of the shutters, be no
secrecy in our love. Then I thought of Stella — 'Why
on earth do you want to watch a slug when you can
watch people?' — and, 'The shore and the sea are only
interesting to you because you are alive'. Supposing I
said to her, 'But I don't want people — I don't like
people — they are always breaking up our loveliest
moods', what would she say? With the question in my
mouth I went to meet her the following night: but with
it, in my inwards, I carried the old devil leech that
gnaws at all men.

This time I met her friend, Marion — a shrewd,
firm-lipped Dublin girl with the features and body of
a man, tall, twice as strong as myself, the type of nearly-
handsome girl who blushes easily, laughs often, to
show her fine teeth, and keeps men at a distance because
she knows her interest in them is greater than her power
to attract, her pride too sensitive to bear rebuff. By
that self-awareness in her, matching another kind of
self-awareness in me, we saw from the first moment
that we could be friends, and yet we found out in ten
minutes that we could not. Our dissatisfactions grated:
our gears did not mesh. It showed itself in a characteristic way. For when I found that she was a Moravian
by religion (her father had been an engineer in Austria),
I began at once, like the typical 'bad Catholic', to
defend what I did not in the least believe, and attack
what I knew nothing about, and in fact heard of that
moment for the first time — the doctrines of one John

Huss, the Bohemian reformer. Naturally she easily triumphed over me, and with so much pitiless crowing that I was cross until Stella told us we were both fools: whereupon we turned on her and rent her because we both derided her beliefs; and as she had no interest in them she was able to tell us still more forcibly that we were foolish to attack her before we had agreed between ourselves. In the end Marion packed us both off, saying that she would follow us when she had finished some letters.

I was alone with Stella. The sea had that coating of silver that comes with the going of the hot sun. The frail September mist and the wan light softened the horizon with fog.

'About people, Stella,' I said urgently. 'Supposing I don't like people, why should I watch them? I don't like them, in fact — they do such hateful things.'

She shut me off quickly.

'If you don't want them you're dead.'

'They do hateful things,' I repeated weakly. 'My grander, Parnell, Christy, Condoorum. People . . .'

'You're one of them yourself. People are you, you are people.'

I felt it was my quietus and I tucked it away in a corner of my brain to tease over when I would be alone. She reverted to our argument about the Reformers.

'So,' she teased, 'you are a good little Catholic after all?'

'I'm not.'

We sat on the sand-dunes and looked at the milky sea.

'You are,' she insisted with a wicked little smile. 'Come, now, aren't you afraid to be with an unsaintly woman like me?'

'I'm not a Catholic,' I repeated more positively. 'It's all over and done with as far as I'm concerned. And you're not unsaintly.'

'I think,' she teased in her feline way, 'that you're a good little Catholic. You think I'm going to be damned, don't you?'

'No, and I think you are a very innocent person. I leave damnation and all that to Marion. I believe life stamps us all out like tin cans, and we can't help much what we do.'

'Thank you, Cornelius.' She snuggled up to me, softly-cruelly, just like a leopard. 'But what about what others may do to the little Catholic?'

I knew she was teasing me to try to make me flirt with her, and though I knew it I could not help myself. After a little while of this foolish talk, I found myself leaning over her, playing with her flaxen waves, and her brown arm stirred me, and the crevice of her arm. She lay and looked at me and did not stir. Was she just examining me with a cold eye, or was she like all women who want love taken from them but will not give? We were not talking now and there was no sound there but the waves and the distant syrup of the merries, trickling away into the moist air. Anyone who spied on us would

have said we were lovers as I looked down into her eyes
and stroked her hair with shaking fingers. But there
was no eagerness in her, and her mouth, soft in a gentle
smile, might have been the mouth of the wind that
blows cold upon us from the north. At last, when I
pressed nearer, she spoke, and it was like a balsam that
stings to cure, she said it so calmly:

'Corney, are you in love with me?'

I sank away. The reproach killed every touch of
desire in me. My hand dug into the sand, ground the
fine grains between my fingers. I could have wept with
rage as she looked sadly at me.

'Come,' I said, jumping up. 'I am just being like
any man. You hate it in me. I am being bestial.'

She rose slowly and touching my arm she said tenderly:

'Corney, why should I? It's just that I have more
control than you, and I know more about the world.
You would be sorry after.'

'Bestial,' I cried. 'Bestial. You're right. I am what
I am, everything inside me, in cores, in cores, like an
onion!'

And though I felt she had done a cruel thing to me,
and I was only half sorry, I tried to ask her to forgive
me, and babbled of the way we had all been brought
up, and, then, perverse as any woman, she wanted to
halt me, and because I had exposed my weakness to
her and she felt sorry for me she would have loved me.
She was too late. I dragged her on to the roundabouts

and looked eagerly for Marion, anxious to escape from
her and from my own nakedness, eager for even a few
scraps of common rags to make me an outward man
again. I saw Marion in the crowd and thrust towards
her, but Stella held me and whispered:

'Please, Corney, don't make love to her — she would
let you.'

I met Marion and because I was humbled she found
something in me that she liked. We talked with our
backs to one of the booths and then we went to the sea-
wall for greater quiet. Yet when we got there we did
not talk at all, because there was between us, we knew,
a chasm over which we had thrown a bridge — the
most gossamer, most frail, next-to-aerial, non-existent,
impalpable. While we kept silent it hung there. Words
would make it fall. We looked at the pale line of foam
and we let the night speak for us, and how long we
might have sustained that silent link I cannot tell, for
Stella ran to us and with her talk we became divided
human creatures once more. Still, we talked as friends,
now, the three of us, and Stella said:

'Marion and I are leaving the cottage this week,
Corney. Would you look at it for us now and again?
We will come back in the spring.'

'Yes, the summer is done with,' I said.

'We thought you might like to use the cottage,' she
went on. 'We'll send you the key. You might use the
place — light a fire there now and then.

I promised I would. We were all smiling. We had

only known each other for a few days (Marion I had
known a few hours), but we felt that we must all meet
when the winter was passed. We shook hands and said
good-bye and I was alone in the train, regretting that
summer brings people into one's life, like that, for so
short a while, and then sends them so soon again to
their own secret ways. And when the train passed the
last light in the last villa-back, and the last farmhouse
glowed in the marshes, I had a feeling that I had said
good-bye not to two women, chance-met, but to a whole
extension of life that I would never really share. Somewhere from my brain, as a man might from some portion
of his clothes, I slowly drew out the last clear note I
had taken of that life, fumbling with it in the dusk of
memory, and at last reading it clearly. 'You,' she said,
'are people, and people are you. Or else you are dead.'
I watched the lights jumping along the hedges beside
me as I tried again to grasp at that broader, easier world,
but with a tired brain and the rattle of the train, it kept
running from me and running from me, and in the end
it became part of the rhythm in my ears, and hammered
out meaninglessly the message of the wheels — Or
you are dead, Or you are dead . . . By the time we had
passed through the long valley, and to the narrowing of
the estuary into the river, and I had been ejected into
the station with its smell of paraffin and steam, I had a
nightmare feeling as if the train were some long surgical
instrument and the valley a canal of the body, and I a
nerve that had been extracted and flung into the dustbin

of the station — already corrupt; truly dead. I sat on a seat and stared at the tin advertisements that I did not see. I felt that I was not 'people'; and that, not being 'people', I was a living corpse.

But, the blessedness of railway stations! So quiet, so full of emptiness that the empty heart does not feel how empty it is; and then as always the sudden bursts of passing life that revive it like an injection. A train drew in, brilliantly lit, and people hurried out, and I saw one or two people I knew, who would not, I knew, pause there to trouble me: and then I saw Elsie in a long coat and carrying several bags. I rushed to her. She took me with her as Orpheus took Eurydice out of the caverns of the Styx. She took me in her arms into the streets. The lights. The cabs. The trams. She was people, and I was part of her. I laughed with such joy in her that she was amazed. I kissed her. She laughed. I was alive.

We were alone in her house among the dark fields and we cooked bacon and eggs in the kitchen among her parcels and her bags, and as I laid the table I would come behind her and, clasping her about her middle, kiss the down at her nape where the little curls floated up into the great curls of her auburn head. And when the tea was drunk and we had sat by the fire of the old kitchen-range — O the loveliness of being alone! — we kissed endlessly. She said, at last:

'Corney, that day . . .'

'Which day?'

'After you left me. I walked around and around the city like a mad woman.'

'But why?' I asked, as if I had not also walked around London like a madman.

'I kept looking at people and wondering what had happened to me. Was I real? Was I in a dream? And then I was wondering if I . . .'

She stopped.

'If you?'

She hid her face in her hands.

'Yes?'

She could not look at me.

'You won't, Elsie.'

'But', she moaned into my shoulder-socket, 'you can't tell, you can't tell.'

She stared into the fire and fell silent and I saw that this was not what was really in her deepest mind. After a while she said it:

'I went to confession.'

I laid her down quietly from my lap and she went across the fire to another chair.

'Well?' I asked coldly.

She shook her head: she was unwilling to say anything more about it. But I knew what was coming.

'What did the priest say?' I asked.

She shook her head as if to shake away what she was remembering.

'I suppose he said I was . . . Well, did he say things about me?'

She nodded.

'And you believe him?'

She shook her head.

'Did he say you must give me up?'

She nodded miserably. We had come to it.

'Well, will you? Do you want to? Did he know anything at all about it? Was he human?'

I was angry. She shook her heavy locks in despair and, leaning to me, took my hands.

'Don't talk about it, Corney. He said awful things. He asked me awful questions. Terrible questions. Going into details.' She leaned away. 'He asked everything. I hated it, Corney. Oh, Corney, I didn't know it was like that. I can't understand that it would happen about me and you. About me, me, me? About somebody else I'd understand it. But you and me. I mean, if daddy knew, if the others knew.' Her voice fell. 'I hated myself, after it. Corney! He wasn't a nice priest.'

The sound of the waters falling on the weir came to us. The trees were rustling.

'You shouldn't have gone to him,' I said.

'I was afraid.'

'Afraid? Of what?'

She went to the window and opened it. The rustling winds through the night came down from the graveyard on the hill. I went over to her.

'I loved you, Elsie, isn't that enough? You are the only human being I know, Elsie. Isn't that enough?

I mean, I am so miserable without you near me. I have
nobody else. Isn't that enough? Isn't that enough?
I mean, isn't all that enough, Elsie?'

'I was afraid,' she wailed.

'Are you afraid, now?'

'He gave me absolution.'

I groaned and tore away from her. Oddly, I remember picking up one of her sweets and tearing off the
tinsel, eating the sweet and hurling the paper from me
into the sink. I mocked:

'He gave you absolution. God! How foul it
sounds!'

'I was afraid,' she wept.

'Are you afraid still?' I asked her, coming to her.

'Yes.'

'And why?'

She looked up at me with the eyes of a pleading dog.

'For fear it will happen again, Corney. Please don't
let it happen again. I'm afraid it will happen again.'

So she was not afraid of the child: only of the sin.
And yet she was pleading now, I felt, with words, as
before with closed lips and silent looks, against her
deepest desire. I took her by the waist and moved
her from me.

'I won't tempt you again,' I said bitterly.

I unloosed her hands and stooped for my coat and
hat. 'But that means,' I said, 'that I can't see you ever
again. I couldn't.'

'But, Corney . . .'

'If you want it that way, I can't help it. You make me promise for you as well as for me.'

'I promised . . .'

'And when we are married, he'll be satisfied. The good priest will smile and tell us be happy.'

'Please listen, Corney. . . .'

'Good-bye, Elsie.' I spat it out.

'Corney!'

'I met your father. He expects you in Youghal. When your brother the priest returns . . .'

I ran out, suddenly horrified to think that maybe it was to her brother she had confessed. Could she? Would it be possible? But when I was out in the fields the night came, blindfolding me. The wind from the hills came crawling over me with inanimate fingers. The weirs were whispering; the ice-cold river's sudden death only a step away. As I walked fast, away from the house, the graveyard hill rose behind me, following me; and as I walked it continued to rise high over me, and the trees became immense as I approached them. Suddenly as I began to make out the alders, more by their crackling than by their shape, I heard a running of feet in the dark and her voice calling, 'Corney, Corney, Corney, Corney', very fast and with terror and tears in the name. I stepped from the path into the bushes. In the dark she would pass without seeing. I saw the pale blouse rush by me and the fear choking her as she screamed out, 'Corney, come back! Come back! Corney! Corney!'

I found her standing alone, sobbing on the path. She leaped at me.

'Corney, come back, anything, Corney, only come back. I'm afraid, afraid.'

We went back. We slept hugging one another as if we would shut away all fear, as if we would clutch our love to us, close as the dark life that had begun to grow within her.

From that on a cold silence came over us. I dared not ask her what I was always wanting to know (if she had gone to the priest again) and she did not dare think, let alone talk of it. That secrecy hid part of her from me, part of me from her. I understood then that even the greatest lovers of the world must have, for all their love, stolen often from one another into the secret chambers of the heart.

Once I visited her in Youghal, to see her priest-brother and, in jealousy, to watch how he received me. He did look at me with a curious glance, but then he joked with me and was so friendly that I thought it was merely because his father had told him I was once in love with her. But for all that and for all their friendliness I would not go again. I had broken with their way of life. I was their enemy. Not even when I thought of Stella and her talk of 'people' could I bear them. Their very conversation drove me off — it was so self-consciously content with life, so smugly happy, even if it was old Sherlock at some trifle like:—

'Oah, there's untold changes in Cork. I was watching

them, there, now, Father Arty,' (he always called his son Father Arty), 'laying that foundations of those new houses on the Mardyke, and I was astounded how fast they did that job. But then, don't you know, I always heard that Cork workmen are the best workmen in the world. Take London, now, for example, I often heard that any man there that says he's from Cork would get a job in preference to anywan else.'

'Still, the air is very sleepy here, father. I notice it, now, coming back to it.'

'Even so, we're the same temperachure as London. Don't you know? That's because we gets the Gulf Stream around the Southern Coast. Of course, now, the building of that Panama Canal is a great blow to Cork. It's deflecting the Gulf Stream.'

Even Elsie so forgot herself as to roar with laughter at him, and they all shouted at him in one voice:

'Father, you're very silly. The Panama Canal and Cork. For goodness' sake, have sense. We ought to complain to the American Government.'

They laughed at that, again and again, amused at themselves and their own self-importance, and yet amused at being amused, and taking good care that neither amusement should be so harsh or rancid but that they could afterwards be equally amused at the memory of both.

'I said it was a pity about the Gulf Stream,' old Sherlock would nod his happy foolish head when he would be sure to recall the incident some nights later on, and with a contented snigger, he would be sure to say, 'It was a very silly thing for me to say in wan way, and they made a hare of me for it. Wasn't it a good wan? Not, don't you know, that I was entirely wrong . . .'

Inbred, I thought as I listened, the veritable Lilliputians. Following their little tails like silly puppies. And all this trifling — how could they keep it up for hour after hour? There was the cleric who went to Croagh Patrick on the pilgrimage, and we had to hear how and why and where he stayed on Monday, and who met him on Tuesday, when and why and where, and how he didn't eat anything on the pilgrimage until he came home, even though he had a bag of chocolate in his pocket.

'Carrying temptation around with you, I call it,' smiled the priest. And they all laughed at the boy; and he said they were 'silly', and they laughed again because he did not see the joke, and two days later he would be certain to laugh over it all when he did.

That favourite word, 'silly', was typical — they were so fond of each other they could not bear to use a harsher word. It was all, in its way — or it used to be when I first met them — very tender and Christian and lovely. But it was all, now, the soft comfort of a world I would not accept.

Instead, I got the key of the cottage in the marsh and I used to light a fire and meet her there in the early dusk. Those were our last days of loveliness: when the frail lightsomeness of the autumn evenings (it was not bright enough to be *light*), the soft clearness of the vanished day, the powderous obscurity of the scanty sun, pearled as the inside of a shell, came over the pools of the sea and made them like floating oil; and over the withering of the land; and over the dying trees, and the hills frozen beyond the railway-line through the marsh, and out of that marsh, spiked with swords, the signal-post rose, vague as a ship's mast in a fog. We would look through the open door of the cottage, from beside a fire whose flames were green and blue, because the wood was sea-wrack, and hear the waves fall on the heavy sand, or the swords in the marsh shiver like tin. Far away, through the bright fog of dusk, there was a lowing of cattle. When they lit the signal-lamp, red or green, it made the air a still deeper blue.

Winter kept us indoors, for it came suddenly towards the end of September with a wreck down the coast, and a storm that leaped over the promenade in waterspouts. The roundabouts were all wrapped in canvas and boarded against the wild winds to come. Then one evening, knowing that I would not meet her so easily when they returned to Cork, I forced myself to ask her what I wanted to know.

'Elsie, is the thought of confession troubling you?'

She looked at me out of her dark world, as if she wondered what precisely I meant: so I went on:

'I mean, you want to . . . tell it?'

'No! I know that it is *wrong*, Corney. But I don't feel it enough. When *you* don't feel it wrong how can *I* say it is wrong? If only *you* would feel it is wrong . . .'

I looked at her silently, turning her own weapon of silence against her, as she used to against me when I pleaded before.

'As you know,' she said with positiveness, 'it is only a bad confession and a worse sin if you don't make "a firm purpose of amendment".'

I looked at her, giving her no help.

'If only *you* felt it was wrong?' she pleaded.

When I said nothing she looked away, defeated. If I could only have believed it was wrong, if I could only have said, 'Yes, Elsie, it is wrong', or 'My love, it is all finished now' — I would have said it: but it was not finished, and would never be finished for her reason. I could not admit what I did not believe — that our love had been evil. From her big eyes the pleading look ebbed away, and she turned from me. Outside was the cold wintry wind and the falling sea — that cry of water and wind that is, they tell us, the cry of the lost souls of the world. . . .

A FEW weeks after, we met in Cork and she told me she was going to have a child. Easily, and calmly, I said, 'We must be married at once', but inside me I felt a quick ebb of strength. I had the same feeling that she must have had — of being caught by an immovable hand. And as we stood and looked over the dreary valley of the Lee where the stripped woods moved dark and claw-like in the wind, I almost felt as if it was in me that something had begun to grow, uncontrolably, leading me to my hour as implacably as time a condemned man to the scaffold. I had said many things to myself, and to her, that had once seemed wise. 'Beauty is all', and 'Our life is higher than the brutes', and 'We learn from nature what life is', and such-like, but — with this fear, this dread sense of smallness, where were they now? I had said and believed it, that 'we discover the meaning of *good*, of the thing that is neither high nor low, divine nor demon, the "golden mean", by watching nature make harmonies out of disharmonies when she sails a moon into a stormy sky.' Now I said nothing. We held hands and saw the fields and trees and the blown fur of the cows and the water noisy in its runnels: and we said nothing. We could only stand near each other and look at it all like dumb beasts — look at our world suddenly darkened by the wintry slope of the sun. The cold was unkind. We stared and shivered.

I went that night to see Mr. Sherlock and we talked alone in the old panelled parlour over the fire. When I said I was fond of Elsie and she was fond of me and we wanted to marry, he began, slowly, to scrape his ravelled tobacco from between the crevices of his fingers into his pipe, and he talked of how he had married forty years ago.

'Of course it was a very small job I had, down in the Harbour Board, the time I got married. A class of a clerk in the customs house I was, a kind of link between the harbour commissioners and the revenue people. Do you know what salary I had? Fifteen shillings a week, and that was good money at the time. And I liked the work, too, don't you know, in and out of ships, up and down the quays, meeting the captains and the customs officials, and all to that and so on. A fine open-air life. Now, Corney! Listen to me! And let an old man give you a bit of advice. The day I married I gave up that job and I took a much harder one, indoors, for — listen to this — for the sake of two shillings a week extra. And damn glad to get it, my boy. And that same day, my wedding-day, I took a vow against drink and tobacco, and not until my poor wife died, and the childer were reared, did I break it.'

Solemnly he laid his withered hand on my knee.

'Corney, boy — you may have children, when you

marry. As I had. And, mind you now, I'm not complaining about it. No man had a betther wife nor betther childer than I had. But, believe me, many and many's the time I'd see my poor wife staying up late at night, and into all hours of the night, after a hard day's work, Corney — may God rest and protect and reward her for it — sewin', and darnin', and knittin' for to dress out them young children. And honest to God, Corney, and may God forgive me, I often wished for her sake that I never married her.'

He lit his pipe with trembling fingers, looking at the leaping flame, talking between puffs.

'Corney, do you know what it is? We often went down on our two knees at opposite ends of the kitchen when the childer were asleep, with aprons around us, to scrub the floors, to save sixpence on a servant. We used to be rivalling one another to see who'd do the most!'

He flung the match from him. His pipe was unlit.

'And then, she'd be up in the morning, hours before the milkman passed in the road, working away on a new day.'

I looked miserably at the fire, so as not to see in his eyes the fog of recollection, the love in him for a woman I had never known.

'Is it any wonder she went young from me?' He leaned to me with sudden fire. 'And do you think I want Elsie to face that same class of a life?'

I looked my reply. But he was adamant.

'Do you want Elsie to lead that kind of a life? Answer me straight out like a man.'

I shook my head.

'Say, no,' he ordered me. 'Admit it.'

'No, I would not, Mr. Sherlock.'

'How much a week are you earning, now, Corney?'

I was earning nothing, and as he asked the question I saw the idle yards, the empty books, and old Tommy Scanlon, our single workman, still called the foreman, pottering around the place trying to earn his keep.

'Ten shillings a week,' I lied. 'But my father would double that if I was getting married.'

He looked at me without belief. He lit his pipe thoroughly this time and then he rose and said:

'I'm still paying back debts I raised for the education of my family. And they'll be paying them back still when I'm in the grave.' Then, while I thought in shame of our spendthrift family, he gave me the blow: 'And yet, Corney, only six months ago your father asked me to go bail for him at the bank for a loan of a hundred pounds. Did you know that?'

I could not look him in the face.

'No, boy. I know you're fond of Elsie and all to that, but . . . Take your time, Corney, and if in two or three years time you get yourself a decent job we can think about it. You're both young. How's your grandfather? I haven't seen him lately. . . .'

I stole off as soon as I could — Elsie was waiting for me in the stables. We whispered together and I told her what had happened. I told her that unless she confessed the truth we would never be allowed to marry. She gripped me and cried aloud:

'No! Not *tell*! I could never face them. Not Father Arty! And Willie going for a Jesuit. They'd turn him from the seminary if they knew. You mustn't, Corney. Promise me.'

'Very well.'

We went out to the river-path, and she halted there by the cold river-pool under the oak.

'I wish I could drown myself,' she murmured, and she shivered at the smooth vat of darkness.

I drew her away, frightened, but she smiled and said I need not be afraid; she was not going to do it. I hurried home, determined to try all other possible ways, and on various excuses I appealed to my grander for money, wrote to Virginia who sent ten pounds, to my sister Vicky, now also in London, and she sent two. That ended my wild hope of gathering a few hundred pounds to impress old Sherlock. I next asked my father to give me a partnership in the business, saying bluntly that I wanted to marry.

'A partnership?' he sighed. 'And welcome, Corney. You're a partner from this day on.'

Then he showed me the remaining books that I had not seen until then, and when I saw them, and saw him ruffle his thin black hair, and saw the scalp beneath its lank ribs, and his eyes smitten by fear and worry, I rose and left him.

Only one plan came to anything, and that was when I got the Crones of *The Blue Peter* in Wapping to invite Elsie over after the winter would be gone. But Father Arty knew his Wapping, and Sherlock knew his Crones, and there was a quick end to that. There seemed to be nothing then to do but wait — and hope, for what we did not know, and in that mood we let the winter steal by.

I confided the truth only to my grander. And he confided it to Virginia who thereupon sent another ten pounds, and then another ten pounds, and then, no doubt, forgot all about us. He was taken ill that December and he kept to his bed and he did nothing for me beyond advising me to say nothing to anybody, and above all to admit nothing to the Sherlocks. I got the idea that he had some experience of such affairs, but they must have been more crude than mine, for his mumblings and astute advice only served to tell me that, if he was the best friend I had, I need expect help from nobody; and as he was very ill I had to sit by him patiently, watching him tapping his nose with his stiffened fingers, winking, and beckoning to whisper conspiratorially.

His whole body had gone dead from the waist down, with a condition of age and arthritis. He was like a rajah in his bed, with his papers and his books all at hand, and his lamp fastened to the wall by a kind of lazy-tongs, and on a little shelf by his side — for he had to twist his whole torso and reach with a cramped arm for everything, in great pain — was his pipe, his feathers for cleaning it, a carafe used as a spittoon, and his ditty-box of odds and ends. There, too, was a bell that he would ring when he wanted something, and being imperious he would ring it often and loudly.

My mother attended to him. Half-way up the stairs he would hear her, puffing and panting, and calling out to him:

'Ah, you ould hathen, now you're come to it. Now, you're on the flat of your back. Now is there a hell and a heaven?'

Down the stairs he would roar:

'Shushush, woman. Trash o' nonsense. Bloody yarns invented by the priests.'

'O God forgive yeh,' she would puff, helping her great weight up the stairs with her hands on her thighs. 'O, wait till your time comes. O, God help me. O, you limb of Satan. O, there's a hot corner waiting for you.'

'Shut up, woman. Hurry up here. I want something.'

In the doorway she would lean to recover her breath, looking at his thin and wasted face. Then, with a motherly deftness, she would do some menial task for her old enemy who was now become as helpless as a child, though all the time grumbling at him for an unforgiven sinner. When it was done she would sit and look through the window at the roofs, or down into nuns' playground, snuffing at her ease, gossiping.

'How's that ould fool of a husband of yours?' he might ask: and she reply:

'Wearing out shoe-leather, looking for contracts. But,' stuffing snuff into her nostrils, 'sure, the poor oinseach, he'll never get them. He's too miserable. Burial vaults is what he should be building. If I was only able to go out and shake a leg — but I'm getting ould, now, and I have no spirit and I have no clothes.'

'Where did I get him?' he'd say. 'If it was only Mel himself, he'd have a bit more go in him.'

'None of that,' she would warn him. 'John worked hard, and he had plenty of go in him, too. But with this thing and that thing, that bloody bitch Virginia, and . . .'

'Now, now, now,' he would roar, and his roar was not impaired by the atrophy of the rest of his body, 'leave Virginia out of it. She's your own sister.'

'And isn't John your own son?'

'Yah, he is, God help me. Look here to me, do you know what I do be thinking? All relations are a curse. Without exception. Sons. Daughters. Sisters-in-law. Brothers-in-law. Mothers-in-law.'

'Fathers-in-law,' she snuffs easy.

'Look. A man should live by himself.'

'Aye, aye,' she sighs gustily. 'Maybe so. And maybe those nuns down there, God bless them, are the best off of the lot of us. Look at them there now, going round and round, like little black ducks in a pond. Happy in this life and assured of the next. Oh, dear!'

'Ha, your daughter Vicky was a nun.'

'Pah! I got a letter from her this morning. Acting up in Birmingham in a pantomime, she is.'

'A pantomime? Ha, that'll be the *cockawalla* of a pantomime then if she's in it.'

'She says she has her death of cold from wearing tights.'

'What? And you permit this to happen? What kind of a mother are you at all, at all?'

'You can keep your guff to yourself! Memories are long. We don't so easily as all that forget things, my dear man.'

His glare would have killed her if she bothered to look at him.

'Is there anything in the paper?' he asks, to turn the subject from himself.

'The divil hoist it,' she sighs, rising. 'I forgot to bring it up.'

'Well, bring it up now!' he ordered. But when she is half-way down the stairs he might shout, 'Hi, Pidgie! Don't mind that paper'.

And when she would insist on lumbering up with it he would thank her humbly.

'You're not a bad ould skin, Pidgie. 'Tis me you should have married and not that son of mine.'

'Ha, you sinner,' she would threaten him with the rolled newspaper. 'When are you going to see a priest?'

A glare would reply. A banging rustle of the paper

between fingers twisted like a thorn tree and hard as stone. She would leave him, with a sigh.

In the end they brought a priest to him, cunningly choosing an old man who had been a great Parnellite in his day. Once or twice I heard their talk through the attic door. It was not difficult because my grander, seeing a feeble old priest, thought he must be deaf, and the priest shouted back at him for a like reason.

'Be content, Father!' he would cry. 'For if I'm struck down I had my day. And if you're an old man, so had you. And what is there left for me to do? Or for you either? Aren't all we knew gone downstairs or upstairs or to whatever place is waiting for 'em? So be comforted and don't be worrying.'

'Any help,' the old priest would wheeze out at the top of his voice, 'that I can give you in a spiritual way . . .'

'Oh, yesyesyes. Of course!' My grander would hurry on. 'No offence. You do your job and I do mine. Look, Father, I want to ask you something.'

'Yes, my child.'

'What do you think of this new Local Government Bill? Do you think the Party could agree on it?'

'One never knows!' from his reverence.

'If Parnell lived, to be sure . . .'

'Aha! True,' the wheezer would say. 'But the past is gone and the future is in the hands of God. You ought to consider your own future, Mr. Crone.'

'Oh, yesyesyes. Of course. As I said forty years ago to Arty Tinsley, in the year eighteen hundred . . .'

'What a memory you have, Mr. Crone.'

'I have that,' he smiles happily. 'There's not a thing I don't remember. Not a thing.'

'Isn't that splendid, Mr. Crone. And now, my child, when you come to go over your own life and how God watches over every act we do . . .'

'Oh, yesyesyes. I agree with you. God is watching over Ireland. I always said it. You know, some people think I'm a bloody atheist. I say it's the clergy . . . present company excepted . . .'

'No offence, Mr. Crone.'

'No offence, Father! I know you're an understanding man. Not like others I won't mention. I say it's the clergy have this country ruined. They think, no offence, now, Father, and present company excepted, they think they're the Pope and the Church and God Almighty all rolled into one.'

'Well, the Church militant, after all, Mr. Crone, is the church created by Christ. "Thou art Peter and upon this rock I will build my church." And it has a difficult and delicate task to perform. Now, take the matter of the Fenians . . . no offence, Mr. Crone?'

'Not in the least, Father. No offence.'

'Well, now, consider that question. Consider the oath taken by the Fenian Brotherhood. Was that, or was that not contrary to the teaching of the Church?'

'Of course it wasn't,' laughed my grander.

'Hold now! Hold now! There's no "of course"

about it. Not, mind you, that I don't agree with you. I don't think that oath was anti-Catholic at all.'

'Oh, well, of course, Father, in that case, of course it's not a matter of course, but still and all, the point is, it's not anti-Catholic.'

'Of course it isn't, Mr. Crone. Or I mean,' he goes on hastily, 'I mean to say that, considering theology, with due care, it appears not to be.'

'Sure, my God above,' roars the old man, 'I could have told you that forty years ago.'

'And therefore, I don't think there will be any necessity for you, Mr. Crone, to mention it in your confession.'

'Oh, yesyesyesyes. I mean, Nonononono! Of course not. As I was saying, Father, the Church is all right. It's a grand Church. It's the finest Church in the world. And I know about all of 'em. It's only the *individuals*. They're the fellows that ruin it for everybody. Do you know that priests have told me that I'm damned?'

'Oh, what nonsense, Mr. Crone.'

'Of course it's nonsense,' cries my grander placidly. But there, that day, I heard no more, for the attic door was closed and in spite of many loud Yesyeses and Nonoes from the sick man, the voices kept to an insistent whispering. And that went on for many visits until one day I went up to him after the priest, sweet-scented from snuff, had taken his slow way down the stairs. The change in my grander was remarkable.

He was lighting his pipe and the match hovered in his stony fingers. The evening was dark and stormy, it was late November, and the match was the only light within the room: outside, the lights of Cork had begun to twinkle like slow-gathering stars. In that light his hollowed cheeks, his strangely mild eyes, gave him the look of a hermit in a cave, smoking his pipe of peace with God. He said:

'Corney, boy. I'm a damn lucky son of a bitch. Here I am at my ease, with plenty of time to consider this world, and the next.'

He saw me smiling quizzically and he shook his head and smiled in return.

'Oh well. I don't expect you to be interested in that. But,' puffing at his ease and looking over the lights of Cork, 'all I wish for you is, that you may have as long a run as me. And as long a pause . . . before the hounds catch you.'

'Have you,' I asked with some temerity, 'cleaned the skillet?' (I meant, made his confession.)

He looked so long out the window that I thought he had taken offence, and I was going away when he said:

'I haven't.' He glanced at me. 'I have to make my terms.' He looked away, troubled and annoyed. 'And the Church is damn tough. But, never fear, I'll best 'em. I'm a bit of a theologian myself, yeh know.'

I left him to it. He sank rapidly when December came in, pitiless to old men. The priest came every second day and they had long confabulations; but every time he went out my mother would meet him at the foot of the stairs and he would shake his head gloomily and she would sigh out a *God help us*. The old man now read nothing, smoked little, ate hardly at all, and slept most of the day, so that when we stole into his room he seemed already dead. But still he would not confess and, while he slept, his mutterings showed that he was thinking of little else: he would mumble the names of Arty Tinsley and Parnell, and Christy was a name often on his white lips. Once he called me to his room, and he made me fish out from among his papers a page bearing the words of the Fenian Oath, written in his own hand. I read it to him — twice. Then he beckoned with one finger to leave it on his breast and go. Before I had gone his eyes were already closed in sleep or in thought.

On December 15th he revived suddenly, as, they say, old orchard-trees will in their last year for sudden fruition before they die. That day the priest had a long talk with him, and the doctor came and said it was doubtful if he would last the week. But at the stairhead the priest shook his head gloomily and my mother made us kneel that night and say the rosary for his immediate recovery or happy death. In the morning he was sitting up, almost as well as he had ever been since he took to his bed — somewhat, I think, to my mother's dismay. That day he said endless rosaries, sleeping with the beads around his limp fingers, waking

to mumble through a decade, falling to rest again.
The doctor gave him some injection that evening and
he was as fresh as paint when the priest came. This
time he surrendered and we could hear the confession
being spoken in such a loud, defiant voice that it was
difficult to avoid hearing it wherever we went.
Repeatedly he interrupted it, however, as if to make
clear that he was still keeping an even balance between
his loyalties, so that what with his *fortissimo* secularities
and the *pianissimo* confession the thing was like an
antiphon between this world and the next. It went like
this:

PRIEST: Sssh!

Fortissimo (as if in anger at the warning): I confess to
    Almighty God, to Blessed Mary ever Virgin, to
    Blessed Michael the Archangel . . .

Interruption: I read a book wanst about the town of
    Archangel.

PRIEST: Sssh, go on, my child.

Fortissimo: . . . Blessed John the Baptist, the holy
    Apostles, Saint Peter and Paul, and to you, Father,
    that I have sinned. It's forty years since my last
    confession. First and foremost, I told an awful
    bloody pack of lies, I can't remember half of 'em.

PRIEST: Sssh.

Pianissimo: (A long mumble from the penitent.) And
    then, a sudden *forte*, both feet on the loud pedals —
    'Oh, that must be thirty years ago. I was down the

249

quays with Batsy Cassidy. We called him Sugar. "Phil," says he, "you're a so-and-so." "Be Jasus, Batsy," says I ...'

The priest's incessant 'Sssh' fell on him like a wave and smothered him, and another long mumbling followed, and then,

Fortissimo again: 'Yerrah, Father, do you remember that meeting Parnell held in Cork in 1890? The chair taken by ...'
PRIEST: Sssh!
Piano: Yesyesyes. *Mumble, mumble.*
Forte: Do you know, Father, who was a great ould bastard, too ... that fellow Healy ...
PRIEST: Sssh!
Piano: I beg your pardon. *Mumble, mumble. ...*

So it went on to the end. The priest left him with a joyful countenance and as he went out my mother knelt and kissed his hand, and she said to us after that he was a saint. I went up to my grander, and I said, cheerfully:

'Well, grander, the old skillet is clean at last?'

He was very weak but he beckoned with the finger and I leaned to him.

'Clean as a whistle. There was only one thing I found hard. He asked me to forgive the clergy for not wanting Arty Tinsley, God rest him, to be buried in

Christian ground. We had a terrible tussle over that. But I said I forgave them.'

'That's right, grander,' I said, and patted his hand. The finger beckoned.

'But, sure, you know, I *don't* forgive 'em. Nor never will. Only you have to cod them blokes of priests, you know, now and again.'

His eyes closed and he smiled like a man who has, in his last years as in his early life, had the best of both worlds and knows it. At his request I handed him his beads and he fell asleep praying on them. He lingered on for a week, and then he passed off in his sleep. We buried him in the old Famine graveyard above the Sherlocks, overlooking the meandering river and the far mountain range. It was his last public gesture — he would not be buried in the cemetery that refused the body of his friend. Barty came from London to the funeral, and Michael and Vicky, and Robert sat in the carriage with my father and mother, and three shivering old Fenians marched behind the coffin.

As we came away the air was dark as with suspended rain or snow, and when the carriages were gone and I walked down the hill with Elsie the sagging wine-bags in the sky released a fall that was too heavy for rain and too wet for snow. It covered the land with dusk and the river became misted. As we walked we thanked each other for our Christmas gifts: mine to her had been a little silk pincushion, hers to me had been a book, *The Thoughts of Marcus Aurelius*. We kissed our thanks and our parting. I noted her upright carriage as she went down the path, and the way she walked on her heels, and once more my fingers counted the months that yet remained to her and me.

IN spite of my grandfather's death it was a happy Christmas with us in the Red House. Several of the family were at home, and they were doing fairly well at their work. They all brought little presents to my mother; and even Maurice, who was in Canada, sent a five-pound note. My father, too, had good news: the church at Blarney, that he had almost despaired of, was to be started in the New Year and the canon had offered him the contract. Even I had fresh hope. I got a card from Dublin, signed, 'From Marion and Stella', and a letter from Marion saying that I must call on her if I ever went to Dublin. With the months stealing on us, and the need to avoid at all costs another scandal until the church was started, I decided to ask Marion's help when the Christmas season was over.

So, early in January, taking the thirty-odd pounds I had gathered from Virginia and Vicky and my grandfather, I went to Dublin. As I entered the city (it was my first time since I raced through it nearly a year and a half before with Christy) and saw the full tide of the Liffey holding the lovely winebrick buildings that burned all along the quays in the winter sunset, and the city glow above their curious level copings, sliced straight across beneath the sky, and passed into the heart and noise of the streets and into the warmth of the

sheltering crowds, I confess that I wished that I could
hide there for ever. The very thought pulled me up
dead. It reminded me of something Donal Condoorum
(the ex-soldier) once told me, that when you are facing
a fight, if you as much think of how you can retreat,
it turns you into a coward on the spot.

After tea in one of those small cheap hotels on the
quays, a place with lace curtains and a dozen sauce-
bottles always on the table, I went straight out to
Marion Gibbons' house. Her people lived in an elegant
terrace on the south side of Dublin, on the canal, quite
near Stephen's Green. Here the night was already rich
and thick. A turf-barge lay moored before a lock,
waiting to finish its long journey across Ireland, the
companion-way lighting the smoke from its chimney,
and a light in a porthole put an eye into its black snout,
lapped by waves sucked by the nightwind out of the
everlastingly frozen billow of the Dublin mountains
still visible to the south-west. Under that same night-
wind, up and across from the plains, the reeds of the
shallows, topfrayed by countless leading-ropes, moved
in the air and moved in the water where a gas-lamp
wavered across them: beyond them, the plates of the
dead nenuphars rode their storm in the same lighthouse glow. The only people abroad were a red-coat
and a girl under a tree, and surely, with that wind of
January, that Irish wind sailing its fleet of stars across
the floes of clouds, it was a night to lift any heart.

Because to me it recalled nights spent with Elsie

on the moors I drove boldly up the steps to the Gibbons' house. I was shown into a room of white marble mantelpiece, white busts and statuettes, slim furniture all white and gold, old paintings, glittering fire-irons. Comfort and charm was so well blended there that even I, who knew something about these things, and could recognize an Adams from a Bossi, could not have said which was foremost in the mind of the person who planned the room.

She came in, and her wide smile and her blush did not make it easy to tell her why I came: it was a greeting for myself alone. And when we sat before the fire I felt immediately a live thread begin to spin itself between us, just as it did one night in Youghal, like a cobweb spinning across the road of a spring day. This was something I had not foreseen, and what with, in her, a shyness that she could not conceal and, in me, that sense of the night outside, suddenly become vast and multitudinous, pitying to no one, according as the warmth of the room and her companionship came stealing over me; what, too, with the memory of the summer that had been so solitary and calm, I felt about us and our talk an atmosphere quite new to me. It was akin to benevolence and far more deep and mysterious than friendship because it was friendship in its first stage when one is giving all, spreading out all one's little riches, not yet having discovered either how much it is vain to offer or expect. That I know now, who have for years tried to live alone, is how people do meet

and join: a first slight bridge, a wavering feeler out of
the shell of self: then a gush of willingness, giving with
both hands: then, when all is given, the secret measur-
ing by each of what — not of what the other has given,
but of what each has taken. The end and measure of
utter friendship, the only release from the cave of
loneliness, is with him who knows how to accept most.
That discovery has meant everything to me. For as it is
with men, so it is with life which we understand and
love in proportion as we accept without question what
it gives, without question as to whether we need it, not
even questioning whether its gift seems cruel or kind.
It is the supreme generosity because we do not even
know who the Giver is; why He has given; or what.

So, here, where I saw through the window of this
pale, silent room, the eye in the snout of the barge, and
could imagine the cold by the way the rough hide of
the water bristled under the lamplight, we were testing
one another all we dared. It did not seem to matter
that at our first meeting we quarrelled over some trifle
that concerned neither of us — was it the Nine Articles?
— or the Eastern rite? — since here we had the obverse
instinct to merge. I mentioned Stella. She gave her
to me at once.

'She is gone back to Paris. She is lovely, isn't she?'

I hesitated, really because of the word she used
rather than the idea.

'She is lovely to look at,' she insisted.

'But she is hard, isn't she?' I protested.

'Hard? She is light-hearted. And she can be very indifferent and too ... oh, too philosophic. But she is very generous and she is wise and she does want to be kind.'

I surrendered, saying only something about Stella not letting things worry her. But then I offered her my Long Strand, and when she wished to say it might be bleak in this cold night, I could not bear that.

'Not with the curtain down and the fire blazing with sea-wrack and the lighthouse hitting the window and the trees over the roof? Then, the sea like a beat of a drum, and you alone, and thinking and pausing and considering. Wouldn't you like it?'

She smiled and accepted my picture, and we went on naturally to what books one would read there, and at each book though we might not be in agreement we never disagreed completely, and we were both eager, so that our chairs drew nearer and we soon had our feet on the fender in complete companionship. At last she said, 'I forgot to tell you father and mother are away ... they are with Stella in Paris. I came back after Christmas.'

She rose.

'I'll get you tea, or come and help me. You were quite useful that evening we met in the cottage.'

We prepared the tea in the basement kitchen: she had let the maid go out, and for the sake of fancy and friendship we took our tea in the kitchen before the red range. But then I had to think of what brought me — to get her to meet Elsie and to ask her to be our excuse for a lengthy visit to Dublin. I asked her, simply, having learned by now that you must take the world as it is shaped, by a roundabout way.

'Would you ever be staying down in Cork a while?'

'I have little reason to. I have friends there, of course. Would you show me around?'

She laughed and blushed until I wondered for a second if my roundabout way had not an unfortunate appearance of being too direct. I said eagerly that I would, and then, to make the visit occur soon, I said quickly that I would be going away within two weeks, and would she be visiting her friends before then? She put it aside at that. But she returned to it later, and when I pressed her this time even more eagerly, she said between laughing and blushing that she might. Soon after, a maid came in and we went upstairs and I left. We were already become old friends when she waved to me from the top of the steps, and I walked back along the canal full of admiration for her; and, as I thought of what I had been doing, I filled with disgust of myself who had so played on her goodness. The following day I pommelled myself again all the way home, so that when I saw Elsie's worried face I felt, indeed, very much like a boxer wearily entering his twentieth round, certain of defeat.

That particular and most elaborate subterfuge, rounded itself to plan when, two weeks after, and just when I was beginning to fear she would not come at all,

Marion visited her Cork friends. I brought her out to the Sherlocks where the old man liked her for her breeding and character, her shyness and her gentle manner, and I walked around the hard ringing roads with her and with Elsie, and they liked each other and became friends. It was easy then to suggest to her that she should invite Elsie to return with her for a week to Dublin. She went, and with the remainder of my thirty pounds she stayed on another month, pretending she was staying with the Gibbonses. Yet, though that took us to the beginning of March we would have been discovered if the spring had not come early, with enticing skies of sailing clouds that carried with them wafted pieces, torn but not detached by the winds. For Marion returned with her and after a single night in Cork the two went to the cottage in Youghal. She said, I think, that she had taken a chill in Dublin and that the seaside in spring would help her to get well quickly.

So far Marion had suspected nothing, though when I met Elsie, pathetically disguising her shape with a little frilled jabot of silk and a loose coat, I thought they must be the two most simple girls in the world, and I was glad that Elsie had no sister at home and no mother and that old Sherlock had no more worldly wisdom or craftiness than a child.

Even so, the old man was at last becoming suspicious.

'That girl of mine,' he complained to me, 'is getting

very restless. That girl isn't sick. Sure 'tis fatter than ever she is. I'm wondering now,' he mused, 'is that Gibbons girl good company for her. I must ask Father Arty about her. What religion is this you said she is?'

'She's a Moravian,' I explained. 'Her father was an engineer on the Austrian State Railways. He was a Protestant to begin but he married an Austrian wife and he changed over with her. As a matter of fact,' I assured him, 'I believe they're very like Catholics. You know the Eastern Church is very near to ours.'

'I have heard the like,' grumbled the old man. 'Leaving me here all alone by myself for nearly three months? I must say I hear there's a lot of those Moravians in Dublin and that they're very good-living people. However,' he consoled himself quickly, 'Lent will be finished soon and she'll be more contented when the boys are back for the Easter holidays. It's lonely for her here with an old man like myself.'

At that I inwardly reckoned the months once again. I believe I must have counted them ten times a day. At the office I would sit looking at the men mixing the dry cement that frayed with the wind, or carrying the planks golden with wet (and, by the same token, damn little seasoned timber must have gone into that Blarney church) and my counting fingers would walk across and across the page of the ledger so that my da, observing me once, said:

'Can't you add up in your head yet? God knows it's not much we have to add!'

It did little good — all the adding: nor the lying awake wondering what would happen between the end of March when she must come home, and May — the month of burgeoning. Once only did I see the humour of it, and that was when I caught my father at his old trick of counting aloud. 'Eight and nine? Eight and nine . . .?'

WHEN I visited Youghal towards the middle of March I found that Marion had discovered everything except my part in the affair. It had eased Elsie a little to share her secret with another woman, but a hunted look caught her when she saw the horror with which Marion heard her confession. It was a foretaste of what must come. A week later I found the poor girl's courage utterly broken, her hands trembling, her face hollowed and pale, and I could scarcely bear to look at her eyes.

That was March 19th, a date I am not likely to forget. There was no effort at concealment now, though Marion could hardly induce her to walk outside the house, and when she did go out she never went beyond the shore or the lonely paths through the marshes, and if she saw anybody on the shore, even half a mile away, she would return at once to the cottage and lock the door and sit there again, for hour after hour, in the awful way of women with child, her little hands across her stomach, looking and sighing in the fire without a word. The waiting had already killed in her all the gaiety and the life that had been such a lovely part of her when we first met. Marion drew me aside that evening to tell me it could go on no longer — the end of Lent was only a few weeks off. As I was without a plan, I agreed.

We were sitting by the fire when I said it, suddenly.
'Elsie, let's tell your father.'

On the other side of her Marion supported me.

'Darling, it's much the best. You will kill yourself with worrying.'

She looked from one to the other of us like a sheep that smells the knife and she took such a fit of trembling that we had to hold her from falling: she clung to us and she begged us in a whisper not to speak of telling, there must be a way out, there must be some plan, we had got so far, she could not tell, she could not.

'But, darling, he is a kind man.'

At that she wept.

'That is why. He is too good, too kind. He couldn't bear it. He has been so good to all of us. He brought us up ... My mother too ... My brothers ... I couldn't, I couldn't.'

Then she suddenly went white as the wall. She almost screamed it:

'Have you told him?'

'No, no. Of course I haven't told him.'

Then, like a thought that spoke itself, rather than something she said, low as the bare twigs rustling on the roof over our heads:

'If I could only drown myself. I look at the sea when I am walking by the shore. And I think of ... No,' she stopped us, 'you needn't think I would do it ... I haven't the courage.'

'Elsie,' I said. 'Your brothers will be home in April.

Lent is nearly over. Easter Sunday will be here in four weeks. You are away nearly three months. It's only March. I haven't a single plan in my head.'

'I can't tell! I must go away!'

She said it fiercely and she rose as if to go at that instant. Marion took her arms and said kindly to her:

'Darling, when it is time ... yes, even now, to-morrow, if it's any help, you can come to Dublin to me. My father has lots of friends who are doctors and they will be very good to you. Nobody there need ever know. But I can't, I couldn't in conscience, do even that much unless your daddy knows. And, soon, when you don't return to him, he must know.'

'I'll go away. Somebody will lend me money. Will you, Marion?'

'I couldn't Elsie. Not unless you tell your daddy.'

'Corney,' she wailed, 'you will get me money?'

'Unless I steal it I don't know where to get it. And even if I did steal it, and I'd gladly steal it for you, how could I let you go? And then your daddy will know anyway.'

She sank away from Marion and she combed her hair feverishly with her hands, and her fingers roved over her eyes and cheeks. Then she sighed that deep, heart-trembling sigh, and again and again she said it like a mad woman, whispering to herself:

'I can't tell. I must go away. I must go away.'

I motioned Marion to leave us and when she was

gone I put my arms about her and drew her head to my side and said to her:

'Elsie, have you told it in confession yet?'

'No, Corney,' she said quietly, as if she were talking to my heart that was by her cheek. 'You told me not to. So I didn't.'

'Little child. Is it worrying you?'

She twisted her fingers and looked at the flames.

'That and everything. I feel everyone is wanting to find it out. And I don't want them to know. And you,' she broke down, 'you don't even want me to tell God Himself.'

'Little one, you must tell everyone!'

I stroked her face and her finger-tips and she stroked my hand and begged me, saying:

'Corney, dear, you won't mind if I do tell the priest?'

'Darling, why should I care?'

'You don't care?'

'For myself, why should I care? Tell him, little one.'

'Will I?'

'Yes.'

She looked at me.

'Yes. And afterwards, you may be able to tell your daddy, too.'

'So you don't mind if I say it was a sin?'

'No.'

She rose and with little steps she wandered over to the bedroom and leaning on the jamb she looked over

the black ocean where the lighthouse beam slowly came
and went. She murmured, tremulously, like a very small
child, her lips and her eyebrows moving as to tears.

'Corney, you didn't say that at first. You didn't
want me to tell daddy. And now you want me to tell
everyone. In the beginning,' she chided, and her eyes
flooded with tears that in the wandering light rose
huge and swelling while she murmured on, 'in the
beginning I said it was wrong. But you said, no . . .
that was it, I said it was wrong. But you said, no.
If I had went to the priest that time . . . maybe this
wouldn't have happened. I don't know, Corney.
I don't know. You tell me . . . one thing at one time . . .
and another thing at another time. . . .'

'Elsie, darling, I did my best.'

The tears rolled slowly but she would not stir her
hand to move them from her tender cheek. The light
came gently and passed gently. Always she looked at
the sea.

'I tried *my* best,' she said valiantly. 'I tried *my* best,
to do what you wanted, Corney. But you want so
many things.'

Her voice broke completely there. 'You want . . .
so . . . many things.'

I would have gone to her but her frail wrist stopped
me.

'The priest will come to-night,' I promised.

She shook her head nervously.

'No, no. Not to-night.'

266

'To-morrow night, Elsie?'

'To-morrow?' she whispered to herself, and then shook her head again.

'How can I tell him?' she shuddered.

'Let it be to-morrow night,' I begged, and she seemed to consider it.

'And then,' she asked me sorrowfully, 'you want me to tell daddy?'

'I have no plan,' I confessed.

'To-morrow night?' she mused, and looked at me reproachfully. 'Very well, Corney. But,' she added as she turned slowly to the bedroom, 'but it *is* a sin, Corney, it is a sin, and it *was* a sin all the time. Now, wasn't it?'

I stared at her and I said:

'It is a sin, for you, Elsie. I didn't understand that for you it would always be a sin.'

Her slow, down-looking eyes looked through me and through me. Then she looked again away at the March sea. By that look she meant, 'How much you would have saved me if you said that when the summer was here! But how hard you were! How vain you were!'

'I'll go now and talk to the priest,' I offered.

'And he will say, "Tell your father".'

'You can think over that, Elsie.'

All the time her eyes were on the wild edge of the breakers, brooding over them.

'I'll go now, Elsie, and speak to him.'

'Now?'

'Will I, Elsie?'

She glanced quickly from the breakers to me, and from me to the shore again.

'Very well. Do. Take Marion with you.'

She went through the bedroom door. I saw there the little pink things she owned, a pink shawl, a piece of smoothly-ironed ribbon, her red tam-o'-shanter hat, and they evoked for me all our old memories, our bruised love. As she closed the door her last words were:

'But it *was* a sin, Corney. All the time, for both of us, it *was* a sin.'

As I stood looking after the closed door Marion came back. Many times, because I hated the task, I said, 'I must go for the priest'. We put on our coats and we went out into the high wind and we clambered under the cliffs away from the tide. Now and again the hidden moon lit up the clouds that moved noiselessly across the stars. It was the wind of the vernal equinox that had distended the sky and sea until the air was full of motion and the sea a torrent over the land. Once I thought I heard a cry and looked back. The shore was a darkness except for the long line of waves.

'What is it?' Marion shouted.

'Nothing,' I shouted back and we ploughed on.

Reminded suddenly of the night she said, 'Corney, come back, come back,' I halted again. Again I saw only the white line stretched for miles into the night. We went on. Again I stopped and this time I told Marion to wait — I must say something to Elsie. I went back to the cottage and as I came near it I saw the wide open door and the light streaming on the sandy grass. I saw her pink shawl on the threshold, caught by a wild rose-bush. I ran to her bedroom. She was not there. I raced to the dunes and howled her name into the wind that sang in my throat like wind in the neck of a bottle. On the wet shore, right, left, around about, I cried again to her to 'Come back, Elsie, come back'. The moon floated from a crevasse, slowly and evenly the beam of the lighthouse swept towards the breakers. She was far out staggering towards the deep sea.

Madly I ran into the surge shouting as I ran, but she could hear nothing with that bellow of waves and wind in her ears and she kept on and on. A little way out and the foam was beating my face. The moon sank away and the beam with its gentle sweep. It was a slow descent but the waves were high and if she fell I knew she might not rise again. I saw her again in the moon and she had stopped. In a nightmare one's legs became leaden. It was like that, slow, slow, through the wind and waves, and the beam that I wanted so madly seemed to move slower and slower like a clock running down. When I howled at her a wave filled my throat. When I was still ten yards away the lighthouse finger struck her and she fell. I was now swimming and the moon blazed full on the sea, and when her body was swept suddenly against me I held her dress. Turning, I floated her, flung along by the waves, her hair over her face, red as blood, and by degrees, more heavily when she lifted out of the water and her gravity increased, I managed to drag her yard by yard until a breaker flung us on the sand. She was neither stunned nor fainted and when she saw me she clung to me and screamed my name and all the time I dragged her inward, was flung inward, walked inward, she just screamed and screamed that solitary word.

I did not understand why she screamed until I had carried her to the fire where she fainted, and Marion, who had come racing back, helped to undress her — her large belly terrified us — and she awoke and began to cry out in pain. We put her to bed and I carried a great fire of turf into the little poke of a whitewashed grate. Marion was in the kitchen as I did so. She rose on her elbow and she faced me through the smoke, and God send I may never again see in any woman's eyes, or hear in her voice, the fear that leaped in her when I said I would run for a doctor. She almost scrambled from her bed as she cried out:

'Corney, don't leave me.'

'But the doctor, Elsie.'

I ran to her through the smoke of the turf and she clung to me, crying.

'I'm afraid. I'm afraid. The priest, Corney, I want him.'

'Then I'll get him.'

'But I can't be alone. Corney, the child. I think I'm going to . . .'

Marion was by her now. The pain made her relax her hold on me and she sank back, groaning. I left her to Marion and I ran, hatless, dripping, heart-thumping, all her fear driving me on, along the dunes and the shingle, staggering, falling, thrusting towards the pier that was a mile away, and, because nobody lives there in the winter, towards the town that was two miles further on. By the time I reached the promenade I had to fall under the lee of it with my heart battering my side and my mouth dry and my tongue stuck in my mouth. I could not see a soul. The waves beat over the wall and over me. The lighthouse beam moved over the purple torrential sea like a finger of fate pointing out the roaring elements. I saw a bobbing lantern. It was an old porter beating his way to the last train. I reached him, and I fell on him, crying out:

'A woman. A woman is dying. Nearly drowned. A priest and doctor. Oh, quick! Quick!'

'Dying? A priest?' He lifted his lantern to my face. 'Nearly drowned? God look down! What is it? What did you say?'

'There. Out beyond the castle. In the marshes.'

'And for God's sake, what took her there? Is it in the marshes? Where is she?'

I hung on him. My knees could not hold me up.

I shook him like a bag of bones. I was in terror. The night was like the Deluge. I thought hell was opening.

'Will you talk and tell me? A priest? Talk to me.'

'Don't shake me. My God, man, I can't rightly say. You see, now, I'm not a Youghal man. Let me think now. Oh, don't shake me, will you. Have patience. I can't think when you're shouting at me. Did you say a doctor? I never heard of e'er a doctor around this part of Youghal. Except in the summer-time of course. There was a Doctor Cassidy there in Homeville. But sure he's gone months and months ago.'

'A priest then. She's dying without confession. It's all my fault.'

'Oh, bless us and save us. Jesus, Mary and Joseph look down on us. The poor woman. If I could only think. Look, run up to the hotel. That's the best . . .'

I ran. The doors were shut and there was only a dim light but I leaned back against the door, and hammered with my heels, and tore at the bell. On the chain, after some rumbling of bolts, the door opened three inches. I saw a man, an elderly man, with a newspaper and a pipe in his fist, looking down at me.

'Who's there?'

'A doctor. A priest. A woman dying on the shore.'

He opened the door wide and I fell at his feet. He was quicker than the old porter. He helped me to a hall-chair complaining that there was no doctor or priest in that part of the Strand.

'But we'll get them. Katey!' A woman came out. 'Ring up the Presbytery. And telephone Sheehy, he's the nearest doctor. Where is she, young man?'

He gave me one look and ran to the bar for a glass of whisky. Its fire ran through me. Holding the glass I told him she was in a cottage in the marshes and was going to have a baby and was nearly drowned and was maybe dying. Before such a piling-up of misfortunes he could say nothing. Instead, being a quick-minded man, he made me sit in the bar where he lit a lamp and took off my clothes. Then he ran upstairs for dry clothes and I changed every rag I had on from the shirt out. The woman came back and spoke through the door because I was in my shirt.

'The priest is on his way. Sheehy is out on a car accident. Will I telephone Doctor Horne?'

'Is she a Catholic?' the hotel-keeper asked me. 'But of course she is or she wouldn't want the priest. No,' he cried to the door, 'Horne won't do.'

'Yes, he will,' I shouted. 'Get him.'

'No,' said the husband. 'Not with the child coming. Ring up Considine, Katey. Hurry.'

She was soon back.

'He's out.'

'Damn them,' shouted the man. 'Is all Youghal having babies? Where's that gom Sheehy?'

'On the Killeagh Road. There was an accident.'

'Then we'll get him. It's on our way. I'll get the pony and trap.'

I told the woman where the cottage was and she promised to direct the priest. Already her husband had the trap out, pulling the shafts with his hands, and a boy was tearing the pony from its stable. Then we had him tackled and we were out in the backlane, grinding our axles against the narrow walls.

'Is she bad?' he shouted.

The wind here was a thin treble to the major roar of the sea.

'Very,' I cried.

The last train was sparkling across the plain of the marshes towards Cork. He lashed the pony to a mad gallop out the road.

'Who is she?'

'A girl named Sherlock. You don't know her. From Cork. A visitor.'

Everything had to be shouted in groups of words.

'What the hell, is she having, a child, out there for?'

He was trying to see my face in the cold moonlight. He was beginning to have doubts about me.

'Premature. There's a friend with her.'

He was silent. He jigged on his beast.

'Where's her husband?' he shouted.

'Cork.'

'My God, the poor girl.'

The clattering hooves, the wild wind — nothing else but the jingle of harness.

'Do you know her?'

'Yes. I was down visiting her.'

'How did she get into the sea?'

'In the dark.'

'It's not dark.'

He shut his mouth tight. He said no more. He was afraid. Suddenly something rose out of the road ahead, but the nag had already seen it and was cavorting on his hindlegs. The group of people rushed aside as we drove into them, and there below me, to my horror, in the come and go of the moonlight, I saw two white faces, two pale masks, staring up at me out of a great dark pool, and it was not a pool of rain — there had been none. Smashed to matchwood, no more than small kindling now, there lay across their bodies the mash of a great country cart. It was as if an elephant stood on a matchbox. The doctor ran towards us as people's hands tore at the pony's bridle.

'Who's that?' cried the doctor.

'Canavan. Can you come with us. A woman is dying.'

'God above,' he shouted. 'Look at this.'

I refused to look again. Even now, stamped on my memory, are those two formless faces lit red by the moon.

'Are they gone?' shouted Canavan.

'Mutton! They're in bits. A terrible thing. They were drunk. God forgive them!'

'Jump in, then. You can do no good here.'

The doctor hesitated. He was a smallish man, very young, thin-cheeked, with crescent glasses.

'Will I wait for my trap? It's gone into Killeagh for the priest. What's wrong with her?'

'A child. Come on, damn it. There's no use waiting.'

In silence, awed by the sight of death, the people watched us turn and gallop away.

'That lad,' said the doctor, nodding at me, 'looks like fainting. It's the sight of the smash. It took a shake out of myself.'

'Thank God I knew better'n to look,' said Canavan. 'Hold up, lad.'

'Leave him alone. He'll over it. Where's this case? God, isn't it bitterly cold. And I left my coat after me. I was down in Mulranny's at a game of Forty-five. I had the bloody Knave and the Ace and seven-and-six in the kitty. Will it rain?'

'Wind is too strong.'

'Who's the woman? Where is it?'

'Out on the Murrough. Behind the rifle-range. One of them cottages of Moran's. How many months, young man?'

'Leave him alone,' said Sheehy. 'He'll be sick in a minute on us if you don't leave him alone. Who is she? Not a visitor surely? In March? Pull up at my house till I get my instruments. I must show them to you.'

I thought he was the most talkative little man I ever met. I wished to God he would be silent. Drops of rain began to fall.

'They're lovely instruments. A new set I got in Dublin. Those premature births can be nasty things.'

The last words I heard, as I fell over in a faint, were, 'I paid eight pounds ten for them'. Then I was in the doctor's house and they were spooning brandy into me.

'Are they gone?' I asked, but I saw Canavan's lean face and I struggled up and insisted on going on to the cottage. I can have been there for no more than five minutes for the young doctor came in just then, struggling into his overcoat, and we left the bright warm room and were once more in the whistle of the wind. We walked the pony down a boreen into the marsh. Then we had to get out and walk. The roar of the sea came louder and louder. We opened gates and crossed stiles. The light of the cottage shone ahead. I kept telling them to hurry. I ran from them to the porch, through which I saw Marion leaning over the fire, tending the boiling kettle.

'Marion?'

The doctor brushed past me and Canavan after him.

'Marion!' I cried. 'Did the priest come?'

She shook her head sadly. I went to the bedroom door but Canavan forced me out.

'Wait,' he said.

I kept going and coming to the door to see if the priest was coming, and back to the kitchen to see if the doctor was still in the room. At last he came out slowly. He looked at us. We stared at him.

'Is she a Catholic?' he asked me.

'Yes.'

'Then,' he asked savagely, 'why didn't you bring the priest?'

'Is she . . . will she last?'

'Where's the priest?' he demanded.

'We sent for him,' said Canavan. 'He's coming on.'

He went back for a second to look. I heard her moaning my name and ran in. She was white. Sweat beaded her brow.

'Are you the father?' asked Sheehy, soft enough.

I nodded. I begged him in a whisper to say, 'How is she?' He just parted the air with his hands, and left us. He closed the door after him. She murmured and I knelt to her.

'Corney,' she whispered, faint as a breath. 'Come back.'

'I am here, Elsie.'

'Corney,' said the breath. 'The priest.'

'He's coming, Elsie.'

I took her little hand. It was damp with perspiration. At the sight of her soft pink-ribboned shawl around her shoulders, the dainty ribbon she had ironed with so much care, I began to cry. I kissed her cheek. Her breath, hardly a breath now, said a word that must have been 'priest'. I thought suddenly of my childhood teaching. I held her limp hand tight to make her aware of me and I spoke into her ear the words of the contrition.

'Oh, my God, I am heartily sorry.'

I watched her white, dry lips and they moved to the repetition of the sounds.

'For having offended Thee . . .' — this I said even louder, and as I watched, I heard the sibilants of the v's and f's.

'And I detest my sins most sincerely . . .'

The wide, gentle lips shaped a word, and I went on quickly.

'Because they displease Thee, my God.'

By her breath alone could I tell that she understood.

'Who art so good and deserving . . .'

The lips opened very slightly for 'art', and there was a tiny hiss for 'so'. With fervour I continued to 'of all my love'.

The faintest, tiniest movement of the lower lip was all I could see.

'And for Thy sake . . .'

Her mouth slowly sank open. I gripped her hand and said it loudly.

'And for Thy sake, Elsie . . .'

I put my ear to her lips. The door opened and Sheehy came in. I cried it aloud — aloud.

'And for Thy sake, Elsie! Elsie!'

He leaned over her while I stared at her. He slipped his stethoscope under her left breast. He was looking at her face. Slowly he drew erect. He patted my shoulder. I looked wildly at him. He made a little gesture with his two hands, and his mouth said, silently, a simple word. I looked at her small hand. It seemed to me to be as it always had been. It was cold, and pale, but it was still *her* hand that I had so often stroked and kissed. Her hair seemed to me to be the same — the deep curls of it that I had played with. Her neck was still as white as when I used love her, her face as gentle, far more gentle, more calm, more kind.

'Elsie,' I whispered: but the thread was broken. The young doctor tapped my shoulder and shook his head. I would not believe him.

'Elsie!' I cried.

I saw her as she lived in that little mole just over her left eyebrow. I had teased her often ... The door opened again and a bald-headed priest entered swiftly. He was panting with running. There was rain on his coat.

'Am I in time?' he asked Sheehy.

He had thrown his stole over his neck: the silver pyx gleamed in his hand.

'Ah, Father Murphy,' said the doctor. 'You're just five minutes too late.'

'She may be conscious,' said the old priest. 'Leave the room,' he ordered.

'Oh, yes. She may be conscious,' I cried, but Sheehy dragged me out and closed the door. Marion sat by the fire, her face in her hands, refusing to look at me. Canavan stood with his back to it. Sheehy sat by the table. I stood in the centre of the kitchen looking at the door. Nobody said a word. In the storm the tree overhead, now without a leaf, squeaked its branches across the tin roof, and the sea rose and fell in its endless roar.

The lamp had been taken into the room and only the firelight leaped on the hearth, or, regular and unbroken, the pale gleam of the lighthouse that came and went like a ghost across the whitewashed wall. It lit each time an old felt hat of Elsie's that hung on a big stumpy nail.

That night, when they were all gone — except for myself and Marion — I slept a little in a chair. Then I saw the morning come up over the sea, a dull gleam as of soiled fish. As I stood and watched that dirty, restless heaving streaked with rain, the lighthouse suddenly went out, and the waves glittered beyond the far headland. It was the risen sun.

Marion stirred and poked the grey ashes of the fire. All night she had not spoken to me. Her face was grey and old. I saw the hat on the wall. The sea-soaked shoes were by the fire. On the window-sill my hand lay on the purse. When I opened it I saw among her pennies and her worn beads a letter of mine, many times folded and unfolded — '. . . so meet me by the bridge, little one, and we can look at the gulls . . . much nicer than Sunday . . .' The rain squall moved away to the south. Beyond the headland was the ghost and the sparkle of the waves. At last I turned to Marion:

'I must go and send a telegram,' I said.

'May I do it?' she asked.

I nodded, and presently I was left alone in the cottage, waiting for old Mr. Sherlock.

I BECAME a Bird Alone. My father would not speak
to me, and my mother would not speak to me. They
locked me out of their house that night and I slept
between the timbers of the timber-yard. But, because
blood is thicker than water, they still fed me, though
after that I used to sleep in the old wooden office behind
the Red House. I became what they call, in Cork, a
charácter.

That means:— a queer fellow walking the streets
without a penny in his pocket, his sleeves frayed, his
shirt and coat crumpled from sleeping in them, not
merely poor but a pauper, and yet with a collar and tie
and a hat like any man: a fellow you glanced at every
time you passed him by and at the crêpe band ostentat-
iously worn around his arm, as if he might at any
moment do some odd thing worth telling to your friends.
For some reason or other they called me 'Third
Person' and said with jollity such things as, 'He doesn't
do a stroke of work. His people support him. Begod,
a grand life entirely he has, a perfect loller.' That
happened within the two or three weeks between her
burial and Holy Week. Not until the first week was
gone did I realize that she was gone. For a week after
I did not sleep one moment of the night which I spent
between thinking of her alive, and thinking of her dead,

praying and praying for her soul in the secrecy of my room. Those silent nights were terrible to me, though, strangely, it was not the thought of her death that moved in me but the terror of those two shapeless, unknown faces, struck down so suddenly on the road — wiped out as by a casual hand. I spent hours and hours, by day, in the chapels of the city beseeching God to have pity on her. Among the old odorous women, the ragged mad creatures, the strange castaways who inhabit the poor city churches, I used to seek for a corner and whisper to the lighted candelabras, endlessly, O God have pity on Elsie, O God have mercy on Elsie. . . . I told myself I was a Faust who had sold his child for his lusts — for now I confessed that our love was a sin, was evil, was bestial. I would have gladly died to make it be that the priest had come to her in time.

Then, by degrees, as I felt that judgment was over, and as they cast me out from them, I fell silent within me and began to hate. Holy Week came and the whole city flocked to the churches, driving me, I felt, out even from them. When the Sherlock family came home for Easter I began to keep out of the very city to avoid meeting them. It was then I heard what people were saying about me and that it was my idiot brother Robert who had called me 'Third Person' — speaking of me as *he*, or *him*, 'Did you see him?' 'Where is he gone to?' as if I had ceased to be a man and had become a piece of grammar. It was Christy Tinsley who told me. He came out of gaol that May, a skeleton without a mind, and since his guardian would not put him into a home we used meet from time to time and go wandering out the fields or around the city. Always he would be chewing the boiled sweets that he loved (four-a-penny), his gob big with them and he telling me that he was the devil. Though always he said it with a pathetic kind of half-sanity as if he hoped I would persuade him that he was not. Indeed it was not so much a statement as a question, and he would put it to me, looking eagerly around the left side of my face as if he thought it was my ear that spoke:

'Corney, I think sometimes that I'm the divil?'

'Well,' I would bully him, 'there's that between us anyway. For I'm the Deep Sea. Don't be play-acting.'

'Oh, then, Corney boy,' he would say to my right ear, watching it and watching my eyes with a wandering look, 'it's no play-acting. I do lie awake saying it to myself. I do be saying, "Christy, you're the divil and what'll you do when God finds out?"'

'Shut up,' I would reply. 'Come for a walk.'

I would trot him up hill and down dale as fast as a lamplighter until he would be too tired and breathless to say it or think it again.

Sometimes, however, to my joy he would become completely sane and then we would have grand discussions lying in the fields, or in the winter I would raid the yard for timber and set a fire roaring in the office-stove and make tea: then we talked and talked until there can hardly have been a soul abroad in all

Cork but the night-police or a night-watchman on the jetties watching the timber-stacks, or a watchman hanging over his smoky brazier where they had opened up a road or the city sewers. We talked always of two things only — the only two things anyone ever talks of in Ireland —Religion and Politics, and he was always a fierce agnostic when he was sane, and a Catholic when he was mad. When he was mad I used tell him there was neither God nor Devil (the sight of him, then, being almost enough to make me believe it) and when he was sane I always took the side of the Church. But, after several months of that, he would suddenly begin to grow worried in the middle of some bitter attack on religion, and say:

'Corney, we shouldn't say things like that. It's wrong. Indeed, I think it's a sin.'

By which I would know that he was wandering once more, and a person to be avoided. Yet, how brilliant he could be sometimes in his atheism! He would take my own old weapons and turn them on me in a flash.

'You say,' he would pronounce the words slowly in his slow emphatic Cork drawl, 'that we ta-a-ake our ideas, of the next world, from what we see-e in this wor-uld? Now, take, the human, body. It's aw-wl tubes and valves and an intricate arrangement between many parts, held compactly, within the human frame.'

'Yes, a wonderful construction.'

'Well, now, take a motor-car. It is just the same intricate, and compact, arrangement of parts. Wherefore I say, that the mind of *your* God, cannot be far different, to the mind of Daimler.'

'But you fool, the very idea of the piston is taken from the human arm. We can imitate that, but no Mr. Daimler has yet made anything like a mind!'

'It is not the ma-aking that matters. It is the matching, by man, of the works of *your* Deity. We can control the mind. We understand how it works; even if we cannot reproduce it. I do not sa-ay that man is a god. I say that there is no such thing as God. And that all the works, of *your* imaginary God, are humanely understandable, are not at all wonderful, and not at all God-like. And I say that the works of nature should therefore suggest to you, a God, very like to a man. If, that is, you must allow them to suggest, to you, anything of that kind.'

'But the mystery of death and life — what your motor-car does not possess — the mystery of where we come from and where we go to. The meaning of it all?'

'A motor-car, that came out of the earth, returns to the earth. So does a man.'

'But we have a brain to ask and a motor hasn't.'

'An unnecessary appendage, that only addles you.'

To which I, of all people, could make no reply, but:

'Well, I think you are using your unnecessary appendage.'

'For the same reason that a dog wags *his* unnecessary appendage. Man will, in time, discard his brain, which must have been, I hold, a relic of his lower nature; and, then, we can live, in happiness, like the beasts of the fields. For it is only folly, on the part of men, that makes them think, as they do, that they are any better.'

Raising his bony wrist, he pronounced:

'And, that should please you, because you always held, to my knowledge, that we learn, by the works of nature, the nature of the supernatural.'

Had he been a sane man and not a lunatic, I think he might have convinced me. Being a madman he made me feel that we were both astray. In silence I would look at him, pondering on that, while he stared into the open stove and saw visions of heaven knows what fantastic perfection of the future.

Finally, when the winter was over, he went quite mad of religious mania and was locked up, and I was at last, truly, a Bird Alone. I visited him once in the home and found him quite happy in his mindless state.

I resumed my wandering. Sometimes I prayed for Elsie. But less and less often. Had I money I might have become a drunkard and a shiverer in every joint. I might, had there been such, have taken to the brothels. Instead it was my brain that shivered and all my lust was in my pride that returned to me, and my solitariness that required it, and my hate that supported it. Slowly the spring came round again and with it I left Cork for ever, a few weeks after the first anniversary of Elsie's death.

It was April, and Maundy Thursday. On Spy Wednesday I had noticed the first budding of spring and it may have been the pink almonds in the sun, or the elder buds, so fat and long and greasy, or the haw-thorn-tips promising their clots of summer snow, that called me. I know it was good weather for work, for I had been contentedly hammering away in the yard, where, since my ejection from the office, I had begun to work as a carpenter, now and again as the mood seized me, under old Tommy Scanlon the foreman. Or it may have been a conversation with him that drove me to leave the place. He was a sour-tongued old fellow, with a marvellous memory, but I had always loved to hear him talk of old times; I had the fancy that with the help of little dredgings from his Well of the Past into my Well of the Present I would, as it were, have a still mirror, brimming to the hour, of what I really was.

This April morning, in a break of work, we sat in the office before a fire of shavings. We were not talking, though after a time I noticed Tom looking oddly at me: when I looked up he would look away: when I looked away I felt his eyes on me again. Finally he out with:

'Isn't it queer that way you're the only one of the family, bar poor Bob, that stopped at home?'

'Well, I'm the eldest, so I was always in the business.'

He sniffed.

'Yes. I know that.'

'Then why did you ask me?'

'Well, you're not a fool. It's not, now honest, it's not much of a bloody business to stay in, is it?'

'It's gone down,' I agreed.

'Do you know what I'm thinking? What will happen you when, God between us and all harm, your old fellow hops it?'

I considered it. Then I laughed to myself, because I found I had never considered my future, in any way.

'I never thought much about it.'

'Huh!' Then after a while. 'You know, Corney, a man could make a good business of this place if he knew how to do it. But your old fellow, God help him, has himself ruinated. There's two things wrong with him. He have no money and he have no connections.'

'Well,' I quizzed, 'there's two of us alike.'

'Aye, you're a poor class of a poor fellow all right, Corney. You haven't much go in yeh.'

I smiled up at him.

'You have me taped all right, Tommy, aw?'

He pulled easily at his clay pipe and he looked me over as if I was a horse.

'I have your measure. And why wouldn't I? Sure I born'd every mother's child of ye.'

He was silent so long that I tapped his knee and said:

'Well, doctor, what do you advise the patient?'

'I'll tell you.' He blinked one eye at me. 'If you're going to make a hand of this business, boy, go out and meet people. Join clubs. This club and that club. Be drinking with fellows. Go into politics, — a bit, you know, not too much. Above all, be in with the clergy.'

I sighed.

'It's good advice. But I'm afraid it's not my nature.

And, anyway, you know as well as I know, that the priests wouldn't come within a donkey's bray of me.'

He leaned over to me.

'I thought so much. I spoke of it because I knew that was on your mind. But you're wrong. For, if you were to marry a nice girl, of good position, all that would be forgotten. You're only keeping it up the way you're going on.'

I rose and went to the window. The little puffs of clouds were small sheep in a blue plain, grazing, hardly stirring. I saw the roofs and chimneys of the city, warmly lit by the climbing sun, and the smell of those chimneys and the smell of the stove mingled in the brain with the humming of the streets. Near at hand the children in the convent-school chanted their numbers loudly and eagerly:

Two and Two are Four. *Soh, soh, la, te, soh.*

Three and Three are Six. *Soh, soh, la te, soh.*

Four and Four are Eight. . . .

Here in this quieter corner of the cathedral I could hear a cart-horse slowly padding up the hill.

'Do you heed me?' said the voice behind my back.

'I'll never get married,' I said quietly to the humming and buzzing outside me. 'And as for clubs and people and drinking — I have no heart for them.'

I opened the window and the clanking came in loudly; a bluebottle flew out high into the sun. I closed the window and went on:

'I get no fun out of that sort of thing,' I said.

'They're all at the same game in this city — they're all out to get money and be rich and respectable. They think of nothing else but what's going to be thought and said of them. It's all pretence and sham and fear and cowardice. They have no guts. Look at the way they treated everyone we know — they've always bit the hand that fed them. Look at the way they're bullied by the priests.'

'All right! All right!' warned the voice. 'That's quite enough . . .'

'All I want,' I concluded, 'is to leave 'em alone and be let alone.'

I watched my breath disappearing from the glass. I could hear him rise behind me, and by the cracking of his bones I could tell that he was rising and stretching and yawning.

'All right, boy,' he wheezed and groaned through his stretching yawn. 'You leave people alone and they'll leave you alone.'

'I wish they would.'

'Oh? Is that a dead wan for me?'

I turned and took him by the lapels, and to show him it was not, I smiled.

'No, Tom. I'm built different, that's all.'

He shook me off.

'Yeh, to hell with you. Ye're a queer, odd, bloody make-up of a family, and anyone that 'ud be having anything to do with ye is as big an ould fool as yeerselves.'

He gave me a sour look, and then a soft look, and he tapped my breast with his old finger.

'But, listen to me, boy. If you're not going to turn to and put your back into this business — take my tip and clear out. Clear out of it altogether. This is a tight little city, and a tidy, small little place, where them that knows how to do it can make good money, and them that doesn't know how to do it might as well be trying to sell crucifixes in Jerusalem. Aye, even the Jews know how to make money here. Going around like pitchy-men, selling us chaney statchas of the Blessed Virgin. But you don't know, and you never will know, how to make enough money to buy dripping for yer bread of a Good Friday.'

He turned to the door with one arm in his sleeve.

'Different? Built different, did you say? Ha, was there ever a Crone was like any other human being on this earth? Ha, that's a good wan. Built different. Oh, no!' he mocked. 'Not at all.'

Out he went, muttering to himself. 'The best bloody wan, hehe, I ever heard . . .' while I looked after him uncomfortably.

That night, Spy Wednesday, the sun sank into a bed of roses. The street was dry and dusky. Cork seemed oddly silent. Not until I was frying my rasher for my tea in the office did I remember why it was so silent. It was Passion Week: the church bells had not rung. I heard the front door bang and when I went into the house there was not a soul from floor to attic. When I went to the window and looked out, the street was as silent as the cathedral graveyard. I idly turned the pages of a magazine, and opened the family Testament. I was wondering whether the old carpenter was not right and what was going to happen me when I grew older — what would happen if my da died. As I turned over the books of the Bible — Kings, Job, Ezekiel — I read: 'So will I make my fury toward thee to rest and my jealousy depart from thee, and I will be quiet and no more angry...' I closed the book with a wry memory of that morning a year ago when He made his fury towards her to rest and He was no more angry. Well, He was not finished with me, it seemed, and I spoke out the sentence I had seen before I closed the book. 'So, I will establish my covenant with thee and thou shalt know that I am the Lord.'

I went out and along the quays. I paused where a stream of people converged towards the old crumbling lump of a church in the side-street. There the only greenery was the green of fungus on the elms that thrust up through the graveyard pavement, and in the daylight the face of the church — how I detest limestone! — very like a tomb. The chanting of the Tenebrae came through the open door, and the grey gloom of the stone was broken only by the bright windows and the lights that shone in the door. For a while I watched them hurrying in, dipping their hands in the immense shells that held the holy water beside the porch, blessing themselves as they disappeared. I wavered. I went in. The lights of the nave were golden in the font inside the porch. The church was as yet only half-filled, for in Lent they always begin the services soon after the day's work. Under the organ loft was a pillared niche. There I could lean on my elbow and watch and listen from a distance.

But by degrees more worshippers came and presently I was surrounded by the smell of a clothes market. Right and left then, close by, I could see the awed faces of the people where they sat, row on row of them, humble and silent. And in all of them, whether they stared at the naked altar, or prayed on their beads with wandering eyes, there was a look of awe that welded them into a oneness that (as I realized) only such as they can ever know.

Slowly, as the surpliced rows of priests swung through the Psalms into the Lamentation of Jeremiah—so old, so familiar—the ancient spell began to fall on me: and when they stopped and the hidden choir behind the bare altar, that was naked but for purple-wrapped candlesticks and brown candles, began without music on that awful cry of sorrow for the sins of Jerusalem, I felt rising in me with the rise in the wailing chant, a trembling matching the trembling of the voices that, at their peak, were like the crest of a wave shuddering before it falls. They sang:

Jer-u-sa-lem!
Jer-u-u-u-sa-lem . . .!
Convertere ad Dominum Deum tuum.

Muttered prayers from the white surplices. A rattle of swift voices in a frightened hurry of speech. Then the antiphonal chanting was resumed from side to side.

Ideo tenuit eos su-pérbia:
Operti sunt iniquitáte et impie-táte sua ...
Posuerunt in coelum os-suum:
et ligna eorum trans-ívit in terra

On the triangular candelabra a brown candle was extinguished, and the dark mass that watched the sacred play seemed to move and sigh. One other apostle had crept from the Master, the last slim candle of all on his peak of Gethsemane. From face to face I could cast my Judas-look, then, seeing in the crusted dust of an old woman's brow, in an old man's sad eyes that rose upwards and fell heart-brokenly, in the lips of a girl who kissed her cross with devotion, all that they all felt, all by which they all lived, so pitying for their abandoned God, so loving of Him who for love of them suffered without a friend.

How wrong I was to have said to the old carpenter, (who was, surely, somewhere in that throng) that men meant nothing to me, now, because I did not believe in them: or that I wished only that we should keep apart. At that very moment, crushed around by them, inhaling their smell, mingling our breaths, I could feel all my solitariness oozing away, and a craving in me, powerful as a lust, to yield up everything that divided me from them in order that I might be swallowed into their universal flesh. Once I felt that only by my wilfulness and my pride did I possess myself, even as I had felt that in a crowd no man can possess himself. Now I could feel my will and pride stealing away, and I longed to kneel and lose those last things that alone were left me to prize. But I could not. For, and the revelation of it drew me erect as a spear, it was not that I did not believe in men, but that I could not believe in what men believed . . . I went out. Behind me the priestly chanting might have been saying:

'I will gather them round about thee and discover thy nakedness to them and they shall see thee in all thy nakedness . . . and they shall stone thee with stones and thrust thee with their swords. And I will cause thee to cease from playing the harlot and thou shalt also give no hire any more. So will I make my fury toward thee to rest, and my jealousy depart from me, and I will be quiet and no more angry.'

They moved aside for me as I went, not heeding me because they were watching one more brown candle go out under the cone. More worshippers were crowding in. From old habit I dipped my hand in the font and blessed myself. Behind me the chanting had once more ceased. The choir had begun its old cry for the fall of Jerusalem.

Old Tom was right. I had better go. But first I climbed up over the city and looked down at it. I looked to the east and I looked to the west, and under the full moon she was lovely: lovely under the faint-webbing of the hearth-vapours of every house, linked from peak to peak into a communal smoke, covering her like a city-under-the-sea. Lit with golden lights in a bottom of mist out to the farthest grey-fogged ridges that bound her in, she was translucent under the riding moon, and looking at her, as with that eye of the night, at all her strange shapes of cubes and triangles, poly-gons and squares, cones and peaks, pyramids, white fields, shapeless twists of lane and gully and street, and the soft shadows of the woods beyond, I could pick out the houses of all I ever knew, the homes that would never welcome me again.

Nor did that sense of regret leave me when suddenly the moon unveiled herself, and in her overbrightness the city was utterly transformed; itself unveiled, unlovely in its nakedness. No longer now a city-under-the-sea, she was the Lilliput she had always been, where the carts trundled to the doorsteps on Saturdays and the cattle dropped their dung on the streets, and the churches were crowded to the doors on Sundays and Holidays. And it mattered nothing to me that she had nothing that one would wish to look at — neither wide streets, nor great houses, nor buildings to catch the breath, nor memories of greatness; that she had no history; or that she was merely a country town filled with half-rich and pauper-poor, and small merchants and petty tradesmen who like my own people fatted the priests, and kept the monks and nuns and starveling beggars alive, and made those half-rich happy in their half-wealth.

Other nights I might have spat on her for all that. But to-night, when I was leaving her, she was my home, and these were my people, and this was their life, rounding itself to-night in tune with my mood to a lamenting for what was lost and what would not return. For if there would be other houses that I might come to know and other moons that I might watch, there is, after all, in every night and every place its own message and it lasts like the rippled sands only until the next wave rises from the centre of the sea to roar upon the shore.

I leaned up and I put my hands on the damp sand-stone slabs of the wall, like a priest on a pulpit. Then I went away, down the hill, into the mist and smoke. The streets were empty. The churches were closed. I lit my last fire in the office and I arranged the tools I had got to know, and that I must use as a journeyman carpenter. And yet, and yet, even as I handled them and laid them in a row, there was a pleasure in the warmth and friendliness of those tools smoothed by the fists of many men — the tools of the first of all trades: a saw, a square, an auger, a level, three chisels, inch, half-inch, and gouge; a mallet, a rule, a small wooden vice, a plane, a hammer, a gimlet, a brace and bit; then a screwdriver, some nails, and those most ingenious objects that, with the cam, are the beginning and end of all machinery —

screws. It was a good manly trade, and I knew I would like it. I put them all into Tom Scanlon's straw bag that for fun I used sometimes to pretend was a sun-bonnet and would put on my head and make a donkey's bray at him to see him swipe at me with a bit of scantling. That done, I slept beside the stove until the night was all but gone and the moisture glistened in the dawn-light on the pane. When I had shaved myself and made my breakfast I put the tea and the sugar and the bread and the utensils into the straw-bag, took the few shillings in the petty-cash and opened the yard-gate.

I struck off up the hill to the west, and when I looked back the unshadowed city was lying cold and pale in its deep hollow: though, already, from below the harbour-lochs great pillars of sunlight hit the sky. It was a fresh morning and the wind had plumed away the smoke-threads from the clean roofs, all in one direction, so that Cork was like an armada steaming out to sea.

I looked at it, for the last time, saying to myself, 'Well, you have me stripped at last, and like a soldier who has been degraded I go in search of a new army, of new clothes'. And though I had a foreboding that before long I should begin to feel the misery of being cold and naked, I was content, saying,' *A man isn't a man until he's naked*': and '*A man's best shirt is his skin*'; so that when the wind over the brow of the hill leaped on me like a dog I only laughed at the shiver of it and strode upward.

At last the first strange horizon leaped up between

the breasts of two fields, rose between them like a glass filling, and expanded into a map of fields. To the west a haze moved into the haze of distance. The birds in the hedges shook the twigs and shook their feathers and chirruped. The grey dew sparkled on the roadside as I dropped downward to my new world, my new faith.

I did not get my last, final glimpse of the city until the darkness fell and when I thought I had left it long behind. Then, turning suddenly, I saw, miles away, its glow upflung on the sky, red as if a house burned behind the near woods. I looked at it for a long time, for as the day drew to a close that coldness I had feared had begun to pierce through my rags of courage and I had felt the indifference of the night long before it came. I had been for hours walking on high land with a dark valley below me to my right, and of the hamlet I was making for there had been no sign; now when I turned wearily to my road, shifting my pack from shoulder to shoulder, and saw at last a dim speckle of lights very far away, I halted to rest and smoke. I would soon be entering a new group, asking for lodgings, telling my tale.

It was dark, and walking had not been easy, with the by-road sometimes roughly strewn so that I had often halted for fear I was making for the ditch, and, where it was smooth, almost invisible because a damp fog hung in the air, blown up from the not far distant sea. Now when I raised my head to see the sky all I could make out was a shapeless blob of shadow, and it may have been not in the sky but in my eyes for when I looked to another part of the fog overhead it seemed to be there, too. In the valley, from time to time, I saw a light, but when one vanished I could not be sure if it had moved or if some invisible obstacle had intervened and I had stirred: for only by distending the eyes and gazing at space did the lights come clear, and whenever I tried to focus on a speck of light it vanished at once. There was no noise other than the sea's many tones, or maybe it was a river, and at intervals a cool — not cold — waft of wind that wandered over me and died away. Once only did I hear a noise of another kind and that was like the sound of firing in the distance: it was a cart somewhere off in the night rumbling over cobbles, perhaps fording a river or trundling through a boreen. I closed my eyes to hear better, and heard no better. When I opened them I could not be sure that I had opened them until the dark shape of the hedges formed slowly and between them the dim lightness of the road.

I stood up. The wind came again, and wandered over me and away. Tired, I remained standing. I did not move. In that indifference of the dark I might have been a cow drooping under a wall, or any brute beast waiting patiently for another dawn.

But the mind of a man is not as the stones that the wind steals about, and even to see a dim light in a fog was an awakening from dumbness. Far away a light did at last move — perceptibly. It was a human being. It threaded slowly, going and coming behind bush or rock, and it became as I watched it, an adventure of the soul. No chill and indifferent wind, no utter dark, no boom of sea, no silence, could destroy the answer of light that stirred in me then, to watch that flicker's patient threading through the night-hills. And when the little wind came over me again, gentle but stern as time's attrition, I did not heed it. Not until the light went out and came back no more did I resume my way.

I was thinking then, as the windows of the hamlet called me, how, all our life long, such flickerings of humanity come to us, and go from us, and not until they go do we shiver at the whisper of the wind.

THAT whisper of the wind I have heard now over many years. For I am become an old man and my friends are few, and that new faith I set out to find I never did find, and because I have sinned all my life long against men, that whisper of God's reproof, who made men, has been my punishment. I have denied life, by defying life, and life has denied me. I have kept my barren freedom, but only *sicut homo sine adjutorio inter mortuous liber* — a freeman among the dead. They call me Crone the Builder and that is all they think of me — as if I were no more than one of the ancient red bricks I put in their houses.

And yet, as I sit here beside my green-globed lamp, and look out over the frosted roofs, and see the stars thicken over the city, and the moon climb over the harbour, slow as an old poem that rises to the memory, I know that before the night is out I shall ask myself, as I have done many and many a night since I came back to live in this empty house — 'Would I have lived otherwise?' and though I may think long over it, I know exactly how my ponderings will end. I shall rise and lower the wick, and blow out the light, saying — 'No! Not one single thing would I change! except that, once, for a week, I was untrue to my sins. But, then, I shall look through the window at the sleeping city spread below, and, after a little while, I shall say, *God rest her:* and I may or may not add, as I turn to a sleepless bed . . . *and God help all the living and the dead.*

So, to rest, restlessly, starting awake whenever a bout of sleep falls on me. Some late reveller may see my light high up in the gable-end — for I can never sleep in the dark — and it comforts me a little to think that it may mean to him a flicker of humanity, as a blind man is comforted to think that by the tapping of his stick he is felt by a world outside his own. Only when the blessed morning comes and the day's work, and I meet people and talk, am I content. I suppose there are many people in the world like that, content enough while they forget; troubled only in the silence of the night by thinking on those little accidents that have prevented them, let us say, from taking part in the affairs of their city, or from marrying a little wife and bringing up a family in the fear and love of God.

OXFORD

MORE TWENTIETH-CENTURY CLASSICS

Details of a selection of Twentieth-Century Classics follow. A complete list of Oxford Paperbacks, including The World's Classics, OPUS, Past Masters, Oxford Authors, Oxford Shakespeare, and Oxford Paperback Reference, as well as Twentieth-Century Classics, is available in the UK from the General Publicity Department, Oxford University Press, Walton Street, Oxford OX2 6DP.

In the USA, complete lists are available from the Paperbacks Marketing Manager, Oxford University Press, 200 Madison Avenue, New York, NY 10016.

BEFORE THE BOMBARDMENT

Osbert Sitwell

Introduced by Victoria Glendinning

Before the Bombardment was Osbert Sitwell's first novel, written in 1926; it was also his favourite. It studies change, both social and psychological, when a world of obsolete values come under the bombardment of a new and harsher era. Set in an out-of-season seaside hotel, it portrays the loneliness of the few remaining guests with a masterly satiric humour.

'It is a book which you will never forget; a book which nobody else could have written; a book which will frighten you, yet hold you with the richness of its beauty and its wit.' Beverley Nichols, *Sketch*

'Few novels that I have read during the past year have given me so much pleasure . . . a nearly flawless piece of satirical writing.' Ralph Straus, *Bystander*